PRAISE FOR THE FR

'Hard-boiled and riveting writing ... A n̶̶̶ crime-writing canon.' *Crime Factory*

'Like Peter Temple, Whish-Wilson tells a cracker of a yarn while wielding language the way Sachin Tendulkar wielded a bat.' *The West Australian*

'Fast-paced, complex and with some excellent twists, this is quality crime.' *The Australian*

'Classic crime noir.' *Australian Book Review*

'A hard-boiled, vivid examination of crime and corruption in 70s WA.' *Guardian Australia*

'Combines the pace of a hard-boiled thriller with a lyricism that makes you pause and catch your breath, before plunging in for more.' *Angela Savage*

'*Zero at the Bone* is a gritty and utterly absorbing read.' *Good Reading Magazine*

'Frank Swann is an attractive lone wolf, and the period is perfectly drawn ... *Zero at the Bone* delivers on a whole series of levels.' *The Newtown Review of Books*

'Unexpected, intriguing and beautifully written, you won't want to put this one down until the very last page.' *The West Australian*

'First rate crime noir.' *Sun Herald*

'*Line of Sight* is beautifully crafted. The characterisation is flawless and economical, the plot has a creeping intensity that grows greater and greater as it progresses to the unexpected conclusion.' *The West Australian*

'Against an intimately realised Perth backdrop three stories intertwine ... gripping and well constructed ... there is a satisfying twist to the end of the tale ...' *The Advertiser*

'Well written and meticulously researched, it's a wonderful piece of hard-boiled writing and an incisive analysis of the changing nature of corruption in Western Australia.' *crimefictionlover.com*

'A tightly plotted, well-textured story of shady figures contesting a lease at the beginning of the mining boom ... fast-paced, complex and with some excellent twists ... *Zero at the Bone* is quality crime.' *The Weekend Australian*

'Like an expert surgeon, Whish-Wilson cuts away to reveal an anatomical dissection of corruption and street level history: Perth's geography, class relations, its tribes and sub-cultures, including the most ruthless tribe of all, the cabal of bent cops who act with impunity. Whish-Wilson's writing is terrific, taut and lyrical.' *Crime Factory*

David Whish-Wilson was born in Newcastle, NSW, but grew up in Singapore, Victoria and WA. He left Australia aged eighteen to live for a decade in Europe, Africa and Asia. He is the author of *The Summons*, *The Coves* and three crime novels in the Frank Swann series: *Line of Sight*, *Zero at the Bone* and *Old Scores*. *Shore Leave* is the fourth. His most recent novel, *True West*, was published by Fremantle Press in 2019. His non-fiction book, *Perth*, part of the NewSouth Books city series, was shortlisted for a WA Premier's Book Award. David lives in Fremantle and coordinates the creative writing program at Curtin University.

SHORE LEAVE

DAVID WHISH WILSON

 FREMANTLE PRESS

For Mark

1.

A midnight easterly blew off the desert, gusting in the higher branches. Swann turned the hose onto the garden that ran alongside his shed, soaking the Hardenbergia whose purple flowers had browned in the heat. Marion was asleep in the front room beneath the ceiling fan, but he hadn't been able to drift off.

Swann aimed the hose into the clumps of wattle, woolly bush and banksia. When the plants were mature they wouldn't need watering, but another day like today and they'd be crisp as the leaves under his feet. Swann avoided squirting beneath the concrete slab where two blue-tongue lizards had taken up residence. Their saucer of water beside the nearest shrub was brimming, and he could see the heavy trace-shape of their tails in the sand.

Swann was glad that the lizards had moved in because they kept snakes away. Last year, he'd removed a metre-long tiger snake who'd occupied the same hole, attracted to the motorbike frogs in the neighbour's pond. Swann had nearly trodden on the snake after looking for a cricket ball knocked into the bushes by his nine-year-old grandson, Jock. Swann immobilised the snake's head with the tines of a garden rake and lifted it by the tail, dropping it into a hessian bag. He took it to the dunes behind South Beach and released it.

Swann put his head under the hose and soaked his hair and face. Gone midnight, and it was thirty degrees. Despite the faint moonlight and the floodlit port working through the night, the sky was a sprawl of stars. The crescent moon sat above the roofline of his fibro shack. He could see its pitted surface and the shadows formed by deeper craters. Above him was the Southern Cross and the Milky Way, like fairy floss across the western horizon.

Swann wiped a hand over his wet hair and flicked a spray of droplets into the bushes. He put his hands on his hips as another wave of nausea rose from his belly. He swallowed hard, and it passed. He was getting better at keeping it down, even if his symptoms weren't improving. The headaches were more frequent and the nausea was worse every day. He was lucky that Marion was a nurse, pushing him to get help. She didn't know what was wrong, but then again neither did his doctor, or any of the specialists he'd consulted. Swann was too sick to work but it didn't matter for now. He'd worked solidly these past years and had enough money to last a few months.

The front gate screeched on its hinges. It was Swann's early alarm system, together with the dog, who emerged from underneath the house, growling. Swann walked to the driveway. He recognised the moonlit silhouette of Kerry Bannister, dressed in her regular jumpsuit and blonde wig. Kerry was the long-term madam of the Ada Rose brothel that was a minute's walk from Swann's home.

Swann whistled to the dog, who ceased her growling. She was afraid of the dark and her relief at being called off was demonstrated by her wagging tail and running back and forth between Swann and Kerry. Swann halved the distance between them and Kerry did the same, shoulders set while lighting a cigarette, her weathered face illuminated by the streetlight.

'Couldn't sleep, eh?' she asked, thrusting out a hand for him to shake.

'Not when there's mischievous Christians afoot.'

Last week, as a favour to Kerry, Swann had installed a security camera on the back wall of the brothel, to dissuade whoever kept painting crucifixes there in fluorescent road-marking paint, which was near impossible to remove.

'I'm a witch, don't forget. Safe from their mumbo jumbo. You and Marion should join our coven sometime. Speaking of, is she asleep?'

'Sound. I don't think she'd be keen to frolic at this point.'

The smoke from Kerry's cigarette turned Swann's stomach, and he felt a convulsion in his belly. If the ripple became a wave then Kerry had better stand back.

'It was you I wanted to see. Glad I didn't have to wake you. We've got a bit of a ... hostage situation in room five. Daniel's off sick. And before you ask, the male person concerned doesn't strike me as the Christian type.'

'You call the cops? Who's he with?'

'Montana. And no, I didn't. Thought I'd try you first. With the Yanks coming tomorrow, I don't want to look like I can't manage my affairs.'

'Is the person armed?'

'Don't think so. He's just refusing to come out. Blocked the doorway with the bed.'

The Ada Rose had been open for as long as Swann could remember. It'd been a Ruby Devine brothel until her murder, when Kerry Bannister took it over. Kerry paid the right people, kept the shopfront discreet, looked after her workers and made sure men weren't involved in the day-to-day. The brothel was a kilometre from the port and only became busy when the Yanks were in town, as they would be tomorrow.

Swann put on his jeans, boots and an old tee-shirt he could afford to have ripped, or worse. On his way to the brothel he stopped to heave behind a hedge. His stomach was empty except for the potato and leek soup that was all he could keep down. His jeans hung loose on his hips due to lost weight.

Kerry Bannister and the three other women on shift gathered in the hallway outside room five. They were all dressed in civvies – jeans, sandals and loose shirts. Kerry moved her workers through the business in three-monthly cycles, paying for them to fly in from Sydney and Melbourne, and Swann didn't recognise two of the newest women. He nodded to Havana, who still worked a room but also filled in as manager when Kerry was away. She was a Noongar woman in her late twenties with short black hair, and Kerry's sometime partner. Her fists were clenched and her large brown eyes were fierce with the desire to get at the man behind the door.

'I think he's got her gagged. She's not sayin anythin,' Havana said when Swann knocked on the door.

'Open the door,' he said firmly. 'We just need to know that ... Montana is ok.'

Swann looked to Kerry. 'Punters in the other rooms?'

'Nah, we closed up, soon as this happened. He came in alone. Small bloke, sunburnt face and heavily freckled. Gave his name as Ron Smith. My guess is a cockie, or a miner.'

Swann knocked again but there was no response. He tried the door but it was wedged shut. 'Carlie, could you get what I left at the entrance?'

Swann had used Havana's real name, and she nodded, returning with the chainsaw cradled in her arms.

Swann took the old machine that he'd inherited from Marion's father. He hoped it'd work. It was primed with two-stroke but he had no cause to use it in his suburban backyard. The last time he'd worked the chainsaw was a few years ago when he'd gone to a friend's block outside the city, to carve firewood off a fallen jarrah.

He nodded to Kerry, who stood back as he opened the choke to full and shouted, 'I'm coming in,' then put the machine on the ground and pulled the starter cord. It caught first time, and the smell of exhaust filled the hall along with the deep chuckle of the idling motor. Swann lifted the blade and pressed go. The blade scythed the air and the motor roared. He gave it a good rev and kicked the door. Immediately the handle shuddered, and turned. The door opened a fraction, then more as the bed was dragged away. Montana fled the room, pulling panties from her mouth. The other women formed a circle around her, Carlie foremost, nodding to Swann to enter the room. Instead, Swann killed the motor, and the sound of the chainsaw died away. A small man with ginger hair and an orange moustache dressed in double-denim stared at him. Wore old KT26 trainers on his feet. He raised his hands to show they were empty. Swann stood away and let Kerry into the room. She backed the man into a corner. 'Empty yer fuckin pockets onto the bed. Every last cent. And yer wallet too. I'll be holding yer licence in case of further trouble.'

The man did as he was told. He had plenty of money: two wads of mixed notes, near three hundred dollars, which likely made him a miner. He opened his wallet and spilled cards onto the bed.

Kerry's right fist hovered beside her shoulder. She shouted behind her, 'Montana, you ok? He do anything?'

'She's alright,' Carlie answered.

The man's face was empty of expression. He didn't appear drunk. He edged around Kerry and didn't look at Swann as he passed. Kept his eyes on his feet as he sauntered past the gauntlet of jeers from Carlie and the others.

Kerry patted Swann on the bicep. 'Thanks mate.'

'Not a worry,' Swann answered. 'Where's the toilet?'

'Down the end, where it's always been. You alright? You look peaky.'

Swann hurried down the hall.

2.

Devon Smith wiped his hands on his US Navy coveralls and closed the lid on the industrial dishwasher, waiting to hear the churn of water. The damn thing wasn't working properly. He and Marcus had pre-washed the thousands of dishes by hand before putting them in the machine. Devon had earlier emptied the clogged drain, then crawled beneath the benchtop to check the plumbing while Marcus, who was a black six-footer, looked on with folded arms.

Marcus was like that. You'd ask him to do something hard and dirty and he'd puff his lips and shake his head. He wasn't lazy, but he also wasn't going to get his hands dirty before some white man had given it a try.

Devon Smith and Marcus were the same rank of Kitchen Patrol shitkicker. There was nothing Devon could do about Marcus because their supervisor, Lenny Arnold, was also black. Devon knew that they played cards together on the rear deck after their shifts, whereas outside of work hours Devon and Marcus lived entirely separate lives. The US Navy was supposed to be a family where the only colour that mattered was the uniform, but that wasn't how it went down. The racial politics on board the USS *Carl Vinson* were no different than back in the US, which was alright by Devon Smith.

Devon looked to the clock and saw that it was 1640. Because of the delay, fresh dishes wouldn't be ready for the dinner service unless they both hauled ass, but he needn't have worried. Marcus and Lenny began to pick up the handwashed dishes and give them a cursory wipe with a tea towel before loading them onto the trolleys destined for the mess.

Smith took a towel and went to work alongside them. It was near a hundred degrees in the kitchen and the months of sweat and heavy lifting since the *Carl Vinson* began its tour meant that his arms were corded with muscle.

A day out from port in a white country, and Devon wanted to look his best. The only thing he knew about Australia came from the film *Crocodile Dundee*, and the excited stories of his fellow seamen from the tour a couple of years ago. Summer whites were being pressed and shoes polished. Plans were being hatched around the best places to get laid. Like every unmarried man on the aircraft carrier, Smith was looking to get his nut, but that wasn't all. A man needed a plan, his father had taught him, and he and his father had devised a strategy that would potentially see him rich enough to quit the service. This fact made it easier to stomach working alongside Lenny and Marcus, who as usual were talking too loud and belly-laughing at things that weren't even funny.

3.

Swann drove his Brougham into the parking space reserved for him and Gerry Tracker. On the passenger seat was the morning paper and a thermos of black tea. It'd just gone five in the afternoon and soon the neighbourhood kids would arrive.

Swann took his roll of keys and unlocked the front door. He flicked the lights and the fans. The gym smelt of foot odour, sweat and Goanna Oil, and he went directly to the roller door and cracked the lock. His illness had made him weaker, and he struggled to drive the door up through its guides. As he lifted, fresh air entered the low concrete chamber of what was known locally as Swann and Gerry's boxing gym. There were no signs out front and they hadn't advertised, but word had spread about the free gym for local kids and by six o'clock the place would be full.

The room beneath the video store didn't cost much to rent, and Swann and his friend Gerry Tracker paid it themselves. Swann and Gerry had fought as amateur boxers back in the sixties, and they had decided to start the gym a few years ago after Swann came out of hospital. The gym had begun with a couple of heavy bags and a few sets of gloves but local sports shops and the Maritime Union had donated equipment and money, and now it was crowded with light and heavy bags, weights and ropes, chin-up bars and a full boxing ring in the back corner.

Swann and Gerry Tracker took turns overseeing the nightly circuit of kids doing exercises and sparring. Tonight, Gerry's son Blake, plus a kid who Gerry was training, Lee Southern, were going to take the class. All Swann had to do was open up and watch in case any of the kids got carried away in the ring. Some of the local bouncers and a few stevedores from the port were regulars and helped where needed.

Swann checked the racks of gloves and arranged the skipping ropes from shortest to longest. The sea breeze didn't look like it was coming in today, and he angled one of the fans towards 'Swann's Couch', which some of the Noongar kids had taken off a verge and carried down for him. It was rain damaged but didn't smell any worse than the rest of the equipment in the room. He sat on it now, unfolding his paper. He kicked off his thongs and lifted his legs onto the cushions.

After returning from the brothel, Swann had slept fitfully through the morning while Marion went off to work, only the sound of the dog's barking punctuating the silence of the suburban street. When he awoke there were three messages on the machine that he didn't bother playing. He ate a piece of toast and butter, and then a bowl of yoghurt.

Following his breakfast, Swann dressed and walked to his doctor on Hampton Road. Now in his early fifties, Swann had been a smoker since he was eleven years old. Swann's GP had organised a chest X-ray at Fremantle Hospital and fortunately the results were clear. His bloodwork was also clean of what his doctor called 'the Celtic disease' – the build-up of excessive iron in the vital organs. Swann didn't know who his biological father was, and couldn't give a detailed family medical history, except that his mother had died aged sixty of a heart attack.

After receiving his results, Swann had returned home and showered. It was on his way out the door again that he listened to the answering machine messages. A Paul Tremain of Lightning Resources had called three times. He said it was urgent. Swann deleted the messages and went out into the dull heat of early afternoon.

Swann returned to his newspaper. He was so out of touch that he had to read the date beneath the masthead – Thursday the second of February, 1989. Five-odd years since his double-shooting at the hands of a Junkyard Dogs assassin and Detective Inspector Benjamin Hogan.

Hogan, a corrupt cop, had shot Swann in the stomach and the injury had nearly killed Swann when septicaemia set in, although it was the other injury that suggested long-term damage, after a shotgun pellet nicked Swann's spinal cord.

Swann's wounds had healed, even though there was a risk of re-damaging his spine should his head or neck take a jolt. He'd set himself a target of six months after the shooting before he started swimming and working some light weights, hoping to put rope in his shoulders to better support his neck. The plan had worked, and he'd built up his strength over recent years, at least until the sickness appeared a couple of months ago.

Swann caught the single column on page five discussing Paul Tremain's Lightning Resources. According to assay reports, and now visual confirmation on the part of invited journalists, the Coolgardie mine site contained one of the biggest gold strikes in recent history made by a 'minor player'. The journalist described the forty-centimetre vein of gold that ran for seventeen metres and likely continued deep into the igneous quartz rock, forty metres underground. According to the article, Tremain himself had guided the journalists down into the earth wearing a yellow hardhat and dusty overalls, letting them run their hands over the visible fortune – an estimated five tonnes of gold.

The article didn't mention the reason for Tremain's unusual media invitation in an industry known for its secrecy. Swann had an idea why, however, based on rumours he'd heard that somebody was stealing Tremain's gold. Not a nugget here and there, but kilos of the stuff. According to one rumour, five ten-kilogram bars had disappeared off a commercial flight somewhere between Kalgoorlie and Perth. There had been more alleged thefts at the mine site. The Gold Squad was investigating and added security had been hired for the mine, but the thefts continued.

Swann had known for weeks that Paul Tremain of Lightning Resources would contact him. The thefts were no great mystery, and there was nobody else that Tremain could call upon. There were other PIs in town, but they were all compromised. Swann, however, wasn't going to bite. He'd made a career over the past decade recovering money for investors ripped off by various corporate scams, but until he got better those days were over. He had promised Marion and his daughters, and he was firm on that promise. Swann was in no position to take on the Gold Squad. Tremain's calls would go unanswered.

4.

Tony Pascoe took shallow sips off the oxygen bottle, knowing that he'd need it later. The private room on the fifth floor of Fremantle Hospital was dark and quiet except for the flickering lights of the heart-rate monitor beside his bed. He was no longer connected to it, although a saline drip still ran into his left forearm. His right wrist was handcuffed to a gurney rail.

Pascoe had taken a big risk to get into the hospital, and it'd nearly killed him. At the nearby Fremantle Prison, while his mate Terry Worthington stood guard by the door, Pascoe had suffocated himself with a plastic bag until he'd gone unconscious. That was part of the strategy, although he didn't plan on going into cardiac arrest. For a packet of White Ox, Worthington then ran to the screws and had them call prison medics.

The assumption was that Pascoe had tried to knock himself. After all, he was sixty-seven years old with stage four lung cancer and chronic emphysema. Pascoe only had months left to serve on his twenty-year sentence, but he had no family and hadn't received a visitor for nineteen years. What did he possibly have to live for?

The assumption was fair, but incorrect.

Pascoe had plenty to live for, even if he didn't have much time. The doctors had told him a year at the outside. Six months more likely.

There was no need to rush. Pascoe had grown up in Fremantle, but he hadn't been on the streets for a long time. He'd questioned new inmates about the place; what had changed and what'd stayed the same. There'd been a building boom before the America's Cup – new groynes and sailing club berths in particular. The inner city hadn't changed much, beyond a bit of tarting up. The Fremantle Prison where he'd spent so much of his life was in the middle of the city. From his cell Pascoe could hear the sound of laughter and music from the pubs, the roar of the footy crowd on Saturday afternoons.

It was in his shared cell that he got to know Mark Hurley, sent down for seven years over the possession of a trafficable quantity of cocaine. Mark was twenty-five, but still a kid in comparison. He'd built himself a suit of armour in the exercise yard and developed the thousand-yard stare, but he wasn't hard and never would be.

Pascoe had only known Hurley for a few months, but he'd developed a sense of fatherly responsibility toward the kid, mainly because of what was waiting for him on the outside. Since last week, Hurley was back in the world, released to an uncertain future.

Pascoe had two sons of his own, but God knows he'd never been any kind of father. He hadn't acknowledged either of them, and had never tried to make contact.

There was no point thinking about any of that. It was too late for him and his sons. He wanted only to look after Mark Hurley.

Pascoe thought of his escape, making the pictures in his head. One thing about doing time – it focussed the will. Most kids that entered the system now accepted the medications that made life easier for the screws. The majority were in for drug offences anyway, and it was natural for them to spend their time doped up and passive, but that'd never been Pascoe's way. He was known instead as a prison scholar, having completed two degrees in arts and law, and an MA in philosophy. He'd written poetry that'd been published in journals. His signature oil paintings on plywood were part of a series of abstract expressionist works that were in private collections. He practised Zen meditation for an hour every morning before dawn, sitting on his bed as the world came awake around him. There weren't many in the system who'd done the stretch Pascoe had, who could say, hand on heart, that in twenty years they'd rarely felt bored or lonely.

The battle was to maintain his sense of dignity within the razor-wire confines of the prison walls. The threat was not external but internal. He had spent so much of his life in institutions that it was easy to become dependent, to become part of it, to let it become part of you.

Pascoe had made a life for himself, such as it was, inside the prison. Outside of the hospital, another world awaited, no more real but one requiring a different set of skills.

Pascoe knew that the derelict camps in South Fremantle behind the abandoned factories were still being used, but that the coppers would look for him there. So too the camps beneath the saltbush and tea-tree scrub at the nearest beaches, or in the remnant bush up on Cantonment Hill. Failing to locate Pascoe among the fringe dwellers, they'd expect him to head east, away from the port.

Pascoe reached for the cannula in his wrist. The skin was bruised and inflamed. The nurses didn't know, but last night he'd taken the cannula out. While a nurse leaned over him to tuck his blanket, he'd unclipped the name tag from her pocket. Behind the hinge of the clip was a length of wire. He had used the wire to pick his handcuff, then removed his oxygen mask. There was no guard assigned to him because he was considered too infirm, and with the impending date of his release, hardly a flight risk. When it became quiet in the corridor he'd gone through the darkened wards and helped himself to clothes and money from the cupboards beside each bed. He now had a knapsack, a pair of ladies' trousers, a windbreaker, seventy-four dollars in change, a male driver's licence and a pair of thongs.

Reinserting the cannula took a while, but he'd watched the procedure many times over the past months, since his first collapse and subsequent diagnosis. Now he removed the cannula in a single movement and put his wrist to his mouth, sucking away the blood. He took the wire pick and worked it into the handcuff, stepped off the bed and began to get dressed. He unclipped the five-litre oxygen bottle from its trolley and lifted it into the knapsack, along with the tubing and mask. It was heavy but well hidden. He walked to the door and looked down the hall. Four am, the time Pascoe usually roused himself to meditate. He felt alert and ready. The old excitement of doing wrong began to work its magic, as it had since he was a boy.

5.

Swann had slept well, head buried beneath his pillow. Not once did he awake to the heaving in his stomach or the acid in his gills that sent him staggering toward the toilet. He ate a breakfast of dry toast and coffee and felt well enough to walk the dog into Fremantle. Mya trotted beside him at her odd angle, leading with her left shoulder, the kelpie in her breeding showing through.

It was another hot morning. The easterly wind blew over him and brushed the ocean flat between the new groynes, built for the defence of the America's Cup. The local sailors had gone down four–nil to the Americans, but the race had kickstarted a home-renovation boom whose echoes he could hear in the streets around him: angle grinders, nail guns, bench saws and cement mixers.

Swann had slept so well that the sound of the aircraft carrier USS *Carl Vinson* entering the port, guided by tugs and the blasting of foghorns, hadn't woken him. He saw a group of US sailors on the pavement outside the Italian Club, looking at a street map. They were lost, but when an elderly Italian woman dressed in black passed them, they looked to their feet. Swann could guess, and he saw the relief in their faces as he approached. They were all young, the oldest perhaps twenty, each wearing their summer whites complete with bell-bottomed trousers, Dixie-cup hats and black neckerchiefs. Swann's friend on the *Carl Vinson*, Master-at-Arms Steve Webb, had told him that according to legend, the neckerchief referred to the Greek myth where a drowned sailor needed a place to hide a coin, so to pay the ferryman to cross the River of Styx.

'Sir, we were looking –'

Swann nodded gravely, which made the young midshipman swallow hard. Mya got busy sniffing at the freshly laundered legs that gathered around them, most of the young men looking off into the distance.

Someone had scrawled *Aiderose* on the top corner of their map. Someone else had tried to scratch out the phallus and breasts drawn alongside the address. Swann didn't try and correct their spelling.

'Keep going along this road until you come to Ada or Rose Street, then turn left. You'll find it across the road from the Seaview pub, which should be open. And, word to the wise, your Shore Patrol puts an undercover officer in the Seaview, just to keep an eye. So behave yourselves.'

The story about an undercover patrolman was a lie but Swann was inundated by thankyou sirs, and wide smiles. The Yanks, they were nothing if not polite – merely one of the reasons they so impressed local women accustomed to the regular blunt, broke, Australian male.

Swann left the men and turned into the city streets. The truth was that he felt uneasy about pointing the sailors in the direction of the brothel. In a perfect world, there would be no brothels and no prostitutes, but Swann had lived long enough to observe the laws wax and wane with regards to the various prohibitions. From his experience, making the sex trade illegal just put more women in danger.

Everywhere Swann looked, American sailors in a variety of uniforms milled about on the footpaths, talking to taxi drivers and buying souvenirs while they still had money. The aircraft carrier was in port for two weeks to carry out maintenance. This news wasn't widely known due to security concerns, not even by the sailors and officers themselves, but Swann's Shore Patrol friend had given him the full story. He'd hinted in a letter that Swann's services would certainly be needed.

Swann's usual dog-walking routine was to skirt the town and take in the Fremantle docks, where he'd grown up as a wharf-rat, hanging around the ships and scrounging food and coins off the crews from all corners of the world. The USS *Carl Vinson*, however, wasn't like most ships. It was part of a nuclear-powered fleet whose presence in Australian ports was fiercely opposed by local activists; Swann's eldest and youngest daughters, Louise and Blonny, among them.

Instead of heading to the port, Swann turned south, toward his home. Marion would return from her shift midafternoon, when they'd head to the beach to cool off. During his lay-off from work, Swann was teaching himself to broaden his cooking beyond the regular meat-and-three-veg that he'd grown up with. Tonight he planned to make lasagne and a green salad. Maria at the local deli would give him instructions on the lasagne, and Swann's neighbour Salvatore had already taught him how to make a standard meat sauce. Swann likely wouldn't eat, but hoped that today might be when his appetite kicked back in. Either way, between that and the latest novel he'd cracked into on Marion's recommendation – David Ireland's *The Glass Canoe* – it'd fill the hours before she returned home.

The Mercedes SE sedan in Swann's driveway was a first. A first for the street, too, and possibly the suburb. Its owner wasn't inside the car and Swann scanned the front seats, saw some manila folders and the hilt of a hunting knife wedged in the leather upholstery. Swann's neighbour, Salvatore, waved his hose across the garden bed planted exclusively with roses. He normally waited until dusk to water his roses, which he laid before candlelit altars to the Virgin Mary in each of the rooms of his house. Like many people Swann knew, Salvatore was haunted by something from his past, and like most people, too, he didn't want to talk about it. Sal was naked to the waist and scratching at the tattoo of Jesus Christ on the cross that began at his belly and finished at his neck and shoulders. He had obviously heard Swann's gate creak open and was keeping an eye. He nodded his head toward Swann's front porch, shaded by the large flowering frangipani.

At the first creak of the gate, the visitor sprang from the porch. Swann knew who it was already, but was surprised by the size of the man. He'd never met Paul Tremain, although he knew him as one of the hundreds of mining speculators trying to climb the greasy pole.

Tremain was short and wiry, wearing a tight blue suit and an artificial tan. His dyed black hair was combed in a ruthless side part. His large blue eyes sat above a long nose and a fleshy mouth. His jaw was small and his chin was dimpled. His striding down the drive reminded Swann of the studied poise of the Terrace legal eagles, headed into court. Tremain stopped at precisely the length of the dog's leash, and thrust out his hand.

Swann dropped the leash and Mya scampered to Tremain's legs, began to paw at his knees, offering her head for a scratch. Tremain couldn't help himself – despite the dusty paw prints on his immaculately ironed trousers, he reached down and fondled her ears, genuine affection in his eyes. Dogs were fair judges of character, and Swann accepted the precisely calibrated handshake of their generation and went to the porch. The day was heating up and his scalp was sweaty. He kicked off his thongs. Tremain sat in the chair opposite, Mya nudging his shins for a pat.

'I know who you are, Mr Tremain, and about your situation, but I'm not taking on work right now.'

'So I've heard. But I've tried everyone else –'

'I know. That's why you're here, but like I say ...'

Swann wafted his hands. Mya moved from Tremain and began to sniff around Swann's shopping.

'Some advice then. Of course I'll pay for your time. Whatever you ask.'

Tremain sat forward and nervously worked his hands, saw what he was doing, forced himself to be still. Swann sighed. 'Who's at the mine site? Who's doing your security?'

'Chemex. They're the third firm I've hired. Same result.'

'You need to go offshore. All of the locals work at the behest of the CIB. Their licences, you understand. Who in the Gold Squad?'

'A Detective Sergeant Dave Gooch.'

There was nothing to say, except for the look in Tremain's eyes – he genuinely didn't understand. 'Let me guess,' Swann said. 'After the early thefts from the site, Gooch was made aware of the first shipment from Kal to Perth. The one that went missing.'

'Yes. Every ounce of it. Near eighty thousand dollars worth. Every cent promised to my creditors.'

'Did you know that Gooch has a gold mine, just shy of Leonora? That he has a part-share in three or four leases with Tommaso Adamo?'

Tremain's face flushed with blood. He'd tried to remain calm, but was beyond that now. 'Yes, I did know that, actually. I've done my research. But seriously? This is *nineteen* eighty-nine, not *eighteen* eighty-nine. What are you saying? That I've struck the big one, but that *every bit of it* is going to be taken from me? That I have to sit down there myself in the depths of the earth, seven days a week, with a shotgun, just to keep what's mine?'

'That's not a bad idea.'

Tremain opened his mouth, the sneer written on his face, but thought better of it. He closed his eyes, kept them closed, swallowed his anger.

'Go offshore, you say.'

'Yes. But even then. The temptation, you understand. The threats. The isolation. The opportunity. It's likely that even were a licence to be granted to an overseas firm, that it'd have certain ... conditions. Delays in approval, that sort of thing. I'm assuming you need to act fast?'

'Fast. Yes. The beauty of the strike is that there's near twenty million, according to the geologists, in the one vein. That's unheard of. It doesn't need crushing, or separating. You can carve it out with a hammer and chisel. Which is the problem.'

Even as they were speaking, reflected heat radiating off the drive, honeyeaters chirping in the frangipani leaves, Swann didn't find it hard to imagine Tremain's workers right at that moment working the vein, stealing for themselves and for Gooch and his higher-ups.

'You need to close it down. Fill it in. Cap it with a mountain of cement, until you've got the situation –'

'That's no good. The vein is near the edge of my lease. The only useful thing that Gooch told me is that if I don't get it out soon –'

'Your neighbour will drill across.'

'Yes.'

'Have you been approached by a potential partner?'

'Yes, many, every step of the way. I've told them no. Was that foolish?'

'Depends who they are. Has Gooch –'

'Yes.'

'Unless you want Gooch to take over the whole thing, you need to find someone at a level of government. A minister. A senior public servant. Have you thought about that?'

'I've had meetings with them all, to complain.'

Swann put his hands on the wings of his chair, made ready to stand. His stomach was churning again. The garden was right there, but he didn't want Tremain to see him sick. The dog read his movements and rose on shaking legs.

Tremain, however, remained seated, his eyes elsewhere. He snapped out of it when Swann finally stood. 'But how would that work? Wouldn't there be a conflict of interest, especially after the recent scrutiny of the government doing business with the Conlans? Talk of a Royal Commission?'

'There are ways. Speak to your accountant.'

'I will. Thanks for your time. What do I owe you?'

Swann shook his head. 'Advice is free. Sorry I can't help.' The churning in his guts had become minor spasms, now short violent convulsions.

Swann leaned over the garden and threw up his coffee, holding back the dog by her collar.

When he was finished, Tremain thrust his hand out, his eyes striving for the right note of commiseration. 'I'm sorry, I didn't realise you were unwell. You've been through a lot.'

He sounded genuine, which saddened Swann, because it was precisely the reason that Tremain was being robbed blind.

6.

Devon Smith scraped gravy and potato crud off the last of the plates, took the water-blaster and scoured the stacks, covering the splashback with pieces of the same crapola before turning the high-pressure hose on the splashback too.

Devon watched the water drain into the massive sink. He took up the handle on the brushed steel dishwasher and lifted, stepped away. The greasy steam that enveloped him smelt of bacon fat, stale eggs and rotten cabbage from where the drain filter was clogged. After he replaced the plates and cutlery in their trolleys, loaded and removed the next wash, he'd have to empty the drain – his least favourite job. He was supposed to empty it after every meal service, but the smell was so foul that it made him gag as he reached his fingers inside the filter and scraped it out. Instead, he changed the filter every couple of days, and never the day before his rostered holiday, which was Monday. It was a small act of defiance, pathetic really, but that was what it'd come to.

The other Kitchen Patrol crewmen were on shore leave, along with three thousand other ranks, the officers staggering the release of personnel into the port. That left two thousand ranks on board – essential staff mainly – the guns manned and the divers still patrolling the vast hull beneath the waterline every few hours in case of a terrorist attack. All of the pilots were on shore leave, as were the pointers and strikers – the staff who made landing and taking off on a moving platform possible.

Devon Smith had joined the US Navy hoping to be one such specialised crewman, but after his ninety days of TAD, or temporary assigned duty in the galley, he hadn't been assigned elsewhere, like all the others from his cohort. He'd wanted to try out as a gunner but after another ninety days he had the same result – kept back in the galley. Even on Kitchen

Patrol he'd failed to impress the team of cooks and their supervisors, who'd banned him from knife and grill work, claiming that he didn't have the temperament to contribute to a team environment. Devon Smith had finally found his level working as a permanently assigned dishwasher in the scullery, something he hadn't told his dad or anyone else back in San Diego. New midshipmen and women came and went, doing their ninety days of shit work before being transferred to more important duties, but Smith was stuck where he was. It took him the full six months to figure out that his nickname in the scullery, *one-dee-ten-tee*, wasn't some nigger word but was instead navy slang for idiot.

That was about to change. With plenty of the KP on shore leave, wandering around in their summer whites pretending they were real sailors, lying through their teeth as they angled for a thirteen-button salute with a local girl, Smith had been reassigned back into the galley to help prepare a special meal service for the officers on shore. Until now Devon didn't know how he was going to get his contraband off ship, but he considered himself smarter than they gave him credit for. It was almost like the amount of shit he'd received was part of a higher plan, designed to get him to this position. He did know one phrase of navy slang, however, reinforced by repeating it over and over, and was something that he was looking forward to saying.

Alpha Mike Foxtrot.

Adios, motherfuckers.

7.

Swann heard a car door slam. He peered from behind the front-room curtain, watched a taxi pull away as the tanned and fit-looking US Navy Master-at-Arms Steven Webb, dressed in tropical whites – shorts, long socks and short-sleeved shirt – took off his cap and opened the gate. The dog crawled out from underneath the house and slunk toward the stranger, trying to raise her hackles but betrayed by her rapidly wagging tail.

It was midmorning and Marion had left for work. Swann had planned on another day of taking it easy until midday, when he was on babysitting duty for his two grandchildren, Jock and Neve. They were both keen swimmers and he usually took them to the pool, or the beach if the Fremantle Doctor wasn't blowing.

Swann cracked the front door and mock-saluted the American.

'Swann. Glad you're home. Been keeping well, I hope?'

'Yeah. Fine,' Swann lied, immediately regretting it. 'I got your letter. Take a seat. You on duty or just showing the colours to the lower ranks?'

'Bit of both. I've got a bottle of overproof Cuban rum with your name on it.'

The idea of drinking didn't appeal, but Swann played along. 'Isn't there an embargo on that kind of thing? The Cold War and whatnot?'

'Not for the finer things. They get traded through the merchant navy, then come to us.'

'Got the brig ready?'

'I'm afraid so. I had some repeat offenders clean it yesterday, as a taste if they screw up again and go AWOL with one of your local ladies. Say, you've lost weight, my friend.'

Swann told him what had happened, adding the part about his new sickness, and Webb nodded attentively. Before joining the navy, Webb had been a Washington beat cop, and later, a detective. They'd traded cop stories over bottles of whisky the last time the *Carl Vinson* was in port. Since then, apart from a voyage back to the US for a refit, she'd been out patrolling the Indian Ocean at the behest of President Reagan, and now President Bush, who wanted a demonstration of American resolve in Iran's backyard.

As the conversation moved to the purpose of Webb's visit, the American looked concerned. Swann put Webb at ease. 'I've got two young men working for me, who can do the legwork if I'm unable. They're learning the ropes, but reliable.'

The last time the *Vinson* was in port, just prior to the most recent corporate frauds whose investigations had supported Swann financially ever since, he had been desperate for work. When Steve Webb had quizzed Kerry Bannister at her brothel about several AWOL midshipmen, she'd walked Webb around the corner to Swann's house. The navy had its Shore Patrol, but they lacked local knowledge. It didn't take Swann long to track the sailors. Webb had the name of their last watering hole, and that was all Swann needed. Twenty dollars to the barman and he had some names, Webb standing beside him looking puzzled. He'd offered the barman the same amount a few hours earlier, receiving a firm 'sorry, can't help ya'. Swann put through a call to a traffic cop friend and then they had addresses to accompany the names. The first apartment-block in suburban Mosman Park was dark, but the next in downtown Claremont was lit up with disco-ball reflections shimmering across the front windows. As they approached, the sound of Prince's 'Kiss' made the windows tremble in their frames. Swann took the front door while Webb covered the back. He'd told Swann stories of men he'd tackled in backyards and stairwells over the years, barefoot and with their pants barely fixed.

The three AWOL African-American sailors looked crestfallen. Swann felt immediately sorry for them. Their new friends pleaded with them to stay. They were all young western-suburbs women with healthy tans, white teeth and ski-ramp noses. Uni student types, being no-strings adventurous. In this they weren't alone. Whenever Yank ships floated into port, the number of women in the city swelled by thousands. They frequented Pinocchios, Rumours, the Red Parrot and other clubs where the sailors were taken by knowing taxi drivers. Sometimes the relationships that started on the dancefloors became permanent, but more often they were one-night stands, both parties looking for a bit of fun. And why not, Swann thought, watching the sailors kiss the Claremont kids goodbye. The lovers wouldn't be meeting again that time, however – the sailors were AWOL, which meant time in the brig, shit-bird duty and a small drop in their rating for the next months, if they were lucky.

Webb took out a packet of Camels from his pristine shirt pocket, offered one to Swann, who shook his head. 'You quit?'

'I haven't felt up to smoking, or drinking for that matter, for a few months.'

'You mind if I?' Webb asked, lighting the cigarette with his service zippo. 'It's great to hear that you've got capable friends, in case I need them, but I was hoping that you could help me this morning. Shouldn't take long. This particular midshipman's friends tell me he's somewhere in Fremantle. Last seen in your local pub, the Seaview, while his amigos ducked into the bordello of the formidable Kerry Bannister. He can't have gone far and it's only a minute walk from here. Thought you might want to accompany me?'

Swann looked at his watch. He had time. The dog, Mya, recognised the signal of Swann shuffling into his thongs. She wrinkled her nose at the smoke coming off Webb's hand but got hopefully to her feet, slinking to rub her face into Swann's shins.

'Sure, I've got a couple of hours. He have any kind of record or history I should know about?'

For Swann, it was a routine question, especially now that he felt physically compromised; his legs and arms gone soft with the months of disuse, his reflexes slow. Webb waved a hand. 'Nothing I'm aware of.'

Webb's answer caught Swann's attention by its tone. Webb was the classic cheerful American, using his charm to open conversations but also to shut them down. He seemed to genuinely like Swann, but was always guarded when it came to questions about his fellow servicemen and women.

'Bring the dog if she wants to come, Frank,' was all he added. 'I miss dogs.'

Webb had shown no interest in Mya, despite her imploring eyes, sniffing at his bare legs all the while. Swann presumed Webb to mean that a loyal dog might be useful in defusing a potentially tricky situation. Swann tapped his thigh and Mya came to heel, slinking beside him as they rounded into the street, smiling at Webb and only ducking her eyes when wattlebirds flew overhead.

The Seaview Hotel was Swann's local. It'd seen better years, back when workers from the local fellmongers, tannery, biscuit factory and the nearby docks flooded in around knock-off time. It still catered to residents loyal to Old Tom, the Serbian publican who'd bought it with a lotto win. Tom ran the lodging house upstairs, although he'd leased the bar to Sydney gangster Abe Saffron a couple of years back. The business was used to launder Saffron's money, who'd refurbished the place and otherwise used it as a money sink, hiring Tom as bar manager.

Tom watched them come, wiping a glass with a dirty towel. The bar was hot with the smell of stagnant air and unwashed beer mats.

Swann made the introductions while Tom delivered his inscrutable Buddha smile. It was a smile suitable for all manner of situations, including the moment prior to wading into a mob of drunken fishermen with his rounders bat.

Swann told Tom what they were after – sailors who'd rented a room for the night.

'Black one or white one?' was all he replied.

'Black one,' answered Webb.

Tom took a roll of keys off his belt and tossed them to Swann. 'Room six. Next to stairs.'

Swann thanked Tom and they took the staircase that rose through the building, the old boards creaking in their carriage posts. 'Economical with words, your friend,' said Webb, who now sported wet patches under his armpits and down his back.

'That was him being talkative,' Swann replied. 'Your Yankee ways rub off on people.'

At the top of the stairs, Swann searched through the keyring. Tom's lodging house was a carnival of scents for the dog. She darted from Swann's legs to the overflowing bins and the stains on the carpet, the sticky substances on the bannister.

Swann nodded to the nearest door, the aluminium number 6 missing one screw and fallen to make a 9. Webb knocked loudly. A toilet flushed behind them in the communal shower. Swann turned and watched a thin hairy man with a neck tattoo and a towel around his waist exit the toilet, clock them and grimace. Tom's rooms were also rented out to the prison service as a halfway house for newly released inmates, and the man had gaol written all over him. Swann ignored him and turned to Webb, who knocked again before asking for the key. Swann handed it over and waited. Webb unlocked the door and toed it wide. A single bed with strewn sheets. Barred window closed, despite the heat. Ceiling fan not moving. Swann waited outside, although he was getting that feeling – some rooms just felt like a crime scene. Webb felt it too, looking carefully at the walls, behind the door, under the bed. Picked up the bin and showed Swann the used condoms. Swann knelt and ran his fingers through Mya's silky ears. She knew something was wrong, and didn't enter the room. Webb lifted the mattress and began looking underneath.

'Locked from the outside,' said Swann. 'But the key not returned. Perhaps your man's already –'

'I don't think so.'

Webb extracted a wallet from inside the mattress. A fat black wallet, stray fibres of mattress-stuffing in its fold. 'Old navy practice, called the Mexican bank. Done it myself once or twice. Every cathouse in every port, you'll find sliced pockets in the mattresses, always on the bottom by the feet.'

'But that's a new mattress.'

'Yes, it is.'

'So sailor boy has a knife, not here.'

Webb nodded, opened the wallet and took out an ID card, looked at it, put it back.

'He might've been drunk, forgot it.'

'Never happen, Frank. Either he's in the wind, doesn't need ID for his imagined new life and wanted us to find it here, or something's not right. Let's go and speak to Mr Friendly downstairs. Gonna need to rent this room for a while.'

'Tom mentioned another sailor – a white one. Should we?'

Webb pocketed the wallet, took a last look around the room. 'Yes, we should, but first let's get the room sealed. Sorry about this, Frank. Thought it'd be routine ...'

Swann had heard that before. He looked out over the balcony, across the carpark to his backyard. His old shed roof, shaded by an ancient white gum. Behind him, Webb locked the door, jangled the keys for Swann to take. Swann turned as the first convulsion rose from his belly. There wasn't time to make it to the toilets. He put up a hand and leaned over the balcony.

8.

Tony Pascoe kept his head down, hoping that the Esso cap he'd stolen and his long white beard would conceal his face. He proceeded down the nearest suburban street, heading away from the coastline and marina.

Pascoe made sure to walk like a civilian. He kept his gait open, like he was innocent of every thought beyond heading home to water the garden or feed the dog, or whatever suburban people did to fill in their time.

Pascoe was nine hours on the run, and the coppers would be looking. It was a risk to leave his hide in the yacht club, where he'd broken into a cabin cruiser off Capo D'Orlando Drive, down the furthest end of a long jetty. The cruiser was a sixty-footer named *Easy Rider*. As he'd hoped, the interior was layered with dust on the sheoak veneer surfaces. It was likely that the super-rich owner only used it occasionally in summer, if at all. There were drawn blinds on the windows and the cupboards were stocked with canned steak 'n' onions, rice pudding, two fruits and baked beans. Pascoe was used to prison food and could eat the rations cold while sitting in the darkness. So confident was the owner of the yacht club security that there was a spare key hidden inside a biscuit tin. Pascoe didn't know how to drive a boat, but he liked the thought of heading west when his job was done. The liquor cabinet was stocked with single malts and tequila. He could steam out into the great wide ocean until the fuel sputtered out, then drift, and drink himself to death.

The only things that Pascoe had taken off the boat were a fishing rod and an army surplus flare gun. He carried the fishing rod in his left hand, hoping to look like a typical old man returning from a day's fishing at the Mole. It was a stubby boat rod and useless for land-based fishing, but he gambled that nobody would look closely. Pascoe wore the backpack heavy with the oxygen tank and the flare gun. He kept a steady pace

33

through the flatter streets, trying to regulate his breathing. The vast open sky and the ordinary smells of restaurant cooking and car exhaust were intoxicating after so many years inside, and he tried to keep his eyes off the new-model vehicles and the fashions worn by the pedestrians headed into town. Even from a casual observation, it was clear that the cars had lost their sixties curves and gone boxy. When Pascoe had entered the prison in 1970, Japanese imports were limited to the rare Toyota Crown or Nissan Cedric – now the plastic bumpers and rice-burner engines were common. The fashions however hadn't changed much. Men still wore their hair long, and flannel and jeans remained the norm. The few women he saw on the street who weren't nonnas in funereal black wore pale blue jeans and permed hair, with bright lipstick.

Leaving the yacht club during the daylight hours was a risk but Pascoe needed a gun. Until the cancer had mowed him down, he'd been as handy as any other prisoner, but now any kind of physical confrontation meant that he was liable to collapse and die.

Pascoe tried to focus his mind on his breathing and his slow, even steps. Walking meditation. Fighting was a useful thing to let his thoughts drift across, however, now he was fighting to survive from day to day. He listened to his whistling lungs and the slapping of his thongs on the footpath.

Pascoe didn't know how the new generation was being raised, but when *he* was a kid, a boy's capacity to explode from zero to a hundred in a matter of seconds was required learning. Until young men mastered the necessary coolness of temperament that came with experience, it was always considered better that they learn how to overwhelm an opponent.

Pascoe had been that young man, but he'd matured out of it. He'd learned that fighting was a cold art, like calligraphy or flower arranging. Meditation had taught him many things about himself, and one of them was that he'd wasted an enormous amount of energy maintaining that explosive simmer throughout his childhood, teens and early manhood. It was exhausting and futile, when set against the clarity of mind that a trained fighter managed even in the heat of a life-and-death struggle. The Zen-trained samurai had it right – Bushido – the way of the warrior. Every time a man lost his temper to win a battle he was closer to losing the war against himself – the only war that really mattered.

Pascoe took backstreets, pausing twice to enter a quiet driveway and take a hit off the oxygen bottle. It was only a twenty-minute walk to the southern end of South Terrace, but he spaced it to an hour. The women's trousers he wore pinched at his ankles, and the backpack was heavy. It was a long shot, but as soon as he rounded into Harbour Street he saw that it'd paid off.

Des Ryan's old worker's cottage was still there, five houses up from the Davilak Hotel. The sight of Ryan's house near the hotel cheered him. Pascoe had grown up in the Davilak, running errands for Con Murphy, the pub's resident SP bookie, watching the fights that spilt out onto the terrace so regularly that you could set your clock to ten minutes before the six o'clock swill. Sometimes the fights were between two men, and sometimes twenty, stopping traffic and the tram service that ran down to South Beach. Sometimes Pascoe and Des Ryan would leap into the fray, throw a few punches and run off laughing.

The stables at the head of the street were gone, replaced with a small park. When Pascoe had grown too big to be a jockey, he'd hoped to be a trainer, but that dream never eventuated. Instead, he graduated to petty crime and helping Des Ryan's father with his sly-grog operation among the brothels of Bannister Street. The Ryans were a big family in the Fremantle racing, sly-grog and gambling games, but there was Des Ryan's house, looking just as run-down as it always did. Piled on the porch was the same rusting BP sign, the same milk crate full of old horseshoes and the same spider webs in the sash-window frames – like the past nineteen years hadn't happened.

Pascoe opened the creaking gate and stepped onto the porch. The front door was open. Inside, he could hear a transistor radio tuned to the racing channel. He put his face to the flyscreen and could smell bacon and cabbage. It looked like he was in luck.

9.

Swann presented his thumb. The American MD pricked it with a needle, then squeezed out a thorn of blood onto a glass specimen plate.

'Done.'

The navy doctor's name was Maria Gonzalez. She had a small round face with almond-shaped eyes, and she hummed while readying the plate under the microscope. Swann had already been CT-scanned. The celluloid images were clipped onto a white glass projector above the doctor's head. Even from Swann's position on the bed he could see the dozens of shotgun pellets still in his shoulders, neck and jaw. There were dozens more scattered through his chest and lower back.

Swann had assumed that after his shooting the surgeons had removed all of the pellets, but Dr Gonzalez had told him that removing each pellet wasn't the norm, at least in the US. It was also unusual to Swann that there were pellets in his back and chest. He'd been shot from behind and above, and the fortunately distant blast had sprayed his head, neck and shoulders. He asked her, and Dr Gonzalez told him that it was common for pellets to migrate through the body. She described her first job interning in a Chicago public hospital ER unit before she'd joined up, where such gunshot wounds were common.

It was Webb who'd suggested Swann see the resident shift doctor of the *Carl Vinson*. Webb had invited Swann onto the aircraft carrier, to shout him lunch in the officers' galley, but Swann was only three feet up the gangway when he'd hurled into the blue harbour waters.

'Worst case of sea legs I've ever seen,' Webb joked, before guiding Swann down through the Minotaur maze that was the ship's lower decks. Even with half of the crew on shore leave, the corridors were crowded with sailors, marines, pilots and officers going about their business. Webb had stopped outside the brightly lit doorway that led into the hospital ward. A young white sailor sat in a chair holding his bloodied head, eyes avoiding Webb's glare, reeking of booze.

'Even navy hospitals have waiting rooms, as you can see. But you can come through with me, Frank.'

The regular hospital smell of soap and rubbing alcohol had made Swann's stomach churn, but he didn't have long to wait. Dr Gonzalez emerged from a nearby office. She was short, even with her bun of black hair and elevated shoes. She shook Swann's hand as Webb described his previous shooting and slow recovery, his recent symptoms of fatigue, nausea, vomiting and abdominal pain. Both Webb and Dr Gonzalez seemed to know what was going on, even if Swann didn't. Dr Gonzalez nodded at each of the symptoms, as though Webb were describing a common cold. Webb joked to her that Swann was his specially appointed deputy sheriff while the *Vinson* was in port, and that because Swann's Australian doctors didn't know what was wrong with him, he'd like Dr Gonzalez to run some tests. He asked the doctor to call when she had results, because meanwhile he had to follow up on an AWOL sailor.

'Take care, Frank. Our facilities here are better than most hospitals on land. I'll bring you back a sandwich. *Doc*.'

Dr Gonzalez gave Webb the peace sign. She had moved to Swann and stuck her fingers into his throat glands, watching his reaction, which was to pull away and retch. She then took a sample of his blood.

'The symptoms are getting worse, or staying the same?'

'Getting worse. What's your call, doctor?'

'My call?'

'If you were a betting person?'

She smiled. 'That wouldn't be a fair bet. I'm pretty certain of a diagnosis, but we'll have to wait for spectrometer analysis of your blood, which needs to be sent to a lab stateside.'

'Don't worry about that. I'll get it done here. In the meantime ...'

'As you wish. I can confirm my suspicions by looking at your blood under the electron microscope, but you'll need that spectrometry done if my suspicions are correct, to get the definitive picture.'

Dr Gonzalez went to a broad desk, shifted aside some test tubes and a steel-cased centrifuge before flicking a switch. The largest machine on the desk, which looked like a space-age coffee machine, came to life with a low murmur that for some reason made Swann even more nervous.

'They keep you busy in here?'

Dr Gonzalez's smile told Swann that she'd picked up on his nerves. He felt like a kid in the VD clinic for the first time, sweating on the results, except that in this case he was beginning to fear the worst. Was it his liver, gone into terminal decline? Swann's stepfather Brian had died of liver failure after copping a beating, and when it came on, the end was fast – six weeks from diagnosis to death – and *his* symptoms prior to the beating had been the same. Like his stepfather, Swann too had been an alcoholic throughout his thirties, struggling to cope with a detective's workload, internal copper politics, a failing marriage and a young family. The truth of course was that he hadn't coped.

Dr Gonzalez nodded, smiling wryly as she loaded the slide containing Swann's blood into the machine. 'Yes. Despite regulations, we get plenty of workplace accidents. Strained backs, wounds that require operations. Sometimes the men fight, as you'd expect. Long hours and cramped quarters. And then there's shore leave, our busiest time. Traffic accidents, muggings, the contraction of tropical illnesses, bar fights and venereal disease.'

The doctor stopped talking as she slipped on her reading glasses, sat astride a low stool, leaned over a brightly lit panel. Swann wanted to keep making conversation, but suspected that he'd get no reply. Dr Gonzalez tweaked a few dials and nodded, looked back at the panel and jotted notes on a yellow pad.

'If you'd come here, Deputy Sheriff. Look over my shoulder.'

Swann did as he was told. The level of detail was incredible. On the screen was a rectangle full of red spheres, squashed on one side, resembling cushions that'd been sat on. Transparent white shapes that looked like jellyfish.

Dr Gonzalez pressed a button that took a photograph of the image. She began to count the transparent white shapes, dabbing the tip of her pencil onto the screen as she counted.

'What am I looking at?'

'The bloodwork of a very sick man, I'm afraid.'

Swann's heart sank.

'You see those red blood cells with stippled blue shades and even worse, blue dots? You'll notice that one in about every dozen cells is so coloured. That is evidence of severe lead poisoning. Like I say, this isn't a precise reading of levels, but what's in front of me confirms that diagnosis. Your white cell count is way higher than it should be, too.'

Now Swann understood. He remembered Webb's and the doctor's knowing looks earlier, as the doctor examined his healed wounds. The CT image and evidence of dozens of shotgun pellets still in his body.

'My doctor told me that lead pellets missed during the operation wouldn't cause long-term damage.'

Dr Gonzalez pressed another button and a printer whirred on a desk behind them. 'Your doctor was correct. Generally, the body heals over bullets and pellets with a form of internal scar tissue, sealing them off from the bloodstream, but that's only in muscles.'

'Meaning?'

'Meaning, most likely, that some of the pellets penetrated a blood vessel or an internal organ. Lead pellets are soft enough to deform upon contact, and because they're small can be passed through the body, settling in organs where they break down and become diffused, ultimately poisoning the bones. The long-term consequences are often fatal, I'm afraid.'

There, she'd said it. Even though the doctor's bedside manner throughout their meeting had indicated bad news, it still came as a shock. She pushed away her stool and looked up at him. Hers were eyes that'd seen plenty. Swann knew those eyes because he had them too. A doctor, like a copper, having to relay the worst kind of news, to a terminally ill patient, or a dead child's mother and father.

'Please, Frank, sit down on the bed. This is serious, but it's also reasonably common ... at least in the US.'

Swann did as he was asked. He couldn't meet her eyes. Strangely, perversely, at that moment he felt fine. No nausea, or pain. He was in shock.

When he finally spoke, his words came from a long way off. 'Is there anything –?'

'Yes, there is, fortunately. You need to begin immediate chelation therapy. It's a substance taken orally or by injection that bonds to the lead, and is passed out of the body by natural means. You're very lucky to have caught this early.'

Swann didn't quite understand. 'You mean that this ... chelation therapy, can cure the poisoning? Entirely?'

Dr Gonzalez nodded. 'Yes, although you'll need to manage it for many years. Regular tests. Monthly, then yearly. It's possible for lead poisoning to occur in gunshot victims, even decades after the initial trauma. The good news is that you've only been sick for a few months. Any damage to your organs or bones is likely to be minor, although potentially significant depending upon underlying factors, such as heart, liver or lung disease. You seem reasonably healthy otherwise, based on the standard indicators – blood pressure, heart rate et cetera.'

Swann hadn't noticed, but Webb was there in the doorway, listening; a plastic-wrapped sandwich in his hand. He shared a look with the doctor that told Swann they were more than friends.

Swann stood, and wrapped the doctor in a hug. 'Thanks, doc. I owe you one. And you too, Webb.'

Webb smiled, but there was strain in it. 'That's good, Frank. Because ...'

Webb looked at Dr Gonzalez again. She understood, and went about her business, placing the printed photograph of Swann's bloodwork into a manila envelope. When she'd finished, she handed it to Swann and wished him well. Webb stood in the doorway, his eyes saying that he was the bearer of bad news.

10.

Devon Smith nursed his beer and watched the police come and go. He'd arrived at the pub early to scope for exits and suspicious-looking drinkers among the dozen men seated at the stick. They had the look of regulars familiar to dive-bars everywhere: middle-aged and lonely, with doughy complexions and soft muscles.

The pub had a quiet atmosphere, even though Devon suspected that it was busier than usual because of all the police. They were mostly detectives in neutral-coloured suits, boring ties and cheap functional shoes. Nothing like the narcotics and vice detectives who worked the Gaslamp district of San Diego – with their gangster flair and loud voices – part of the street theatre of the area he called home. Smith could easily imagine the local detectives seated at the bar alongside the local drinkers, who were barely energised by the police presence, eyes darting from their beers when they thought it was safe to look.

There was a uniformed officer at the foot of the stairs, which led up to what was presumably a boarding house for wet-brains. The cop was a big blond unit, wide across the shoulders with paws the size of baseball mitts. He was a fine example of Aryan manhood, although his blue cotton uniform was also on the plain side, and made him look like an oversized boy scout. At a holster on his belt was a six-shot .38 S&W revolver, another point of difference. Last year, the police at home had all switched to the Glock 17, a lightweight mostly polymer pistol with a large magazine and no external safety or hammer – meaning a fast draw and easy repeat firing. Smith imagined himself in a shootout with the policeman. His Glock versus the Aussie cop's S&W. Smith would prevail because of the Austrian pistol's safe-action feature, and also because the cop had probably only fired his weapon down at a gun range, unlike

Smith. The thought made Smith happy. He'd have to work that into his sales-pitch – the fact that with a Glock in your hand the local police were outgunned.

Smith had no idea what the police were doing upstairs and he didn't care. He hadn't been off the *Vinson* since Yemen, having had his shore leave revoked for the most recent port of call in Mombasa, Kenya. The black sailors taking leave in Mombasa had been thrilled at the thought of banging whores of their own kind, and hadn't shut up about it when they got back from the bars and cathouses in what looked another sweaty and stinking port. Fremantle, however, looked more like Smith's kind of place – clean and mostly blue-collar white. On his way from the *Vinson* to the Seaview Hotel, he'd seen a few examples of the local blacks, all of them poor looking and some of them clearly homeless, hanging around a soup kitchen. To Devon Smith that was another tick on the positive side of the ledger – a sign that the Aussies had their social pyramid the right way up, unlike what was happening back at home.

Devon Smith looked at his cheap-ass watch, a fake Rolex bought in Yemen. The biker was due in ten minutes. Devon hoped that Barry Brown wouldn't be put off by the presence of police in the bar. They looked like they were leaving anyway, one detective in a beige suit and tan tie with a ginger moustache carrying a fingerprint kit in a plastic suitcase. There were no other sailors in the bar at this hour despite the brothel across the road. Smith checked himself in the mirror behind the bottom-shelf spirits – Jim Beam and Jameson, Beefeater gin and Smirnoff vodka. Something called Stone's green ginger wine, and Brandavino. Captain Morgan rum.

Smith wasn't in uniform, despite the regulations. He'd worn his summer whites off the *Vinson* but changed in a toilet block at the edge of a park, stowed the uniform in a haversack.

Smith straightened the collar on his freshly ironed Fred Perry polo, which showed off his tattoos. His father had become a member of the California Aryan Brotherhood in San Quentin back in the sixties, and had brought Devon up in the life. Devon hadn't been to prison himself, so wasn't officially entitled to wear the shamrock, Celtic cross or the numerals 88, but they'd both figured that it was a matter of time. Devon's father had done the tattooing himself, a trade he'd learnt while locked up. It was Devon's father who'd made contact with the Aussie biker when he learned that Devon was going out on the *Carl Vinson*. The meet was difficult to organise, done by letters and aerograms. It was made more complicated by the fact that a shit-heel sailor like Devon wasn't informed of the *Vinson's* route on its world tour, let alone the possible dates and duration of his arrival. But a meet had been arranged and Devon received a name and phone number to call. He'd dropped the twenty-cent piece from a public phone in the same park where he'd changed into his civvies of polo shirt, khaki Dickies trousers and Converse high-tops. The voice that answered was male, and middle-aged, the Australian accent broad and deep.

Smith looked around at the drinkers a final time, wondering if one of them was his man. None of them looked likely, although it was hard to tell – his father, for example, had gone to seed because of the beer and crank. There were a couple of Mediterranean types which he could discount, and the white men looked too weak-chinned and hokey.

Smith looked to his watch again. The final policeman had left and the bartender reappeared: a fat Slav-looking thing with a sweaty face and monobrow. Smith followed the man's eyes as a shadow fell across him. He heard the voice, and turned in his seat.

11.

Webb dialled in the zoom of his Minolta, waiting for an opportunity. They were parked in a picnic ground on a rise above the Canning River. Beneath them on the river's edge, three homicide detectives walked the riverbank while two forensic staff in white jumpsuits and waders stood thigh-deep in the water, largely hidden behind a clump of reeds. The tea-coloured water was barely ruffled by the wind. Pelicans floated further out and cormorants sat drying their wings on guano-basted pylons. To their left was the nearest headland, the choke point straddled by the Mount Henry Bridge, loud with commuter traffic.

Swann took a swig of lukewarm tea and capped the thermos, dropped it on the floorpan. 'I'm ready. You ready?'

'I don't see anything in the water.'

Webb had received the courtesy call from the chief of the CIB, relaying the news that he needed to get down to the park. The matter was in relation to a US midshipman. The CIB chief hadn't mentioned anything about a homicide or forensics squad. Swann and Webb tried ten minutes ago to enter the crime scene but were waved back by a surly uniformed constable too young to recognise Swann.

'Oh no.'

Webb's voice carried the full horror.

Down on the shoreline, the two forensics staff in waders floated out a corpse from among the reeds.

It was a woman, a civilian, facedown.

'What the hell?' Webb hissed. 'Who's the senior detective? Why was I called here?'

Swann felt sick in his stomach. 'How many female navy staff on shore leave, last night?'

Webb shook his head. 'I don't know. Forty? Fifty?'

'Let's go down there.'

Webb looked ashen as he climbed out of the car. The police photographer began taking pictures of the woman's corpse, following the pointed fingers of the tallest forensics officer and using his zoom for the finer details.

A taped perimeter had been set, but Swann and Webb wandered down to the three detectives who this time turned to watch them come. Swann recognised one of them, an old-stager by the name of Mike Cassidy – not an enemy, but not a friend either, judging by Cassidy's reaction. Swann thrust out his hand and introduced Webb.

Cassidy looked away from Swann to the river, where the two forensics staff were gently cradling the young woman, lifting her towards the plastic sheet on the shore. Cassidy made the sign of the cross, wiped a hand over his rough brown chin. As an afterthought, he introduced Swann to his two peers, ignoring the American officer. Swann shook their hands and nodded in turn. They were British imports, part of the new recruitment drive, with clear blue eyes in faces undamaged by the sun.

The five of them watched the body placed upon the plastic sheet, wet strands of hair concealing her face.

'Is she American?' Webb asked tentatively. 'I don't recognise her.'

'No, she isn't,' replied Cassidy, looking for Webb's reaction. 'She's a local.'

'Then I don't mean to intrude, or step on toes,' Webb said quietly. 'But do you mind telling me why I'm here? I was told that it had something to do with a naval serviceman.'

Cassidy grinned like a wolf. 'There was a witness. Last night, walking her dog. An old woman but with good eyesight. Said she saw a sailor here, canoodling with a young woman, who had an Australian accent. This morning doing the same walk, she saw the body.'

'Did she describe the serviceman?'

'She did. Big tall American negro. Scar on the left side of his face. Shiny scar, reached from his ear to his mouth.'

'I'd like to speak to the witness, if possible.'

Webb couldn't possibly have wrung more politeness out of his words, but Cassidy wasn't impressed. 'No, you bloody can't.'

Swann cleared his throat. 'If this is what it looks like, Cassidy, then you're going to need access. Webb here is going to be your liaison.'

Webb looked uncomfortable. 'That's not entirely true,' he said. 'A potential felony crime like this will need to be investigated by a NISCOM special agent.'

There was more, but Cassidy lacked the patience. 'But? Spit it out!'

'Our resident special agent flew out this morning, back stateside, to complete some training. It'll take days for a replacement to be sent here from HQ. So yes, it's me for the time being. Liaison, and able to assist with –'

'You're not assisting with anything, my American mate. Not if I can help it.'

Swann lowered his voice. 'Webb is an ex-cop. He can be of help.'

Cassidy looked Swann up and down. 'Never too far from trouble, are you?'

There was a lot of history in that statement – history that Webb and the two Brit detectives weren't privy to, but Swann let it slide.

'I never had a problem with you, Cassidy.'

Cassidy didn't hide his contempt. 'What's your role here? Working for a foreign power? You helping the Septics do what they always do? Hold, delay, cover up until they set sail again? By which time it's too late? I've still got two unsolved rape cases on my desk from when I worked sex crimes – the last time these pricks were in town.'

'Now hang on, fellas.' Webb put a hand between them. 'There's only so much we can –'

Swann looked hard at Webb. 'Is that true?'

Webb shook his head. 'That wasn't the *Carl Vinson*. I can assure you –'

The American fell silent at the look on Swann's face, who stared at the murdered woman being carried past them on a sling.

The riverbank was steep, and Swann hadn't been able to see her clearly until now. He felt his stomach tumble. It was Montana. Swann had last seen her at Kerry Bannister's brothel on South Terrace, after the weirdo had taken her hostage.

There was a clear ligature mark on her neck. Her eyes were open, and bloodshot. Her face was throttled blue, teeth bared.

'I know her,' said Swann. 'I saw her a couple of days ago. I don't know her real name. She works in a Fremantle brothel, for KB.'

Every detective in the force knew who KB was, but Cassidy was having a deal of trouble believing Swann.

'When did you see her last, exactly?'

'The night before the *Vinson* arrived. I'll give you a full statement.'

'How helpful of you, Swann. Course you bloody will.'

'The midshipman,' Webb said. 'Tall, strong, African-American with a scar on the left side of his face. I think, we think, we know who it is. His name is Charles Bernier. He's currently AWOL.'

Charles Bernier was the man they'd searched for earlier at the Seaview Hotel, who'd left his wallet stuffed in the mattress.

'That's why you were called here,' spat Cassidy. 'Start speaking.'

Webb was about to speak until he saw Cassidy cross himself again as Montana was slid into a nylon body bag, the sound of the zipper ugly in the still air.

12.

Des Ryan sprawled his long legs over the pine coffin he'd made for himself, a dusty pillow supporting his back, watching Pascoe prepare the lathe.

'It'll never fucken work.'

Pascoe laughed. 'Oh, it'll work. This flare gun is an antique. Made of iron.'

Ryan finished with his makings, put the packet of White Ox on the floor and gave fire to the racehorse-thin rollie at his lips. It was cool and dark in the shed where Ryan traditionally spent most of his time. Pascoe had already established that Ryan's wife, Leonie, had died five years ago of a stroke. No fairness in that – not when Pascoe remembered her as fair and fit-looking, compared to the leather-skinned skeleton beside him now. As though reading his mind, Ryan tapped ash and repeated himself. 'I'll say it again, Tone, you look pretty good for an old bloke.'

'And I'll say it again, that's the difference no sunlight makes. You still lie on the beach in your jocks, all hours of the day? You're supposed to be Irish.'

'Black Irish mate. Or just black. Either way, take a compliment why don't you? Even if it's from a bloke who hasn't had a root in five years. Unlike yourself.'

It was like the sixty years since they'd first met as boys were merely a week or two ago – Des Ryan reverting to the humour of their childhood.

'And I told you I'm done for,' Pascoe replied. 'A few months at the outside. These blades sharp?'

'Course they're sharp, Paz. What else I got to do? You gonna move in with me?'

Pascoe shook his head, tightened the lathe blade and turned the crank. He'd been called Paz all his life until about a decade ago, when even the screws started calling him Tony, in deference to his new status as a geriatric.

'I haven't been arrested for nine years,' Ryan continued. 'They won't trouble you here.'

'What was that for? The last arrest?'

Ryan's charge sheet was nearly as long as Pascoe's own, although he'd only done shorter stretches. He'd gotten away with the serious stuff, including being Pascoe's driver at the armed robbery that put him away for what amounted to a life sentence. When things had gone south inside the central Perth bank, and Pascoe and his partner Ben Davey were trapped and outgunned, Ryan had wisely escaped in the stolen Torana, torching it south of the power station. Ryan wasn't there to see Davey get shot down, or the security guard bleeding on the faux-marble floor.

'Makin an arse of myself. Dispute with a dickhead over the back fence, decided to settle it with me shotgun. Just to scare 'im, of course. That's the problem with getting old and your reputation fading to nothin, the weasel had no worries dobbing me in. Though the judge took pity on me, gave me community service planting trees in Kings Park. Beats breathin the stinkin air of Three Division like all the other times, I'll say that for it.'

'I'm ready, flick the switch.' Pascoe nodded toward the powerboard that was piggybacked with double adaptors and cords splayed everywhere. 'Bloody fire risk in here. You ever think about getting power laid out from the house?'

Ryan pinched his rollie, tossed it through the door. 'The next owner, whoever that is, can do it. While they're busy wiping out the memory of me an Leonie. Knockin down the house and whatnot. Makin it fit for habitation by yuppies and their kids.'

Des and Leonie Ryan hadn't been able to have children, which was a sadness they carried their entire lives. Des dealt with it by joining up with the infantry, like most of his friends, including Pascoe, before being sent off to North Africa for the war. He'd seen and done terrible things over there, but he reckoned he got the good end of the stick compared to Leonie. She was a loving woman who died carrying the disappointment of never having a child to love.

Ryan flicked the switch and the old lathe came to life. In the bracket facing the blades was a length of solid iron pole, used by fencers and road workers to loosen the ground before digging. *Measure twice and cut once.*

Pascoe remeasured the inside mouth of the flare gun's barrel with a pair of steel callipers. Once he'd shaved off the outside of the pole to the required width, the next step was to bore a precise hole down its centre. Des Ryan's shotgun had been confiscated by the police, but he still had his .303 rifle and plenty of ammunition. The gun was registered, and so unsuited to Pascoe's purpose. He didn't want his plan to boomerang on his old friend. The new barrel would be bored to carry a .303 cartridge. He wouldn't worry about rifling the barrel, so to make the bullet spin accurately on its passage from flare gun to living body. He planned to shoot the gun once, close in.

True to form, Des hadn't even asked Pascoe why he'd broken out so close to his release, or what the weapon was for.

Des Ryan was old-school.

'If you don't want to live here, despite me needin the company, you're welcome to come and die here. After you've finished doin what you need to do.'

Pascoe knew that one day in the coming months he was going to drown when his lungs filled with fluid. It wasn't going to be pretty, and he thought about Des's offer. Des would do the right thing and help him along, if that's what Pascoe wanted. Pascoe grinned. 'Might do that. I get to go quick, and you get to blow a hole in my head, like you always wanted to do.'

13.

Swann pulled the Brougham into his drive, parked two feet ahead of the hanging bottlebrush. Wattlebirds nested up there in the foliage and liked to paint his car with streaky shit.

Webb had been silent until they reached Fremantle, weighing his options. 'Swann, what did he mean by trouble following you around? You understand, in the circumstances, I've got to limit our exposure to potential –'

Swann had nodded and turned into the street. 'A colleague of Detective Sergeant Cassidy's, and a good friend of mine, a kid I always thought of as a son, was helping me on a case a few years ago, got murdered over it.'

Swann let it hang there, hoping that the answer would be sufficient to Webb's needs. He had no desire to get involved in Montana's murder, although because of the diagnosis made on the *Vinson*, he felt a degree of gratitude that he'd repay with assistance, if needed. But Webb didn't comment, and so Swann asked his own question. 'The rape cases that Cassidy mentioned. What he was hinting at – the US Navy running off before an investigation was complete – that standard procedure? Because, if so –'

'I'm not aware of the details, Swann, but I can promise you, never on my watch. It's been known to happen, I won't lie, especially in countries where the gaols are atrocious and the legal system's a bad joke. It's highly likely that there weren't actual suspects, in which case no commander is going to linger in port for the duration of a drawn-out investigation. You'll appreciate that US Navy vessels are sitting targets when in port, for terrorists and protestors. But in return for ... fair treatment in the matter before us, I'm happy to follow up on Cassidy's cases through my own channels, if that'd help smooth the waters.'

Swann had never served in the armed forces, but he'd done fifteen years as a beat copper and detective, before returning to uniform as a superintendent. Webb's answer was persuasive, but once again there was something in his tone that made Swann wary. Webb was a policeman with a duty to uphold the law, but he also had an institution to protect, an institution that served the most powerful and wealthy nation on earth.

Webb wanted to speak to Kerry Bannister before Cassidy and the other detectives arrived, and so they'd driven straight home. Swann had agreed because Montana was one of Kerry's staff – a young woman whose life had been stolen. He wanted Kerry to hear the news from a friend, rather than from Cassidy.

The day was still hot and the street trees on South Terrace drooped. Swann approached the brothel's side entrance. He could hear the sailors talking before he turned the corner, noticed Webb straighten up his uniform, place on his officer's cap. There were five rooms inside the brothel and ten sailors waiting outside. Those in groups smoked and chatted among themselves while the few men who were alone leaned on the wall and stared at the clear blue sky. It was a narrow entrance, and when Swann moved to pass the group of four sailors at the head of the line, a strong arm reached out and barred his way. Swann looked into the sailor's eyes, waiting for the response as the sailor recognised Master-at-Arms Steven Webb beside him. Webb cleared his throat, the man gulped, dropped his arm, stood away. When Swann and Webb didn't move along, the young sailor reluctantly saluted, as did the others.

'As you were,' Webb said formally. 'Although I think you need to find something else to do.'

The sailors looked at each other, started to leave.

Swann led the way into the brothel. 'You didn't want to ask them about our missing sailor?'

Webb paused inside the front door. 'They were all white, Asian or Hispanic. They likely wouldn't know, and besides, they're fresh on leave as of oh eight hundred this morning. I could smell the soap powder in their clothes. You sure about this, Swann? I'm having second thoughts. Those detectives will be here any minute. You sure that coming here won't put Cassidy's nose out of joint?'

Swann shrugged. 'It might upset Cassidy, although at this stage your investigations are separate. You're trying to track an AWOL sailor. He's trying to track down a murderer. We don't know if your man was with Montana, and even if he was, his being seen with her is still circumstantial evidence. Would you mind waiting here for a minute? Kerry doesn't know that Montana is dead. Better she hear it from me.'

Kerry Bannister was as tough a person as Swann knew, but the news made her reach for Swann's arm as she slid to the desk. She sat there, legs sprawled, tears falling down her weathered face. 'Oh, the poor dear. The poor, poor girl.'

Swann crouched beside her. Down the corridor, the rooms were all occupied. It was a Federation building with solid brick walls but from Kerry's office you could hear every creaking bedspring and murmur. She'd told him previously that the women didn't mind the Yanks – most of them were polite and all of them were generous. Some of them just wanted to talk to a woman, smell a woman, hold a woman.

He wondered if the missing sailor was such a man, or whether he was the other kind.

Now Kerry looked up to him, wiping her eyes. Swann waited for the question. He'd broken similar news to dozens of people over the years – mothers, fathers, husbands, wives, and children. First came the shock, then the cruel pang of hope.

'You sure it was her, Swann? Could it be some other woman? Plenty of ordinary women tart themselves up when the Yanks are in town.'

Swann shook his head, squeezed Kerry's hand. 'I got a good look. It was her. She have family, a partner here?'

'She's from Sydney. Came over for a month, two years ago, then stayed. Don't know much about her family. She's into men, only. Got regulars, but never seen her with a steady partner. Montana ... her real name's Francine McGregor.'

Kerry looked over Swann's shoulder. Swann turned, and there was Webb, where he wasn't supposed to be. Webb's posture was appropriately apologetic, hat at his waist. He'd combed his hair again.

They knew each other. Part of Webb's job was communicating with local madams in every port, making sure that his men behaved.

'What're you doin here?' she asked him.

Webb made to answer, but Swann held up a hand. 'What time did ... Francine work until last night? You see her leave with anyone?'

Kerry answered, looking at Webb. 'She worked the four-to-midnight. Didn't see her leave with nobody.'

Webb took something from his shirt pocket, leaned into the room. 'Did you see her with this man yesterday afternoon, or last night?'

Swann looked at the photographs of Midshipman Charles Bernier, broken into four frames – hat on, hat off, front view and side view. His name and rank were handwritten at the base of the image. Big dark eyes and cropped hair. The glazed-looking scar that stretched from his ear to his mouth.

It took a moment for Swann to register what Webb had done, or hadn't done. Back at the river, he hadn't supplied the photograph to Cassidy, despite the witness statement identifying Francine McGregor with an African-American sailor who wore the same distinctive scar.

Kerry sniffed, shook her head. 'No. He wasn't here yesterday. But I do recognise him. He was here last time. I got a good memory for faces. Why? What's he done? He got anything –'

'We don't know, Kerry,' Swann said. 'So he was here two years ago when the *Vinson* was in port. With Francine? He one of her clients?'

'Yeah, he was. She was new then. Don't remember anything other than that.'

Swann asked Kerry where Francine lived. Webb wrote down the address.

There was a long male sigh in the closest room, followed by relieved laughter.

'Kerry,' Swann asked, 'did Francine ever work off the clock?'

'Not that I know of. She wouldn't be working here if I caught her, but being straight, it's possible she took a shine to one of her blokes.'

'If she did, or if she wanted to meet a client, a regular. Not for business, but for fun, where would she go?'

Swann knew the answer, picturing the single room upstairs in the Seaview across the road, its slashed mattress that contained Bernier's wallet.

'Tom rents out short-time singles. You know that.'

The door to the nearest room opened. Swann looked at his watch. Five seconds before five o'clock, the flushed-looking sailor making use of every moment, leaving the buttoning of his smock and the tying of his neckerchief until he was outside. In the context of what'd just happened to Francine McGregor, the sight angered Swann. He felt like wiping the satisfied look off the sailor's face.

The sailor saw Swann's expression and the smile slid away. He made a perfunctory salute to Webb and scampered for the door. Behind him, one of the new young women who Swann didn't know emerged from the room, a shawl draped over her bare breasts and shoulders, making for the toilet. She was a redhead with a hard face that scanned Swann and Webb. It wasn't until she saw the tears on Kerry's face that her eyes softened.

'Dakota,' Kerry said. 'We got to close up. Knock on all the doors. Get the blokes dressed and outta here, then lock the front door. We got to have a meetin.'

14.

The GTS Monaro coupe was Devon Smith's kind of car. Barry Brown gave him the specs as they drove north across the river. Beside them in port was the *Carl Vinson*, looking like a floating shoe in the glare coming off the water.

'Gotta 308-cubic-inch V8 under the bonnet. All the LS features – chrome rings and four headlights, bonnet and boot standard paint-out and a big-arsed rear window. You really never heard of the Monaro? Designed and built here in Australia – the best muscle car ever put rubber to road.'

Devon Smith had to agree. He'd grown up peering over the dash of his father's Barracudas, Camaros, Caminos and Panteras as they headed out to the desert for a run. Every time his father was locked away, it fell to Devon to reluctantly sell the car and take his father the cash, to get it put on his commissary. The Monaro had that same deep chuckle when it idled, like a purring lion.

Barry put his foot down as they turned past some gas silos and blocks of shipping containers onto the coast road. The light and the beach and the port reminded Devon of home.

The Aussie biker was the same age as Devon's father, although unlike his father, the beer-gutted and moustachioed man beside him didn't mind conversation. He'd happily filled in some missing information about how he'd met Devon's father, back stateside. Barry Brown rode with a local outfit called The Nongs. He wasn't in his colours but instead wore the universal Harley tee-shirt, biker boots and oily jeans. The biker clubs in this Australian state were homegrown and unaffiliated, although that was changing. Barry had travelled to California, where it all began, to do some research about possible allies. He'd partied in the main, but one night at an Angels clubhouse in San Diego he'd met Devon's father. Devon Smith

Snr wasn't a patched member but had been there since the beginning, had served time with plenty of the hierarchy and shared the same politics. Barry was put onto him, as a gesture of goodwill, because of his trade in guns. Barry returned to Australia with the promise of contraband sometime in the future. That time had arrived.

Devon hadn't talked much. Back outside the dive bar, before Barry Brown climbed into the Monaro, he'd stared across the roof at Devon, who was waiting for the door to be unlocked. The stare was long and hard. Devon knew that stare – it was the look of a man breaking through another man's eyes. Devon knew that Barry Brown saw beyond the pasty skin and tattoos. The scars on his face and arms. The attitude of fuck-you-all surliness in his eyes.

Barry Brown's face settled into the same look Devon's father gave him in every prison visiting room and when he got out of gaol. The same look of disappointment, and knowing.

So when Devon asked the question, 'Hey man, where the Nazis at in this burgh?' his voice reedy above the throaty roar of the Monaro accelerating along the coast road, he wasn't surprised by the answer. His game was already up.

Barry Brown smirked, like he was in on a private joke. 'There's a fair few of 'em in the city. Runts, mostly. *Pommies.*'

Devon didn't know what that meant but he assumed faggot. Despite himself, he began to talk. How some of what he was doing related to the Aryans back home. Kind of like what Barry had been trying to foster in California. Build the network, the movement.

Which made Barry smirk again.

'You think that's funny?'

Devon's tone was a provocation, but he was clearly so unimpressive that the biker didn't bite, at least not hard.

'Your business is your business, son. I got me own tribe, me own colours. I'm a simple man. For me and me brothers, it's The Nongs versus the rest. I might be white, but that don't mean I feel kinship with some pasty fucking German or Norwegian or Pommie, 'less he's gonna be my brother and wear the colours. Righto, let's get this over with.'

The Monaro pulled into a parking lot with a view over the ocean. Kids out there on a reef break riding shortboards, hands shielding eyes as they watched for the next set.

'Show us what you got.'

Devon lifted the haversack and opened its neck, began to extract the Glock pistols one by one, all ten of them, and then the magazines.

He began the spiel. 'Glock second-generation safe-action. Polymer framed for lightness. Short recoil for repeat shooting. Ideal for concealed carry. Self-loading. Takes a nine-millimetre parabellum. Got the rail for adding laser sights, or a torchlight.'

Beside him, Barry Brown snorted, lit up a cigarette. 'You come all this way to get yourself murdered, son?'

'What? No, sir. I –'

'Just cos we live way over here, other side of the world, you think we're fucken idiots? That's not a second-gen model. That's the original seventeen. Hasn't got the checkering on the front and rear straps, or on the trigger guard.'

'No sir, it ain't. My father told me –'

Barry Brown gave him that stare again, breaking him down, again. Saw that he was telling the truth.

'Yeah, he struck me as a shady fucker. But what kinda dog sends his son into a rip-off gun deal without tellin him?'

'I didn't know, sir.'

'I can see that. Though your payday just got cut in half. I was promised second-generation seventeens. You're lucky I'm givin you anything.'

Brown took out a roll of crisp Benjamins. 'Ten grand, now five grand. Take it and get the fuck out.'

It occurred to Devon that he didn't know how to tell counterfeit money from real, which only added to the shame.

Barry Brown wasn't going to ask him again. He was putting the pistols in a leather bag, the cigarette dangling from his lips.

This wasn't how Devon imagined it'd play out. First, they'd do the deal, then he'd be invited to the clubhouse, to celebrate. Then, cashed up and partied out, he'd head off to find his people, the others of his race who'd welcome him.

Brown had finished stowing the pistols. He flicked his cigarette out the window. Devon mustered the last of his pride. 'I can get more, if you want. AR-fucking-fifteens. Maybe an M-sixteen. But only if the price is right.'

Brown looked him in the eye. He lit another cigarette and watched a seagull float down in the sky, threatening to land on his polished bonnet. Brown beeped his horn and the seagull arrested its flight, cut and turned over the cliff's edge. 'Why didn't you say that right off, son? But that's above my pay grade. I'm gonna have to run this up the chain.'

Devon kept his eyes level. 'I got nothing better to do. Take me to your president, right now, and we'll talk.'

Brown smiled, but his eyes said – *so, you want me to make you feel important.*

'Alright, I can do that.'

Barry Brown cranked the ignition and the Monaro roared to life. As they reversed onto the coast road, Devon whispered to himself, 'I ain't no punk, no sir.'

15.

Old Tom passed Swann the roll of keys. He leaned forward and scratched his nose.

Webb craned his neck to listen. For such a big man, Tom had a very quiet voice. 'They was here, Frank. Not in room six, but the detective asked for the keys.'

Tom put his hands flat on the bar. His work was done. Swann would have to spell it out.

'Tom, what were the police called for?'

Tom thought about it, his big brown eyes fuzzy with confusion. Hadn't he just said that? 'There was a bloke in room three. Anglo man. He got fighting with a young bloke in room one. Another Anglo man. Still haven't cleaned up the blood. The coppers wanted to check all the rooms.'

Tom drew in a deep breath, his verbosity exhausting. He gave Swann a shy smile and nodded.

'So the police being here had nothing to do with any navy personnel?'

Tom put up his hands and backed into the shadows.

Swann picked up his soda water and drank it down, crushed ice in his teeth, felt the shards slide down his neck. Webb drank the shoulders off his stubby of Export, not hiding his distaste. He opened his wallet.

'You let that warm too long,' Swann said.

Webb frowned. 'I bought it a minute ago.'

'That's a minute too long. Now you can taste it. My buy.'

Webb nodded, pushed the stubby away.

'Tell me though,' Swann said. 'Why didn't you show Cassidy and the other dees the photograph of Bernier? I know you value mutual respect between the Shore Patrol and local authorities, especially in a case like this. You *trying* to get Cassidy offside?'

A hint of anger in Webb's blue eyes, some clenching of the jaw. Product of being an officer, Swann presumed – not used to being queried, or asked inconvenient questions. 'There's history, Swann. Nothing to do with Cassidy, but from my experience of other organisations, other ports, other jurisdictions ... our men are innocent until proven guilty.'

'I understand that. The history. But if you get to Bernier first, what are you going to do? He's still only a suspect. Hand him over, or take him back onto the *Vinson*? Which is American sovereign territory.'

Webb played along. 'I'd advise him of his rights under Australian law. Secure him a lawyer. Hand him over. I do it all the time.'

Swann looked over Webb's shoulder. 'Looks like your hearts-and-minds opportunity just arrived.'

Webb turned and watched Cassidy and the two younger detectives climb out of the new-model Commodore, lifting jackets from seats. Cassidy straightened his tie and corrected his shoulder holster, as did the others, before heading down the side entrance of the brothel. They returned a minute later, stood looking about the street, taking off their jackets and wiping sweat from their faces. Kerry Bannister had locked the front door and wouldn't be opening it for anyone.

'All yours,' Swann said.

Webb stood and moved to the entrance, taking out the Bernier photograph. It was hot in the bar but even hotter outside. Webb straightened his cap and crossed the street, Cassidy watching him come. They talked for a few minutes. Civility in their postures, until Cassidy looked across at the Seaview. He placed the photograph on the Commodore's bonnet and wrote Bernier's details and Montana's real name and address in his notebook. The three detectives and Webb crossed the street. Cassidy's face when he entered the pub was puddled red with the heat. He rolled his cuffs and took out a ten-dollar note, passed it to the youngest detective.

'Frank Swann,' said Cassidy. 'One step ahead, as always. Can I buy you a drink?'

'Off the grog, Cassidy. Just headed home.'

'Yes, on that. Could you please do me the favour of staying here for a bit? Want to talk to you, when we get back from the room upstairs. A *personal* favour.'

Webb shrugged like he didn't know, then held up the roll of keys. The four of them traipsed up the creaking stairs. They returned five minutes later. Old Tom was snoring in his office. The youngest detective peered down the bar.

'You'll have to serve yourself,' said Swann. 'Just keep a tally.'

Across the road, another group of young sailors stood on the footpath, took their bearings from the Seaview and headed down the brothel's side entrance.

The young detective passed three stubbies over the bar, placed the ten note on the till and rejoined them. Tom snuffled away in his office. The three policemen cracked their beers and took long swigs. Cassidy looked to Webb's stubby. 'Sure you don't want another one?'

Webb glanced at Swann. 'Thanks, but sure.'

Cassidy nodded. 'Frank. I just learned that you're crook. Not surprising, really. And that you've only been helping Officer Webb as a favour. I want you to keep doing that, on Webb's dollar. We've established some trust, but he trusts you more than he trusts me. That right, Steve?'

'True enough, Mike.'

'So, you're already in the middle of it. We don't know what *it* is yet, but, as more comes to light ...'

'Our first priority,' said Webb, 'is to find Midshipman Charles Bernier. Then we'll know what *it* is.'

'You got good reason to say no,' said Cassidy, wiping froth from his lips. 'Given recent history. I've told Webb, Smart and Moylan here some of that story. But I want you on point, Frank. Webb does too. Just as a liaison, until we locate Bernier.'

Swann hadn't emptied his stomach for more than three hours. Something about the promise of a cure, helping his symptoms. Right at that moment, part of him *wanted* to feel sick, so that he could walk away. But Francine had worked for Kerry, and he felt obliged to follow through, at least for now. On top of that, Swann never thought that he'd see the day when a Western Australian CIB detective would make a peace offering to him, let alone ask for his help. Despite himself, that mattered.

'I can do that,' he said. 'But first I need to see my GP.'

Cassidy looked relieved. Webb squeezed his shoulder. 'From what I just heard, Swann, it's a miracle that you're still alive. Can't believe you never told me about all that – the Royal Commission, contracts out on you, bad cops and gangsters wanting you dead. Gonna have to start calling you Serpico Swann.'

Cassidy nearly choked on his beer. 'For Swann's sake, Steve,' he said, 'please don't do that.'

Swann avoided Webb's gaze.

It had never felt to him like he'd defeated the men who'd tried to kill him, most of them dead now.

Just outlasted them.

16.

The lathe was noisy and obstreperous, its motor shorting every few minutes, although it did the job. The iron on the outside of the rod peeled easily enough; it was the coring that took time. So much time that Ryan fell asleep on the coffin, a dead rollie hanging from his lips, the transistor radio plugged into his ears. He had a smile on his face that made him look like the boy Pascoe remembered, dreaming of jockeying a Melbourne Cup winner, coming from five lengths back with a furlong to run, the crowd bringing him home.

The length of tempered iron had been cored to the width of a .303 cartridge. Pascoe took it off the lathe and slipped a cartridge down its mouth. It was a snug fit – not too tight or loose. The problem was fitting the new barrel inside the flare gun's existing barrel. He could use the single-point lathe to carve a thread onto the outside fitting of the new barrel and an internal thread on the flare-gun barrel, but it'd take time. If the bloody thing shorted out during either operation then the ratio of distance to the spindle rotation might be compromised, and then he'd have to start from the beginning with another length of iron.

Pascoe took a long draw on the oxygen bottle. One alternative was to groove out an internal thread and use superglue to fill the grooves and hold the barrel inside. After all, the way Pascoe had planned it, he'd only need to test the weapon once, and use it once before throwing it away.

Better to do it right. He took another lungful of the cool sweet oxygen and put the bottle aside. Ryan had told him that he could get more, if needed. No call to ration what he had.

Pascoe worked out the gearing of the lead screw and put on his safety glasses. He was working in his jocks because of the heat, and his slack muscles were silvered with sweat. He turned on the lathe and got to work.

An hour later, both parts were threaded. Pascoe wiped the internal barrel with an old rag, used a rod to push the rag inside the flare-gun barrel to remove any shavings. He began to screw in the iron barrel, lubricated by spit. It fitted perfectly, and the length was right.

Ryan awoke with a cough. He lit his rollie and clapped his hands. 'All those hours we spent makin gidgees paid off, eh? That looks a nice snug thread. Pass it here.'

Ryan looked down the unified barrel, examining the hammer position, appeared satisfied that it'd strike the percussion cap of a .303. 'Nice work, old boy. You got yourself a pistola. Now, to test it.'

Pascoe was one step ahead. He'd already found an old steel garbage bin. It was home to three red-back spiders, whose silky egg pods were too numerous to count. Pascoe got the hose on them and blasted them out into the pile of grey dirt that was mounded by the back fence. 'Get me a couple blankets?' he asked. 'Let's make us a silencer.'

'You mean a suppressor?'

'You know what I mean, smart-arse.'

Pascoe began to smash out the bottom of the bin with the remainder of the iron pole. It was heavy and he felt his chest gurgle and his heartbeat begin to slip before Ryan took his arm. 'Stupid old bugger. You ain't dyin here. Not till we've had a farewell session.'

Pascoe watched Ryan's shoulders rise and fall with the weight of the rod. He was a proud old rooster and hadn't let himself go.

'There. Done.' Ryan turned and twisted the bin into the sand pile. He took an old grey army blanket and folded it until it was the circumference of the bin, before packing it around the inside. He did the same with a moth-eaten red blanket. The same with another army blanket.

Pascoe leaned over and peered inside. Just enough room for the flare-gun barrel.

'Here goes nothin.'

Pascoe put in a .303 cartridge, pointed it at the ground. It was heavy with the new iron barrel but the shell didn't fall out, and therefore didn't need packing.

'Kinda like a reverse musket,' Ryan added. 'You're gonna have to use a rod to get the casings out, each time.'

'Yep.'

Pascoe had a good listen to the neighbourhood. His hearing was ok, and there were no conversations in the houses on either side. He put the flare gun into the bin and looked to Ryan, who was waiting with a rusty old fire-extinguisher, probably been in the family for fifty years.

Pascoe held the flare gun with both hands and pressed the trigger. The flash and bang was loud but it was the recoil that took him by surprise, throwing his hands over his head and toppling him backward onto the sand.

Ryan put down the fire extinguisher, but only so he could laugh better. Pascoe's ears were ringing. Ryan put his hands on his belly and slapped his thighs, hopping about on the spot and laughing his arse off. Gradually, Pascoe's hearing returned.

'Ah, you silly old bugger. Funniest thing I seen in ages.'

Ryan helped him up.

'Least it didn't blow up in my hand. Not like that mortar you made, remember? Nearly took out a wall at school. You looked like Wile E. Coyote with yer smokin hair, yer singed eyebrows.'

Ryan slapped Pascoe on the back. 'Yeah, that was too funny.'

Pascoe gathered himself and went to the oxygen bottle. He put the mask over his face and took a long draw, the flare gun on the table beside him.

It was only then that he looked at the neighbour's fence, saw the young bearded longhair watching him.

Pascoe held the man's stare until Ryan noticed and quit sweeping the lathe. 'Tone, meet Sat Prakash. Satty, meet an old mate of mine –'

'… Tony Smith,' Pascoe finished.

'Oh yeah,' Ryan said. 'Tony Smith.'

The bearded man nodded, looked to the smoking bin that had acted as a silencer. 'Sorry, Des, thought I heard a gunshot. Sounded like a forty-four Magnum, my old gun.'

Des Ryan leaned on the broom. 'Satty's a Sannyasin. Follower of the Bhagwan. Mob of them live next door. Feed me sometimes when I'm broke.'

Pascoe didn't know much about the Rajneeshees beyond what he'd read in the morning paper, which characterised them as a dangerous sex cult. He didn't believe any of that – it was the kind of thing that the paper regularly served up to its largely old and conservative readers. Pascoe had been the target of misinformation in the same paper, back when he was free.

'You knocked off for today?' Ryan asked the bearded man, clearly knowing the answer. 'Tone, Satty's a bricklayer. His crew have renovated half the homes on this street, half the neighbourhood.'

The bearded man looked at Pascoe strangely, then past him to the shape of the adapted flare gun, hidden beneath a hessian sack. 'I know who you are,' he said. 'You were on the front page of the morning paper. Just wanted to get that out the way. You've got nothing to worry about. Des trusts us, I hope you will too. Both of you, come over for dinner in a minute, if you're keen. I'll put the paper in the chook cage, where it belongs.'

Pascoe was about to speak but Des cut him off. 'Sure, mate. That'd be good. I could eat the arse out of a horse.'

17.

It was early evening by the time Swann returned from his GP, who'd sent him to Fremantle Hospital for blood tests. Lefroy, his GP, was excited by the diagnosis made on the *Vinson* – the first case he'd discovered of shooting-caused lead poisoning. He consulted his manuals and made notes and wrote the scripts for the blood tests. Tomorrow, he'd put in a call to a Sydney laboratory to place an order for the chelation therapy medications. The medicine consisted, apparently, of doses of something called dimercaptosuccinic acid, otherwise known as succimer. It'd been used in Australia to treat lead poisoning among children in Broken Hill, after dogs living near the smelter started dying. Lefroy told Swann that he was curious to chart how he responded to the treatment. The average Fremantle home contained hundreds of kilograms of lead in the coats of paint on the walls, and in various plumbing solders and leadlights. It was a public health disaster in the making, he said, and if it was acceptable to Swann, he'd like to record the changing blood levels, with a mind to writing a possible paper.

Swann didn't mind at all. He just wanted the medication quickly, and paid for it to be couriered to Lefroy's office. It was due tomorrow or at the latest on Monday morning.

Swann sat in the rattan chair on the front porch. Marion had taken the dog for a walk. She would be happy to hear about the diagnosis.

Swann relaxed his shoulders into the chair, watching the light drain out of the pale blue sky, shadows building in the garden, a hush falling over the street. He thought about following Marion and the dog to the beach, felt like he needed to be with them.

The doctor had given Swann good news, but he didn't take any pleasure from it. He'd seen a lot of death over the course of his career, and each new victim brought the ghosts out from the grave-dark rooms of his memory. Swann had felt a spike of pity and anger at the sight of Francine's violated body, the purpled face and bared teeth, but also a haunting that he knew would shade his thoughts until the person responsible was identified, then taken down.

In the old days, on nights like this, Swann would reach for the bottle. He felt the familiar need that he focussed on, examined, then pushed away.

When the phone rang, Swann was eager to answer it. He went inside and took up the phone, walked it out the door.

Webb sounded tired and frustrated. He told Swann that Cassidy had brought in a forensics team to fingerprint and take samples from the Seaview room that Bernier and Francine had rented for the night. Cassidy and his detectives, together with Webb, had just returned from Francine's home address, where they failed to find evidence of Bernier's communicating with her over the past year.

Swann hung up the phone and stared into the darkening sky, considering what Webb had told him. He felt the old relief at the thought of work, a distraction from the memory of Francine and a movement toward making things right.

It was possible, he supposed, that Bernier remembered Francine from his last shore leave and sought her out, although according to Kerry he hadn't entered the brothel. What Kerry's workers did in their own time was their own business, but for financial and safety reasons she discouraged their meeting clients off the clock. It happened, of course, and plenty of prostitutes Swann had known over the years had exited the industry this way, hooking up with a long-term partner.

But Francine had worked her full shift before knocking off and meeting Bernier at the pub. The probability was that the meeting had been arranged prior to the *Vinson*'s arrival in port, and there were likely letters and telegrams to give an indication of the nature of their relationship. Even a detail like who the letters were addressed to would speak volumes. If Francine had confided to Charles Bernier her real name, then that suggested a degree of intimacy that would be absent if she kept to Montana. According to Webb, Bernier had no priors for sexual assault or deviancy, although he was double-checking at the level of Bernier's neighbourhood police jurisdiction. It was possible for a sex offender to slip past the military's vetting process, especially when, as was the case with Bernier, he'd signed up having been offered a choice by a judge – gaol time or military service – following his arrest in Houston for burglary.

The mystery was why, if Bernier was the killer, he'd allowed himself to be seen. Why had he rented a room across the road from Francine's workplace, if his intention was to hurt her? If Bernier had indeed murdered Francine, this suggested to Swann that the crime wasn't planned, and that instead he'd killed her, panicked and run.

Swann continued to think about Francine McGregor while he showered and changed. His thoughts turned, as they always did, to what her final moments had been like. He had interviewed rape victims and had seen first-hand the trauma that would never leave them. It wasn't hard to imagine his daughters in Francine's position, or to maintain the desire to hunt down the man who'd taken Francine's life. Swann pocketed his keys and stepped into the night.

18.

It only took one line of crank for Devon Smith to get his head up. He swiped the mirror with his index finger and put it to his tongue. His father had worked as a speed cook back in the day and this Australian shit tasted like caviar compared to his father's crank that burned the nose and was dangerous near a flame.

One of the things about being on the *Vinson* was the strict no-drugs policy. They hadn't introduced drug testing yet, but it was coming. Up on the deck you occasionally smelt weed when the blacks played basketball while their boom boxes pumped Niggaz Wit Attitude, Public Enemy or Grandmaster Flash. Smith couldn't help it – he loved that shit, especially NWA, wished more white bands carried that loading of malice and cool. Devon Smith liked to whistle and sing, and once, in the galley, Marcus and Lenny caught him belting out 'Fuck the Police' over the ceramic clanking of the industrial dishwasher. He never saw them laugh harder or longer, slapping their thighs like old minstrels, picking up the lyrics where Devon left off, Marcus beatboxing while Lenny sang – *Devon the kinda vanilla ice nigger that built to last, fuck with him he put his own damn foot up his ass*. Then more slapping and wheezing laughter, fist bumping and wiping tears.

Fuck them, *and* the police.

Devon had five large in his pocket. That was half what he was owed, but it was still three grand profit. Not enough for him to avoid the ridicule of his father for failing to bluff the biker, but there it was, in his pocket.

And now here *he* was, taking care of business, in an ordinary-looking office with titty calendars and filing cabinets, with his head up and a glass of Jack in his hand. Devon knew what they were doing, leaving him alone with a gram packet and a freshly cracked bottle while they deliberated outside – testing him to see whether he would show restraint. He could hear their murmuring behind the sounds of AC/DC's 'Hells Bells', a hastily convened meeting of the governing council. Devon had assumed that Barry Brown was the bikers' sergeant-at-arms, but he was just another gang member, older than the rest. It made sense, Devon supposed. You send an older biker to make the deal, someone whose kids have left home, who's probably single and can do the time easily if caught, whose family won't need supporting from the club coffers.

Devon hadn't met the club president or the sergeant-at-arms. Barry Brown had forced Devon to crawl into the front seat floorpan of the Monaro for the drive to the clubhouse, told him it was either that or the boot. Devon didn't know what a boot was, thought he'd meant a literal kick in the ass, until Brown pointed to the trunk. After a long and silent drive, Barry Brown honked his horn and Devon heard iron gates clank open. It occurred to him in a moment of fear that nobody knew that he was there. He could go missing, and nobody would find him.

Depending on what happened next.

Devon cut out another line onto the mirror and used the razor to pat the packet so that it still looked full. He put the crank up his nose and sipped on the Jack and it was only when he rolled his head to look at the ceiling that he noticed the black eye of a surveillance camera staring down at him. He smirked and shook his head. He should, he supposed, feel heartened that they were so careful. If given the go-ahead, he was about to commit a crime that would see him locked up for a very long time. The Aussie bikers were careful, and so *he* needed to be careful, but it was hard with the speed now surging through his body, tingling his balls and making him feel happier than he'd felt in months. Devon wiped his nose and closed up the packet, capped the bottle, waited for them to come. He kept his hands steady and his face blank, occasionally sipping from the glass, lighting a cigarette while staring at the tanned curves of the calendar biker chick, sat astride a Harley with her ass reared in the air.

The door opened and Barry Brown indicated that Devon should follow. His eyes scanned the desk and cabinets to see if anything had been disturbed. The bar room had been noisy with Nongs members when they'd entered, patched men in leather and prospects in denim, but now it was cleared of all but five men, seated at a table underneath a fluorescent light. Barry Brown dabbed his toe at the one empty chair and went over to the bar, began to pull bottles out of a misted fridge.

The smallest of the five men cleared his throat, put a half-smoked cigar into the ashtray. He had a scraggly red goatee and fierce green eyes. His ginger hair was cropped on top and long at the back. He had Asian tattoos of goldfish, samurai warriors and slant-eyed demons up his bare arms. When he smiled, his teeth were surprisingly white and even.

'My name is Gus Riley. Club president. We talked about your offer, but want to hear it from you. How you plan on getting the weapons off ship without being detected.'

The four other men smoked and watched Devon through slitted eyes, reading his weakness as though it was a sign hanging from his neck. Stone-cold killers, each of them. No tension in their bodies. No need to put on an act.

Devon had known plenty like them. He had always feared his father, sure enough, but alongside hard men, his father seemed a yappy dog. Devon had turned out no different, but still believed that his association with outlaws meant that it was only a matter of time before some of that gravitas was passed to him. He just had to show them.

'I got a buddy. He's in the bunk next to mine. Three gradings higher than me. He's just a storeman, but he secures the rooms where the ordinance and weaponry is kept. It's a big room near the top deck. Got the marines' stuff there. Even stuff for resupplying submarines. Like a supermarket, he reckons. Everything got to be combat ready, in case.'

'Have you been in there, yourself?'

'No, sir.'

The redhead smiled at that. Took up his cigar and flicked open a zippo, put fire to the stub end, huffed himself a shroud of grey smoke. 'Go on.'

'I got a way to get whatever I want. I got a plan to get it off, too. I just need to pay my buddy his cut, up front.'

'That ain't gonna happen, son. Nothin to stop you takin our money and hiding on the carrier – nothing we can do to get you off it. And I don't wanna know anything about your ... buddy, or what your arrangement is. You got to grease the wheels, you pay it out of your end. The five K in your pocket, for starters. I just want to know that you can deliver, and how you plan on getting it to us.'

Despite his best attempts to mirror the men around him, Devon sensed the tension in his shoulders, his hands wringing like a little boy under the table. Hated the sound of his reedy voice, too. He pulled his hands apart, set his shoulders and leaned forward. 'You want to hear my plan? Well, this is what I figure on doin ...'

19.

'Is this him?'

Swann showed the photo of Bernier to the squat, muscled man with a shark tattoo across his bare chest; teeth to tail, shoulder to shoulder. He was a scallop-trawler fisherman from Carnarvon on two weeks leave, renting a room at the Seaview. His shoulders were tanned and his face was burned. His long brown hair was sun-bleached at its tips.

'Yeah, that's him. No doubt. I ran into him comin out of the dunny. Not used to lockin it. He called me sir. Never been called sir before.'

'What time was that?'

This was more difficult for the fisherman. He was down for a spree. Swann could see the heroin in his eyes, hear it in the flatness of his drawl. He stank of mildewed sheets and stale bourbon.

'Dunno mate. Reckon it was well after midnight. Early hours. He was all dressed up. Smelt like a flower shop. Had one of them negro combs stickin in his hair. Was brushin it while he walked into the dunny. Last time I saw him.'

'The fight yesterday, that brought the coppers. Were you here when it happened?'

'Sure I was. I'm in town, I don't leave this place. Got everythin I need right here. I keep to meself though. Heard the crunch of some blokes goin at it, bashin into the walls while they wrestled. Just cracked the door to take a look. Fists, kicks, one of 'em nearly went over the balcony.'

Swann looked over the balcony to the concrete apron that fed onto the carpark. That would be a lethal fall.

'You sure neither of them were American? There was another white sailor here. He left a fake name with the manager.'

'Everybody does that. It ain't a crime, is it?'

Swann pursed his lips. 'No, it isn't.'

'But they were locals. The swearin, you see.'

'Did you get the feeling they knew each other?'

'I got the feeling they wanted to kill each other. Couldn't tell you anything else. The guy who got the better of the other bloke. Choked him out. He cleared off in his white Holden ute. An HZ it was. Burning oil. Slow to start and blowin black exhaust. Rings must be goin.'

Swann knew already that the injured man had been interviewed by the detectives, before being taken to Fremantle emergency with head wounds and concussion. Swann would get to him later.

'You didn't see a bloke up here, round the same time? He was shorter than you. Looked like a miner or fisherman. Red hair and a ginger beard. Handy-looking.'

'That sounds like the fella made off in the HZ.'

'He ever come back? You ever see him after that?'

'Nope.'

'Last question. I know that the door at the bottom of the balcony stairs, sometimes it's left unlocked. Means that anyone can come up here, without being seen in the bar. Do you know if it was unlocked the night before the fight took place? The night the sailors were staying?'

The fisherman scratched his hairy belly, wouldn't meet Swann's eye. 'Might've been. Sometimes, people come up here ... I dunno.'

People like the fisherman's dealer.

'I can't remember. Been a bit of a blur, mate, this past week. Got one more week left, before I head north again.'

Swann shook the man's hand, could feel calluses formed by hauling rope, thanked him and moved to the next door, knocked twice.

Swann's wife, Marion, and his eldest daughter, Louise, were seated on the front porch, drinking beer from tall glasses. Louise's partner, Karen, and another young woman Swann didn't know, drank glasses of iced water. Swann leaned over and kissed the crown of Marion's head. Louise stood and Swann squeezed her in a hug. She smelt of cigarettes and cocoa butter. He stood back and took her in, a couple of weeks since she'd last come to dinner. She wore cut-off denim shorts and a tank top, thongs on her feet. Her black hair was cut short, just like she wore it as a girl. Spray of freckles on her nose. Clever, mischievous blue eyes. Louise worked in the public service as a lawyer, the first in either Swann or Marion's family to go to university.

'You remember Karen?' Louise asked.

'Sure I do,' Swann said, smiling. 'Good to see you again.'

Karen nodded and smiled, but didn't meet his eyes. Swann hadn't made up his mind about Karen. Louise loved her, but she was older, much older, and she rarely smiled. On the few occasions she came to dinner, her eyes constantly wandered around the house, always seemed to be making judgements, didn't appear to like what she saw. She worked part-time as an academic and as a staffer for a state MP. Swann knew that Louise's instincts were good. He supposed that his reservations were the normal ones due to a father wanting to see his children happy.

'Dad, this is Maddie. She works for the *Daily News*. The reason we're here. And also, because Mum told us you have something good to tell us?'

Swann gave Maddie a small wave. He sat on the arm of Marion's chair. He told them about the diagnosis made on the *Carl Vinson*, the likelihood of a cure. Karen knew the story of how he'd sustained the shooting injuries, and he assumed that Maddie did too. 'Should be able to start on the medication soon, all things being well. Can I get you another beer, more water?'

Louise and the two women shook their heads. Swann was waiting for it, was ready when it came. After all, Karen had looked disgusted when he'd mentioned the *Vinson*, and Maddie was a journo.

'Dad. You and Mum don't need the money. But you've got your notebook in your pocket. You're still sick.'

Swann tried not to feel defensive. One thing about his family, whenever Marion or Louise challenged him, it was always with his best interests at heart. 'That's something me and your mother will talk about. No offence to Karen and Maddie.'

Marion squeezed his hand, a suggestion to continue. 'It's only temporary. And I'm just a liaison. Just legwork. I promise.'

'Dad, Maddie's been working on a story. The story about the murdered prostitute –'

'Her name was Francine.'

Maddie took out her own notebook, held it up. Swann nodded.

'Do you have a surname for her?' Louise asked.

'McGregor. MC, with no a.'

'Maddie's also writing about the sexual assaults, last time a US Navy ship was in port.'

'That wasn't the *Vinson*, or so I've been told.'

Now Maddie spoke up. She had a good voice for the trade – deep and clear. 'Mr Swann. Can you confirm that ... Francine, was in the company of a US sailor, before she was murdered?'

'You know that already.'

'But can you confirm it? For the record.'

Swann looked to Louise, who looked right back at him. 'No, not for the record. Sorry.'

Karen cleared her throat. 'Because you're working for the Americans?'

Swann ignored the contempt in her voice, caught the brief look of hurt in Louise's eyes. 'Well, yes, I suppose I am. We're trying to locate an AWOL sailor, who might have nothing to do with Francine's murder. If he does, he's going to cop it, I promise you that.'

Maddie leaned forward, tried to restore the ease lost by Karen's comment. 'Thanks, Mr Swann. Sorry for the questions. I'm getting nothing from the US media advisor. But I think it's in the public interest, if you know what I mean.'

Swann nodded, because it was true. Louise stood and embraced him, whispered in his ear. 'Sorry, Dad, but it's important.'

Swann looked into his daughter's eyes. 'Yeah, it is,' he said quietly, looking to Maddie. 'You'll get more details from Kerry Bannister around the corner. That's where Francine worked. Tell her I sent you.'

Maddie smiled at Swann and Louise, put away her notebook.

20.

Pascoe had tried to get away but Des wouldn't let him. Insisted that he come next door for dinner. While it was being prepared, Pascoe had fallen asleep, worn out by his labours. He'd woken up the next morning, nearly midday, on a mattress on the Sannyasins' back deck, hooked up to his oxygen bottle. He must have fallen asleep again because he was still there now, seated in a verge-collection armchair, pergola roof and ceiling fans turning slowly. Mosquito nets wrapped above more day beds in the corners. What he thought was incense burning on a nearby fire-pit turned out to be sandalwood sticks, broken from branches of the stuff, piled in the parched backyard. Des was inside chatting to the cooks, who were working up some vegetarian chow that smelt good. There were five of them living in the house, two men and three women. One of the women, whose name he couldn't remember, had helped him move from the bed to the armchair, remarking upon the prison tattoo that Pascoe had done on himself, rubbing her fingers over his wiry forearm, correctly recognising the Sanskrit symbol for Padma. She was the first person he'd met who understood its significance, beyond its translation as Lotus.

'You've been through a lot,' she said, looking into his eyes. 'But risen above it. Like the lotus flower, sitting on the muddy lake water.'

Pascoe didn't know anything about her guru's teachings, but she was practising acceptance, right there. He smiled.

'You're dying, aren't you?' she added. 'I'm a nurse. Des asked me to get more oxygen, which I'm happy to do.'

Perhaps it was the sandalwood, or the kindness in her eyes, but Pascoe was momentarily lost for words.

'Your lips are bluing,' she said. 'Stay on the bottle for a while. Dinner won't be long.'

Pascoe did as he was told, kept the mask over his face. He could hear Des cackling in the kitchen. A funny pairing, earnest middle-class kids like the woman and her friends, and a hard case like Des Ryan, but there it was.

The young woman returned with a plate that she placed in his lap. Vegetarian food, which was all that he ate. Curried pumpkin and chickpeas. Saffron rice. A couple of puri. Black dhal.

Pascoe removed his mask and took up his spoon while Des and the young hippies sat on stools around him, eating and watching him eat.

Sat Prakash, the bearded bricklayer, began reminiscing about his time on the Rajneeshees' Oregon ranch where he was a sworn member of the commune peace force. He'd trained at the Oregon police academy in his maroon uniform, learned to shoot and make arrests. On the commune he carried a .44 S&W Magnum as his sidearm, strapped to a hip holster. Learnt how to shoot Uzis and shotguns. Trained others to do the same. They were peace-loving folk, he said, but not the kind to turn the other cheek. They all laughed about it now. None of them wore the orange, maroon, pink or purple. There was no need for any of that.

As darkness fell and more of their friends arrived, Pascoe kept to his armchair, at a distance from the dancing and drinking crowd who'd gathered on the deck. Beside him was the young woman who'd given him the pill. 'It isn't medicine,' she said. 'It's a drug formerly used in psychotherapy, called MDMA. Always been a bit of a community secret, but good for occasions such as this.'

Pascoe swallowed the pill and the woman drifted off to her friends. Soon, he felt himself melt at the margins of his body and mind. He felt the music. A creamy warmth rose up inside him that made him smile, despite wearing the mask. There was Des Ryan, on the dancefloor with the others, doing the rockabilly moves of their youth while women gathered around him and clapped. Pascoe closed his eyes, still smiling, let the warmth overwhelm him.

21.

Francine/Montana's full name was Francine Amy McGregor. DOB 15/05/64. Last known address in Darlinghurst, Sydney, but born and raised in Applecross, Perth. Some juvie arrests for possession and shoplifting. In Sydney, for soliciting and possession of heroin.

Her mother had died around the time Francine first migrated across the country to its biggest city. Francine was listed as Mary McGregor's only child. If Francine had inherited money there was no sign in her one-bedroom flat, in nearby Hamilton Hill.

Swann pulled away the police tape from across the doorway of flat number seven. Behind him, he could smell the tannic waters of the nearby wetlands. The strong scent of tea-tree, algae and waterlogged paperbark.

Swann knocked out of formality, knowing the flat was empty. Cassidy had already told him that there were none of Bernier's prints inside, or anybody else's besides Francine's for that matter. It was odd that Francine hadn't brought the sailor back to her home, if their relationship was more than business. The block of flats was quiet this time of night, the same hour that Francine had likely met Bernier at the Seaview Hotel. Swann turned the key Cassidy had left him and entered the incense-heavy atmosphere of the main room. He flicked the lights and scanned the kitchenette, with its three stools set along the formica benchtop, the washed dishes in the drying rack, covered with a tea towel. In the sitting room was a couch and television, a record player with a banana box full of vinyl. He knelt and flicked through them, out of interest. Found one of his daughter Louise's punk band, from back in the late seventies. It was their sole release before the band broke up. Louise played bass and there she was, with two other young women and the only male in the band, Justin, the lead singer. They were sitting on the rocks of South Mole, all of them in black, storm clouds above their heads. Two of the band members were now dead – the drummer from a heroin overdose and the lead singer, Justin, from suicide.

Swann looked around the walls of Francine's apartment. It felt like she'd only just left, and was soon to return, reminding Swann even more of how lucky he was. There was something about being a father of daughters that terrified him. As an ex-cop who'd often been in the position he was now, looking over the possessions of a murdered woman, usually from a domestic violence incident, it was impossible to pretend that he could keep his daughters safe, however much they were in his thoughts. They were all street-smart – he and Marion had given them that at least – but being wise to the nature of men hadn't saved Francine. So much came down to luck.

Swann began to work the room, looking for the letters, aerograms or telegrams that Cassidy hadn't been able to find. There was nowhere at the Ada Rose for Kerry's workers to store personal items, and even if there was, given Kerry's rules about meeting clients off-duty, it wasn't the place for Francine to keep correspondence that might compromise her position there.

Swann went into Francine's bedroom. He could see that her drawers and cupboards had been gone through – some of them still out and the wardrobe doors ajar. Swann skimmed through the hanging dresses in mostly primary colours and looked through her shoes, finding nothing. Swann knelt at the chest and started pulling out the drawers, placing them on the floor beside him. Sure enough, there it was inside the gutted chest: a stuffed manila envelope stapled to the back surface.

When Swann entered the flat he'd noticed the jemmy marks around the front door lock, the fact that the lock-face was loose. Letters had no financial value to a thief, but they were personal enough for Francine to decide that they needed securing. Swann pulled away the envelope and tipped the dozens of aerograms and cards onto the floor. He opened them all and placed them in order, starting with the oldest, sent by 'Charlie' a mere three days after the *Vinson* had last been in port. Bernier was a regular correspondent, writing fortnightly and then monthly throughout the two years of his absence. He wrote in a spidery hand, much like Swann's own, that suggested someone who didn't write much. He was forthright in his expressions of desire for 'Frannie', both physical and emotional. The most recent letter was dated a month ago, postmarked Mombasa, Kenya. It described how he'd secured shore leave among the first group allowed to leave the *Vinson* in Perth, and that he intended to book a room at the Seaview on that first night, just like they'd done last time. How he would buy wine, candles and flowers. He didn't know how long he'd be in port and so wanted to see her as much as possible. He wrote a short, rhyming poem that was nakedly sentimental, describing her eyes, the softness of her skin and the smell of her hair. To Swann, it didn't sound like a man using confected charm to get what he needed.

Swann drove home through the empty streets, the manila envelope on the seat beside him. The nausea he still felt was made worse by his fatigue, the fact that he hadn't slept. He thought about where Midshipman Charles Bernier might be hiding, aware that Cassidy had gotten word out to the train stations, airport and bus stations to keep an eye out, while Webb was monitoring the *Vinson* in case Bernier returned to base. Bernier's description and picture hadn't yet been published, and Bernier's name hadn't been formally released – a compromise that Webb and Cassidy had arrived at together. The arrangement would hold until Bernier was either captured or more evidence linking him to the crime could be secured.

There weren't many places for Bernier to run. If he didn't know anybody except Francine, and had nowhere to hide, it was always possible that he'd show himself at night, hoping to find a woman to take him home. If he was Francine's killer, then that woman was in danger. Swann, Webb and Cassidy had to make sure that didn't happen.

The dog was waiting for him at the front gate. Swann knelt and rubbed her ears while she wriggled closer to him. She was cold and he let her follow him inside. There was a message on the answering machine, which he'd turned to its lowest volume.

Swann pressed the button and the red light ceased blinking. He leaned down so that he could hear without waking Marion. The caller didn't leave a name, but Swann recognised the voice. It belonged to Detective Sergeant Dave Gooch of the Gold Squad, warning Swann to keep away from Paul Tremain and Lightning Resources, or there would be problems.

Swann clenched his jaw. Perhaps he hadn't been clear enough with Mr Paul Tremain. He could see why a man in Tremain's position might want to use Swann's name, spread false rumours that Swann was on the Lightning Resources payroll, but that didn't mean Swann would be giving the businessman a pass.

He pressed his finger and the message was gone.

22.

Devon Smith put his hand to his jaw and pried it open, made sure to feel the hinges stretch. The headlights of the Monaro illuminated the ocean road lined with silos and shipping containers, the giraffe-looking crane structures hulking over the port ahead. He lit the last cigarette in his packet of Luckies. He always chain-smoked when he got his head up.

Barry Brown yawned beside him, rolled his neck and kept the chugging V8 on course, windows down to keep himself awake. He hadn't drunk, snorted or smoked a thing. He was on shift, and it was Devon that he'd been working. It'd taken a lot of pleading for Barry Brown to agree to take Devon to his nephew. Barry wanted Devon back on the *Vinson*, to get preparations underway. He was worried that Devon might make some kind of side deal with the skinheads once the introduction was made.

Brown cautioned Devon that he'd hear about it if that happened, but didn't know that there was one more Glock in Devon's haversack. They were a light weapon, and ever since he was a child Devon had been schooled to keep himself armed. Most sailors carried a switchblade when in port, despite the weapon being illegal. This was tolerated because US sailors were targets for thieves and terrorists. It didn't seem right that the fighting men of the most powerful military in history should go unarmed in public, especially in foreign countries.

'Just around the corner.'

The headlights dipped as the Monaro cut across train tracks and began to climb a stone hill. The moon was above them. Devon could smell the ocean and freshly watered yards. Dogs barked as they turned into a dead-end street, passing small factories and warehouses, a wrecker's yard and a brewery that loomed like a church in the semi-dark. Barry Brown double-clutched the Holden as they passed an old bungalow built onto the top of the hill, making the engine roar. They swept around the cul-de-sac at the end of the street and returned to the bungalow.

'What time's your shore leave end? You can probably see the port from the back windows. Get one of these fuckheads to drop you back. You could even walk from here. Don't know why you want to hang out with these morons but I guess it's a free country.'

Devon put out his hand, but Barry ignored it. 'I got until nine am tomorrow morning,' Devon answered. 'That gives us two days until the officers' party. Just make sure you got the van there, unlocked. I'm gonna want my money, right away. If it ain't there, I don't leave the M16s.'

'We're cool, kid. You call us beforehand to get the van licence plates, we'll do the rest.'

Devon put out his hand again, and this time Barry Brown shook it, the pressure fierce.

The Monaro chugged down the hill. Devon waited until its tail-lights were gone before flicking his cigarette and knocking on the door. It was answered by a shirtless kid about Devon's age but ten pounds lighter. Devon had made sure to push up his polo shirtsleeves to show his ink, and the boy's eyes wandered over his arms and across his face.

'You got the sulphate?' was all he asked, still not moving aside or inviting Devon in.

Devon was still powered up on the crank and decided to play the role. He put a little pimp in his voice and smiled. 'Suurre, brother. If you got me a cigarette? You Aussies call that a durry, am I right?'

There were footsteps in the hall and the skinny kid moved away. A taller, meaner version took his place, head shaved and shirtless beneath the red braces, wore the bleached jeans and boots, swastika tattoo over his heart; the whole nine yards.

Devon put out his hand. 'You be the daddy bear, am I right? Barry Brown's nephew, Antony?'

The skinhead looked at Devon's tattoos and nodded. 'Come in, Yank.'

'Don't mind if I do.'

Devon followed the two men down the hallway into a lounge made by knocking out a brick wall. The work had been done recently, judging by the dust on the floorboards and the jagged bricks beside the kitchen sink. The sledgehammer was stood in the corner on a mound of swept drywall.

It was quiet in the house but out in the backyard Devon could see a group of young men gathered around a sawn-off drum, fire shooting sparks up into the sky.

The truth was that Devon had hoped to meet some women. He'd been told that the local women were crazy for Americans, and was hopeful that with a bit of charm he might get lucky – something that would shut up the clowns he worked with. Lenny and Marcus had been teasing him all week about it. Saying, hell, even Devon Smith could get laid in the Australian port. 'All you got to do is smile and ask 'em to dance. They beggin for it. Don't even have to pay. They so desperate for some chocolate candy bar. Though Devon got his happy sock, so he alright. Devon you know you go into port you got to leave your happy sock behind?'

Devon was so deep into the memory that he hardly noticed when the taller skinhead told him that he needed to be searched. Devon just nodded and put his hands up. The taller man was silent while the smaller man searched Devon, patting him down and rifling through his bag. The smaller kid didn't even notice the compartment at the bottom of the bag that contained the Glock. He handed over the bag and focussed instead on the packet of speed that Devon waggled in front of their noses.

'Night's old, fellas, not long till dawn. US Navy's in town though, yo! Booyaa!'

He said it with just the right amount of swagger, but it didn't go down like he hoped. The taller man gritted his teeth, took the packet of powder and said nothing. Nodded with his head toward the table made of a door placed over two tea chests. The smaller skinhead returned with a black plastic box and a spoon. Opened the black box and took out two syringes with orange caps. Offered Devon a third, who shook his head.

'Naw, I don't do like that, fellas. I gotta be back at base in a few hours and I ain't gonna sleep as it is. But you go right ahead.'

They already were. Neither of them had spoken, but they exchanged glances. Devon got that anxious feeling again, rising up through the fake speed confidence. He tried to clear his mind, focus on what was happening. It wasn't that the two Australian skinheads were any kind of threat. There was nothing in their postures or in their silence. They didn't appear to be jonesing either. There was something else going on that Devon wasn't privy to, some kind of secret that he didn't know. That was a good thing, he realised. He didn't want in with any kind of cowboy outfit. He was looking for real players. He decided to let the two men take their shot before breaking into their silence. If they were the right kind, then he'd reveal his trump card – the Glock in his bag. He hadn't decided whether he'd charge them or present it as a gift, with the offer of more. The latter, most likely. He wanted them to get some girls around, to liven things up before his artificial mood wore off and he was due on deck.

23.

The morning sun rose to the rim-line of the brick wall above them. Swann and Webb sat in its shade, waiting for Cassidy to arrive. The boxing gym was open but only Blake Tracker could be heard inside; the steam-press hisses of his exhalations as he worked the heavy bag, the thudding of his sixteen-ounce gloves hitting leather, and the bag creaking on its chain. Swann had set up the card table outside and made a pot of filtered coffee for Lee Southern, who'd been up all night working the door at Kerry Bannister's brothel.

Lee Southern lit a cigarette and exhaled sideways, aware of Swann's sickness. That morning, Swann had gone to his GP's home and received the first injection of the chelate solution that would bond to the lead in his bloodstream. Swann had taken three months worth of glass vials home with him. The solution wasn't covered by Medicare, and it was expensive, but he didn't have much choice. Daily injections for a fortnight and then weekly after that. He looked forward to the first sign that the poison was abating. Right now he hadn't noticed any difference. Even the smell of coffee made him want to hurl.

'This is your place?' Webb asked, genuine surprise in his voice.

'Long as we keep paying the rent. Everything else is donated. An old friend and I started it up a few years ago. Philosophy's simple. Make it the kind of place that we would've liked when we were kids, but didn't have. Better to work it out in here, than out there.'

'Amen to that. Shall we begin?'

Swann nodded and Webb turned over the crime scene and autopsy photographs, spread them on the card table. Cassidy had done a good thing by sharing them. He'd left the file with Webb for an hour while he went to canvass Kerry Bannister's staff, who'd all been summoned for that reason. Webb had worked as a county detective before joining the navy. Swann had worked homicide too, but not for many years. The two men looked closely at each of the photographs, which were in turn photographed by Lee Southern. Webb picked up the fifth photograph and pointed out the bruise to Swann. It wasn't a big bruise, but it was clearly visible on Francine's lower back.

'That's the first odd note,' he said. 'She's been strangled from behind.'

'Odd for a crime of passion, which is what we've been assuming.'

Lee Southern put down the Minolta, scanned the picture with his grey eyes. 'What do you mean?'

Swann pointed to the bruise. 'We know that Bernier and Francine were intimate. Most cases where a man strangles a woman he's familiar with, particularly if he's angry, he does it from the front, usually with his hands. You strangle someone from behind when your attack is a surprise. It's as impersonal as such a horrible thing can be.'

'What if he was ashamed? Couldn't bear to look?'

Webb leaned forward. 'That's possible, but unlikely. Why do it at all then? As far as we know, Bernier doesn't have a motive. Crime of passion, fit of rage, men usually revert to impulsive methods like attacking with a blunt object, or choking from the front. This, however, suggests a degree of planning, which in turn suggests a degree of coldness – the kind of coldness that doesn't usually look away. *Wants* to look. The whole point of doing it, for such men, is to look.'

Lee Southern met Swann's eyes. He'd picked up on it too – the hopeful note in Webb's voice. If Bernier was involved in the murder of a civilian ally, then the murder was also political. It would therefore be politically expedient if Bernier could be ruled out.

'That's all true,' Swann agreed, still looking at Southern. 'But it doesn't put Bernier in the clear. And we still don't have the ligature used to kill Francine. From the bruising on her neck, it doesn't look like a wire, or even rope. The bruise is too diffuse. There's no broken skin. She suffocated, slowly. Not the work of a professional. More like a first-timer.'

Webb flicked through the autopsy photographs until he came to close-ups of Francine's hands. He put the two photographs in front of Swann. None of her artificial and painted nails were damaged.

'We'll have to wait for the bloodwork,' Swann said. 'To find out if she was already unconscious, on the nod, or knocked out with something stronger.'

'There's always the other explanation,' Webb added, passing the photographs to Lee Southern, that hopeful note in his voice again. Lee scanned the images and looked to Swann.

'What, it was accidental? Part of some sex act?' Lee asked.

'No, this wasn't accidental. It took too long, and there's the knee at her back. What else is odd in those photographs?' Swann prompted.

Lee nodded. 'There were maybe two people. One holding her hands, so she couldn't fight back.'

'Precisely,' said Webb. 'But like Frank said, we'll have to wait and see.' Webb looked at his watch, began to read deeper into the autopsy report, the gruesome truth of Francine's surgery at the coroner's office hidden behind language describing stomach contents, dental anomalies, the size and weight of organs.

Lee's friend Blake Tracker emerged from the gym, lathered with sweat, peeling off his leopard-skin wraps. He looked over at the table and did the Noongar hand gesture, little curl of the wrist, indicating a question. Swann shook his head. Blake's mother had been murdered by an abusive boyfriend when Blake was still a child. It was Blake who'd found her, crumpled in a bedroom corner. Blake didn't need to see the contents of the folder, and he nodded and turned back into the gym.

The sound of tyres on the steep driveway, coming too fast. Swann and Webb stood, Lee taking up the Minolta. Cassidy's Commodore, driven by one of his underlings, speared into the small carpark and slammed on the anchors when the driver saw their table. A cloud of dust rose over the skidding car.

Cassidy cracked his door and stood one foot on the cement, the other on the chassis. 'I got to go. They've found another murdered woman. Strangled. In the city. Sounds like our man.'

Swann necked the rest of his coffee, nodded to Webb. Gone was any sign of hope in his eyes.

24.

Tony Pascoe looked at his reflection in the rear-view mirror of the Toyota van. He was parked across the road from Mark Hurley's home in suburban Floreat Park. It was a two-storey affair made of faux-limestone bricks with pale blue cornices and black tiles. The front lawn was bowling-green quality. The soil in the garden beds that skirted the house looked good enough to eat.

Back at the Sannyasins' house in Fremantle, Pascoe had sat on milk crates with a shower curtain draped over his shoulders while Sarani, her baby sleeping in a crib beside them, had taken the shears to his head and face.

The front page of the *West Australian* was laid on the floor beside her feet. It contained a blown-up image of the last mugshot taken of Pascoe, back in '70, when his beard was red and his hair was long. Pascoe's beard was now white and his hair had thinned out, and Sarani wanted to disguise him the best that she could. She carefully ran the shears over his scarred scalp, moving down through the blades until he had a buzz cut. She removed his beard altogether and shaved him with a disposable razor. When she held up the mirror to his face, he got a shock. Despite the weathering on his face he looked twenty years younger.

He had said too much at the party. The drug that they'd given him seemed to open his lungs and bring energy into his old body. He hadn't danced, unlike Ryan, but had been effusive for most of the night. Now however his voice was gone and his lungs were congested and painful. He remembered telling the men and women gathered at his feet the reason why he'd broken out of gaol. None of them seemed to judge him, perhaps because he hadn't told them the full truth. Sat Prakash, the bearded bricklayer, had offered Pascoe the use of a van that he'd recently bought from a house-painter. It had *Bill the Painter* in large letters on its sides, and a picture of a clean-shaven old man. Pascoe now looked like Bill the Painter, complete with his government-issue Buddy Holly–like prescription glasses. The likeness was pretty good. Sat Prakash had filled the van with old buckets and sheets, and a couple of rollers and tins of paint. The van was part of his disguise and it ran well enough. If Pascoe was arrested, then Sat Prakash would claim that the van was stolen from the street. There was no way to prove otherwise.

Pascoe ran a hand over his cold smooth chin. He was used to hair on his face and now his skin was soft and pale. He could feel his cheeks burning in the thin sunlight of late afternoon, parked under a gnarled old bottlebrush. His ribs hurt and his lungs crackled every time he breathed, and he sipped water and timed his hits on the oxygen bottle to once every fifteen minutes. There would be another fresh bottle for him back in Fremantle when he returned, assuming that he didn't finish the job tonight.

There was no sign of Mark Hurley inside the front rooms of the house. It was a condition of Mark's parole that he live with his father for the next six months. Mark's father was a builder and was likely out at a site. There was no condition placed upon Mark's work, and it was probable that he was working for his father too. It wouldn't do Mark much good in terms of the problems he now faced, but it might take his mind off things.

The kind of business that Mark Hurley was imprisoned for, and was being forced back into, was part of a night-time economy. Mark's problem was both the buying and selling sides of the equation. He didn't have a stake, and he didn't have the trust to receive credit. He'd lost all of his contacts due to the time he'd served. Mark would have to start near the bottom, where it was always more dangerous. Unless something could be done. The reason Pascoe was there, waiting.

He didn't have to wait any longer. A small convoy of trucks and vans rose over the nearest hill. A bobcat on a flatbed truck and another carrying pallets of corry iron. One van was being driven by Mark Hurley, sitting beside his father, a thin-looking man in overalls, already climbing out, dusting his boots in the gutter before stepping onto the pristine lawn. Mark Hurley looked around the street, but didn't see Pascoe's van. He looked healthy. His bulked-up prison-body had worn down to what was useful to do real work. He was tanned and his face was rimed with plaster dust. He kicked off his workboots and like his father walked in his socks to the front door. His father, according to Mark, was a good man, but didn't know the kind of trouble that Mark was in. Hurley Snr pointed to a bucket by the front door. Both of them stripped down to their jocks and tipped their clothes into the bucket, before slipping inside.

25.

Swann parked the Brougham in the Northbridge alley, behind what used to be the Zanzibar nightclub. He used his police radio to monitor the arrival of police and ambulances to the alley across the other side of William Street. Not many people knew about the alley beside the Brass Monkey pub, mostly used by punters eager to smoke a joint, or by couples looking to engage in a good old-fashioned knee-trembler.

Swann and Webb stood at the edge of the crime-scene perimeter, along with print and TV journalists and locals keen to rubberneck. Down the end of the alley they could see forensic staff in their white jumpsuits, hovering around an unseen figure; a photographer flash-lighting the scene so rapidly that the figures of the police, ambulance officers and forensic staff appeared like characters in a clumsy animation.

Webb had changed into civvies – jeans, boots and a windbreaker. Sunglasses and a Chicago Cubs cap. He and Swann weren't talking, in case one of the nearby journalists got too curious. Not many people knew that the *Vinson* had its own Shore Patrol and investigative officers in the city, and that was how Webb wanted it to stay.

Cassidy's great silver head rose above the crouched forms of the forensic team, his face bleached by flashes of light from the photographer's camera. He looked down the alley and saw Swann and Webb, but didn't acknowledge them, knowing that this would set the journalists off. He looked angry, however, muttering to his junior colleagues who stood against the wall and took notes. Now Swann could see the tipped-over wheelie bin and the rubbish strewn across the rough paving. The pale form of a young woman, still dressed in a platinum disco singlet and leather skirt. Black leather boots and silver bangles up her arms. Peroxided hair covering her face.

'Holy shit,' said one of the journalists beside them, a young man peering into a long-distance lens. He passed the camera to the young woman beside him. 'Is that what I think it is?'

Webb raised the Minolta to his eye, dialled in the focus. Swann saw his Adam's apple pump as he tried to swallow. Webb shook his head grimly, passed the camera to Swann.

Swann spoke for the first time since they got to the alley. 'What am I looking at?'

Webb leaned close, whispered. 'The ligature around her neck. It's a midshipman's neckerchief.'

Swann saw the neckerchief tight under the woman's purpled face. He saw movement beside her and took the camera from his eye. It was Cassidy, approaching them, removing something from his pocket. The anger in his eyes and the set of his jaw made the journalists begin to snap and film. He arrived at the perimeter tape and ignored Swann and Webb. He stood in front of the flashing cameras and held up the photograph of US Midshipman Charles Bernier.

'This is the man we're looking for, in connection to the murder two days ago of Francine McGregor. She was last seen alive with this man. We want anyone who has seen him to contact the police. Do not try to engage with him. Do not harbour or shelter him. We have reason to believe that this murder behind me is linked to the first. Our investigations are ongoing. The identity of the deceased woman has yet to be established. She appears to be between twenty and twenty-five years old, with bottle-blonde hair and black nail polish. She is wearing a metallic singlet and black leather skirt and boots. Anybody who can help identify her please contact the police. She is without identification, money, or car and house keys.'

Cassidy passed the picture of Bernier to the most senior journalist, Brian Hunter, who'd just arrived, still panting from his exertions. Hunter took the picture but didn't put it away.

'Brian,' Cassidy continued, 'I want the midshipman's name and photograph shared with every media outlet that asks for it.'

Hunter nodded to the eager faces around him.

Cassidy cleared his throat. 'But in the meantime, if you have any further questions about the midshipman in that photograph, then I suggest that you address them to Master-at-Arms Steven Webb of the USS aircraft carrier *Carl Vinson* over there, beside Frank Swann, who many of you will know. That is all.'

Cassidy turned on his heels and went back to his grim task. Webb took Swann's elbow and made to leave, but Swann shook his head. They were surrounded and it wouldn't be right to run away. Webb clenched his jaw but he took off his cap and squared his shoulders, looked into the faces of the dozen men and women leaning toward him.

26.

Devon Smith placed the final breakfast plate, smeared yellow with congealed yolk, in the tray and pulled the handle. The brushed steel box engaged the dishwasher electronics and began to churn. Steam seeped from the edges and condensed on the box. The steam reeked like a dumpster and Devon wiped his face on a clean tea towel, tossed it into the scullery wash-basket. Somebody the same rating as him would come later to collect the towels and dishcloths. Someone else whose career in the US Navy had gone the way of Devon's.

It was late Sunday afternoon, and thirty-six hours since Devon had slept. He'd forced himself to eat cereal when he returned to the *Vinson*, five minutes before he would be declared AWOL. He'd walked back from the skinheads' house on the hill above the port to where the *Vinson* was moored. He had anticipated the time it'd take but not the armed guards searching everyone returning from shore leave. Devon didn't have any contraband so had nothing to worry about. He got changed back into his uniform in an abandoned storage shed on the docks. Two Shore Patrol officers gave orders to six or seven underlings who made the returning sailors line up before entering the gangway, patting them down and firing questions. The men returning at this hour were the lucky ones who'd gotten laid, and none of them complained, just stood there with half-smiles and bleary eyes while the sun rose above them and the cement expanses of the dock began to radiate heat.

Devon took his place in the line, opening the neck of his rucksack for inspection. He'd gifted the final Glock to the skinhead leader, Barry Brown's nephew, whose full name he'd learned was Antony 'Ant' Wallace. It was the only time the tall guy showed anything in his eyes, which grew large with appreciation. Devon showed him how to eject the magazine and clear the breech of its cartridge. 'I don't want nothing from you guys,' Devon added, just in case they thought he had an ulterior motive. Some of the other skinheads were already eyeing his haversack, in case it contained more treasure. 'I just want to help out. Uncle Sam wants to help out. There's hundreds of thousands of guys like me stateside. We got to reach out to each other, before it's too late.'

'Too late for what?' one of them asked. He was a skull-head with piggy eyes and the posture of a doorman; menace in his poise even when stood quietly against the wall, arms folded against his chest. His knuckles were skinned and his wife-beater was stained with what looked like gravy, or blood.

'The apocalypse of the white race. Perhaps you guys, where you live. It's a small city, a long way from everywhere ...'

Ant Wallace took exception to that. He scoffed, sneered, sighted down the Glock's barrel at the ocean across the highway. 'Except that you Yanks keep bringin the frontline here,' Ant said. 'AIDS and VD and whatnot. You just told me the last port you visited was in black Africa. And now you're here, same dicks been dipped in black ink, puttin AIDS in our women.'

Devon couldn't argue with the logic, but didn't understand why the Australian wasn't seeing the bigger picture, forcing Devon to repeat himself. 'Well, like I said. I was in the brig that whole Kenya shore leave. For insubordination. Got thirty days for speakin back to a nigger officer.'

It was a lie, but they didn't know that. Devon hadn't been in the brig and he hadn't been in trouble for insubordination. He'd been late for his shift three days in a row.

Devon's words didn't appear to have any effect. He'd tried to play the role of the brash US sailor but it hadn't worked. Soon as he started on with his tales of fighting in ports, or telling them stories he stole from his father's life, their eyes glazed over and they shared looks that made Devon feel even more on the outside. There was something dangerous about their silence, too, as though there were secrets behind it that involved him. Which was impossible. They hadn't known that he was going to contact them. Bringing out the Glock had changed things but not as much as he expected. They still wore that worked-up look like they'd been out fighting, when according to Ant Wallace they'd spent the night around the fire 'sinking piss'. They took turns hitting up the crank until the packet was gone, their needles laid out on the dirt next to their cigarettes and car keys. It was only when the sun rose and some of them started dozing on the old couches around the fire that Devon nodded to Ant and indicated that they should go inside.

Ant followed Devon up the stairs into the house. The feeling of Ant behind him made the hairs on Devon's neck stand up. It was in the kitchen that they drank glasses of water and Devon splashed water onto his face. He leaned closer to Ant and whispered his plan, watching the Australian's face and hoping for signs of excitement or gratitude, of which there were none – just the same cold stare.

When Devon Smith approached the front of the queue leading onto the *Vinson* it became clear that the navy police were merely looking for uniform code violations. Devon knew that most of them were police back on civvy street, and he wondered if they resented turning their hand now to checking the square knots of sailors' neckerchiefs. One by one the men fronted the Shore Patrol sailors and showed their neckerchiefs and were allowed on board. Devon hastily retied his own neckerchief and made it neat and square. He felt like a fool for doing it but couldn't risk another infraction, no matter how minor. He stood to attention in front of the Hispanic policeman who, because he was a senior rank, and also an asshole, made Devon salute. While Devon's hand was still at his forehead the officer showed him a picture of a black sailor and asked if he'd seen him on shore leave. Devon acted like the question itself was insulting, and the spic officer glared and nodded Devon toward the gangplank. There was just time to change out of his uniform into his service coveralls, eat breakfast and get to the scullery. He wasn't looking forward to hearing about how much booty Lenny and Marcus had hit or being questioned about the size and quality of Australian cock. It was going to be a long day. All Devon had to do was get through it and secure some shut-eye, then catch his bunk-mate Scully when he returned from his shift in the armoury.

27.

Swann led Webb up the beer-smelling stairs of the Brass Monkey and onto the second storey where the floorboards creaked beneath carpet laid during the gold rush ninety years earlier. Back then, the second storey was a brothel; now the old rooms were used for storage and offices. Swann knocked on the door of the furthest room on the north side. As he'd hoped, he heard the gruff voice of Richard Hand, the unfortunately named hotel manager, telling him to come in.

Hand was perched over the open window leading onto the alley. Cassidy could be seen below conferring with a forensics officer, standing over the murdered woman. The contents of the garbage bin were being spooned into ziplock bags, clearing the space around the woman prior to her removal. Hand got a surprise when he turned and found Swann inside the door, rather than one of his bar or cleaning staff.

'Swann. What the fuck?'

Hand was a handsome man in his forties, still sporting a quiff of blond hair. His face shone with the moisturiser he'd just applied. The open jar of Pond's cream sat next to a lit cigarette on the desktop laden with bills, invoices and orders.

'Nasty business,' Swann said. 'You been watching the whole time?'

The question wasn't an accusation but Hand's reply was testy. He screwed the lid on the moisturiser and put it in the top drawer. 'Since I got in, about an hour ago. Why?'

'No reason. Dick, this is Steve Webb. He's an investigator with the US Navy.'

There wasn't space in the room for Webb to do anything except lean around Swann and show his face. 'Sir. Thanks for seeing us.'

'Seeing you? Not like you asked first.'

Webb looked a little shocked. Swann angled his head and Webb stood back into the hall. 'I'm assuming it was one of your staff found the poor woman. That's your row of bins, no?'

Hand put his elbows on the desk, took up his cigarette and rolled the glowing end into a point of fire. 'Yeah, sure is. They got Kylie in a paddy wagon somewhere. What do you want?'

'Before Cassidy gets up here and asks the same questions, I want to speak to your bar staff who were on duty last night. Or, even better, you call and ask them, put the phone on speaker. We're looking to ID the murder victim.'

Hand took a good hit off the cigarette and flicked it over his shoulder, out into the alley. 'I don't have to speak to you, Swann. Those days are over. Why the fuck would I?'

Swann was prepared. He took out the twin hundred-dollar notes that he'd extracted from Webb's wallet, held them up. Webb hadn't needed convincing. Cassidy had publically shamed him, and by extension the US Navy. He was now on the outer and needed a way back in.

'Give 'em here.'

Hand swiped the notes and put them in his desk drawer. Squinted at the duty roster beside him and squared up the phone. Lifted off the handset and punched the numbers.

Dick Hand let them out into the alley by way of the pub's back door. They were now inside the police tape perimeter and Swann walked toward Cassidy with the note held up. Some of the journos down the far end of the alley noticed and raised their cameras. Cassidy pulled out his handcuffs and strode to cut the distance, his hand on the revolver at this hip.

'You're under arrest, Swann, for impeding an investigation. The Septic Tank can leave, but you're –'

Swann stopped and waited. When Cassidy was in his face and reaching to turn him to the wall, Swann offered him the note. 'The young woman's name is Jodie Brayshaw. She lives alone in a flat at the Bayswater address there. I just spoke to a barman who knows her well. He noticed her drinking with two friends and three white sailors before midnight. He then noticed her talking to a black sailor in the corridor leading to the toilets, beside the cigarette machine, just after last orders. He said hello to her and she replied. She didn't look scared. He didn't get a good look at the black sailor and wasn't able to identify him as Bernier because it was too dark, although the man's size and height are a rough match. The barman's name and phone number are there too. Do you want it or should I give it to the journos?'

Cassidy relocked the bracelets, put them into their pouch on his belt, reached for the note. 'If Bernier's at this address, and he resists, I don't want your Yank copper mate getting in the way. Wait until we're gone before heading there yourself. You got it?'

Swann put up his hands, nodded, retreated back to where Webb was smoking, looking up at Dick Hand in the offices above them, his face shining in a box of sunlight, pale fingers on the lintel, enjoying the show.

28.

Tony Pascoe took a long draw off the oxygen bottle. The taste was metallic and he knew that it was near empty. He could feel the blood in his head, a simmer rising to a boil. He had been sitting in the van for fifteen minutes, watching the spectacle while trying to calm his breathing.

Pascoe's plan of taking Jared Page by surprise might succeed, but would also mean the end of his life. Page's security was discreet but couldn't be ignored. The adrenalin in Pascoe's bloodstream was a response to the imminence of his death, should he choose to cross the street and enter Page's restaurant; 'Big Salty' a reference no doubt to the businessman's opinion of himself as an alpha predator.

Pascoe didn't recognise the two men in tan suits who lounged behind separate tables. They were stationed out of earshot of Page but close enough to come to his aid should it be required. Page sat at what was probably his favourite table in the corner near the plating station. The restaurant was only half full, but the two elderly waiters were busy rushing from the customers to the steel counter where the hands of a chef could be seen adding garnishes and wiping plates.

Pascoe had no trouble identifying Jared Page. Once Mark Hurley had pointed him out in the society pages of the shared prison newspaper, attending a fashion opening, a young blonde on his arm, Pascoe had seen him in the pages on a weekly basis. The same jet-black hair with a widow's peak, the same crow-eyes and cynical grin. Always fashionably dressed. A thin dark man who made up for his lack of stature with conspicuous displays of wealth, on his wrist, on his fingers, in the suits and ties that he wore. He was among the wealthy now but still carried the bad-boy attitude that had gotten him there.

Pascoe was interested to see how it went down, and he was rewarded for his patience. A young man in loafers and a cheap jacket entered the restaurant and took a table. He didn't acknowledge Page or the waiters. One of the bodyguards got up and went into the kitchen. One of the waiters returned with a paper doggy bag folded at its mouth. He passed it to the young man who nodded and made for the door. The bodyguard resumed his seat, looking at his nails.

Pascoe knew that Mark Hurley was another such young man, also on the string. When he was busted with the drugs that ensured him a long sentence, those drugs were destroyed. Unfortunately for young Hurley, however, the drugs hadn't been paid for. When he was imprisoned, his debt to Page remained, but with five years of punitive interest added to the principal. Hurley now owed Jared Page something in the order of two hundred thousand dollars.

Thus far, Mark Hurley's father was in the dark, but if Mark didn't come up with the money soon, then Page's heavies would be put onto him. If Hurley Snr chose to cover his son's debt then he'd lose his house, and likely his business too. This was how Jared Page had acquired so many assets over the years. He owned a trucking company and dozens of commercial properties alongside his mining interests.

Hurley had always suspected that Page put him in. Hurley was a heroin addict and at that age, a fool. He didn't see the way things would go for him. Cocaine was a rich kid's drug, and he enjoyed the dealing lifestyle until he found himself in Fremantle Prison. Now he had little choice but to return to a dead-end life, a trap of Page's making.

Pascoe took a final hit off the oxygen bottle. It echoed as he inhaled. The bottle was empty now. He closed his eyes and calmed his breathing. This was the moment where everything he'd done in life reached its culmination. He said a silent prayer to himself, apologising to the women he'd loved and then left, the two sons he'd never known. The world wouldn't miss him, but that didn't make it any easier.

The moment had come. Without opening his eyes, he reached under the newspaper beside him and felt the crosshatched grip of the modified flare pistol, now a sawn-off rifle. He had one shot. There was no point waiting until Page returned to his home in nearby Subiaco. His goons would see him to his door. They would clock Pascoe as he entered the restaurant, too, but as an old man dressed in painter's clothes – a harmless worker wandered in off the street. By then it would be too late for them. Pascoe would pretend to be the man he'd once been, young and strong and storming a bank, voice loud, power in his movements.

29.

Darkness wasn't far away and Swann followed the convoy of unmarked Fords and Commodores, cherry lights flashing without sirens, to the Bayswater Bridge rendezvous where they were joined by a TRG van. Cassidy was in the lead vehicle, no doubt formalising a strategy to be enacted when they reached Slade Street. So far Cassidy had maintained radio silence, but that would soon change. Each of the police vehicles had left the crime scene separately, some heading into the city and others turning north toward Mount Lawley, but had met again at the servo just inside the Bayswater Bridge. This was Cassidy being old-school, and Swann admired him for that. Plenty of other detectives would have leaked word to the gathered press in the hope of getting their picture on the front page – that flash-lit moment as the suspect was led to the waiting panel van. Instead, and justifiably worried that the press might get there before them and alert Bernier, Cassidy had put policy before self-promotion.

'What do you think Cassidy's problem is?' Swann asked. 'He's onto something more than a suspicion of Bernier's guilt.'

Webb was unnaturally still. He'd finished talking into 'the brick', the Nokia Cityman mobile phone that was the first Swann had seen, allowing Webb to communicate with the *Vinson* by way of the ship's own cell tower. He was careful not to talk too much, using formal code to designate what Swann presumed to be procedures and protocols. This signalled to Swann that despite Webb's earlier cheerfulness there was a developing trust issue, which led to Swann's question as soon as he hung up.

Webb lit a cigarette and scrolled down the window. The late afternoon was hot and bright, the smells of exhaust invading the car. Up ahead, the ridgeline of the scarp carried the last rays of sunlight reflected from windows and corrugated-iron roofs, making the heat seem worse. Webb ashed into the wind as Swann caught King William Street, making their turn right.

'I don't know, Frank. My guess is that through whatever channel, he's learned that Charles Bernier has a sex crime conviction, back in Texas. What he mightn't know, and the reason I didn't bother sharing it with him, is that it was a stat rape charge, laid when Bernier was sixteen and his girlfriend was fifteen. The girlfriend, it must be said, was white.'

Swann nodded but didn't reply. He followed the police convoy and turned the Brougham across traffic into Slade Street, headed toward the riverside block of flats where Jodie Brayshaw lived. Now the radio crackled to life as Cassidy directed the lead vehicle to cut its cherry lights. He ordered the TRG troopers to take up positions in the entrances, stairwells and second and third floor balconies of the five-storey block. He told the uniformed officers to keep out of sight, but to scout the carpark and nearby streets looking for a brown Datsun 120Y, registration number 6BC 456.

Swann's knuckles were white on the steering wheel as he pulled the Holden to the kerb. They were uphill from the apartments, with a clear view of the plainclothes and uniformed men and women swarming to their task. He killed the ignition and pulled the handbrake.

'Yeah, that might explain it,' he said to Webb. 'What else haven't you told him?'

Ahead of them, Cassidy looked up the street and saw Swann and Webb, made a point of ignoring them, taking out his Smith & Wesson revolver, checking the load.

There was no contrition in Webb's voice. 'I didn't share that Bernier is something of a loner. That the navy shrinks have had their eye on him. Regular attendee at Sunday services, across two denominations. Skips meals. Was treated for venereal disease three months ago, clear for HIV. Nearly failed his last physical, as a result of congenital asthma. Should be wearing glasses but refuses, out of vanity. No discipline issues. No gang affiliations. No likelihood of promotion anytime soon. He performs his role as a boatswain's mate well enough, maintaining mechanical equipment, related to his civvy job as a diesel mechanic. He has a high IQ, based on tests done by the shipboard shrinks, who feel that Bernier's withdrawn nature is the result of frustration at his current position, although he shows no ambition to retrain or reskill himself. When his belongings were searched there was nothing untoward, no women's possessions or lewd material –'

'Any letters?' Swann asked. 'Francine kept every letter from Bernier.'

'No letters. I'm not sure what that means, precisely. Whether he didn't value the relationship as much as she did –'

'Or he didn't want to leave any evidence of their knowing each other.'

Webb looked at Swann for the first time. Swann felt the voltage in the look but ignored it, watching the TRG troopers secure every escape route from the building while Cassidy and two other plainclothes officers crept toward the flat on the second floor, pistols drawn.

'Do we have a problem, Frank?' Webb's voice was quiet, but there was steel in it.

'Not if you share everything you just told me with Cassidy, and anything else you think might be useful to the case. Meat in the sandwich, that's not where I want to be. I'm not taking sides. I just want to help catch Francine's killer, Jodie Brayshaw's killer.'

'Fair enough.'

Cassidy stood next to Brayshaw's bedsit, gun raised as a prequel to assuming the firing position. He nodded his head to the TRG officer in a visored helmet, who slammed an orange battering ram into the door, just above the lock. Cassidy went inside, followed immediately by three other officers. Swann and Webb waited for it, the sound of a gunshot, but there was only shouting, and then silence. A minute passed before the TRG officer returned to the balcony and signalled to his troopers to stand down, inverting a thumb before holstering his pistol.

30.

Devon Smith sat on his rack and thumbed through an old hunter's magazine. On the cover was a picture of a Tennessee hog the size of a small car, surrounded by two bearded men and the dogs who'd brought it down. The men grinned like kids gathered around a birthday cake; the dogs panted behind bloody snouts.

Mike Scully would come off shift soon, and then Devon would make his pitch. Scully was one of the lucky ones. As a storeman his responsibilities included transporting weapons up to the deck, where the men and women of the air wing undertook target practice by firing at paper targets hung over the ocean. Mike occasionally got to feel the sun on his face while he waited and watched, handing out ammunition and checking off the pistols as they were returned. Devon's ordinary duties meant that he lived, worked and slept below deck for weeks at a time, never seeing the sunlight or taking in a view over the ocean.

Devon had the rack closest to the floor. Mike had the rack above Devon because he was a six-footer in a bunk too short for him. If he were on the bottom rack his feet would trip up everyone as they squeezed along to the head, or the stairs that were the only exit to the berthing floors above and below. On the top rack was a Montana cowboy called Winter. Used to wide-open spaces and a big empty sky, now he slept with an iron ceiling one foot above his face. He snored and grunted and his knees cracked the ceiling when he turned over in his sleep, although he never complained. Another dope fiend who'd chosen military service over prison time.

Devon and Mike Scully had joined up at the same recruitment intake and were both from San Diego, although back home their lives were different. Mike was a surfer from La Jolla with a steady girlfriend who he called when he had the chance. Devon on the other hand grew up south of Interstate 8, moving from house to house until he hit the Gaslamp district to live on the streets when he was fourteen.

Devon shared the berthing room with fifty-one other men, two-thirds of whom worked the day shift. There were only a dozen or so men in the room now, some sleeping, others reading or staring at the ceiling. The room smelt so bad that he only returned there to shower, change or sleep. No matter how much deodorant or powder was used, the stink of feet never dissipated and the air was particularly stagnant in the corner where Devon was bunked. He needed to sleep but didn't want to miss Scully, who'd return soon to change for his daily session in the gym before hitting the mess and rec areas.

Right on cue, Devon heard the trampling of boots on the steel steps that rose through ten floors before reaching the open layer beneath deck level. Devon straightened his blankets and tried to look like he wasn't waiting for Scully, instead setting about relacing his boots. Ten or so men began to thread their way through the different aisles and then he saw Scully, unbuttoning his shirt as he walked, bent over as usual in the low space. He saw Devon and mock-saluted, tossed his shirt onto his rack, leaned toward his stowage bin and drew out his kicks and shorts.

'Hey Mike,' Devon said. 'See that *Terminator*'s showin tonight. You gonna catch it with me?'

Scully shook his head, breaking into a grin that showed his straight white teeth. 'Nah son, got shore leave tomorrow. Gonna work out then hit the rack, get me an early one. Don't aim to be sleepin tomorrow night. How'd you go? You look all wrung out, son. You get some?'

Devon had hoped to accompany Scully to the movie room, where it got so loud before the lights went down that you could talk about anything without being overheard.

'Naw, bro, strike one for Devon Smith. I was doin business, though, like I told you. What I want to talk to you about.'

Mike Scully's smile dropped, but Devon knew that didn't mean much. Scully was from a good home and didn't need the money, but there was something about him that told Devon he could be worked. Scully was into the thrill, and it'd brought him trouble back home. It was Scully's father, an ex-marine, who'd convinced his son to sign up, believing that it'd straighten him out. Scully had failed to get into the marines, but still had four of his five contracted years left to serve, when he was planning on working in his father's auto yard. Scully was into cars, and they'd talked about vehicles they'd stolen for joyrides and, in Devon's case, for breaking down and rebirthing. Scully had that look in his eye when he talked about his small-time criminal history, and Devon knew that he could play with that. Devon had an instinct for corruption that he figured had been passed down to him. You wouldn't rely on a straight like Scully to make any serious moves, but if you had it all planned out, like Devon did, and if the excitement was there, together with a little pay-off, then you were a chance of getting your way.

All Devon had to do was point out that the trolleys the galley staff used to transport plates and bain-marie trays between floors were the same trolleys that Mike used to transport weapons to the deck for target practice. Mike Scully had told Devon often enough that the storeroom where he worked was like a giant supermarket, and that they only did stocktake when the *Vinson* returned stateside. There were no cameras and the CO was quartermaster to several other kinds of store, and so was rarely in his office. They could meet in the lift where there were no cameras and switch trolleys and nobody would know.

'Sit down, Mike.'

Scully looked nervous but did as he was told. Half of the stories that Devon had told Scully were bullshit but the surfer had no way of knowing that. It was part of a seduction routine that began when Devon saw that light in Scully's eyes, talking about stealing a cop car and setting it on fire at the beach one night. That was a dickhead move in anyone but a middle-class suburban boy's book, but Devon had played along and laughed and bumped fists. Scully was eager for some street, and here was Devon offering him a taste.

'Told you I had business last night. Look what I got here. Just the beginning, bro.'

Devon Smith fanned out the five grand, laid it on the bed. 'This five large is yours, you do me right.' Devon swept up the bills and with a snap of his wrist had the money banded, ready to pass over. 'You're gonna party tomorrow, right? You sure are now.'

31.

Swann wasn't used to injecting himself but he gritted his teeth and stuck the needle in his thigh. Pressed the plunger and wiped the denim trouser-leg to catch any of the chelate solution that seeped. Twenty-four hours since his last dose and twelve hours since he'd been sick. He hoped that there was some correlation because he'd been told the medicine took a week to have any effect. Still, he had his appetite back, drinking a bowl of soup with buttered bread before he heard the front gate squeal and the dog bark.

It was Louise and Maddie, her journo friend. The nose of Louise's FB Holden was turned into the drive, catching sunlight on its windscreen. When each of his daughters turned eighteen, Swann gave them the keys to a car that he'd bought cheaply and refitted inside, resprayed with original acrylic and fixed up at Gerry Tracker's mechanics workshop. He'd taught each of his daughters how to service their vehicles every ten thousand k, swapping out the oil and petrol filter, changing the spark plugs. Louise's white-over-green FB looked clean, waxed and polished against the harsh West Australian summers under the salty sea air.

Swann hugged Louise and shook Maddie's hand. She already had her notebook out and Swann waved her to a seat on the porch. Louise followed him into the kitchen where he took out a jug of chilled water and lemon juice. She had grown up eating in the kitchen and Swann caught her eye wandering over the rough surface of the small timber dining table. The table still wore the pen marks, paint splotches and carved divots from when she and her sisters had done their finger-paintings and art projects for school. Swann leaned over and kissed her ear, passed her two glasses.

'Yes, I'm feeling better,' he said in answer to the question he could see in her eyes. 'I've been passing the lead out in heavy water, you could say.'

Louise smiled and pretend-kicked his bum. 'You look better. Some colour in your face. But you've got to start eating.'

'Lasagne,' Swann said. 'Tonight, I promise. Maria's recipe. Made it a few days ago. Froze enough to see us through a nuclear winter. What's your friend doing here?'

Louise followed him down the hall. 'Nothing for the record. But I asked her to come. She's been digging around. You'll see.'

Louise's voice was gentle, but he recognised the tone in it. It was part of his daughters' job to educate him on matters important in their lives. For Louise, that was often political matters. He didn't always agree when he felt that his experience outweighed her idealism, but Swann saw it as one of the best things about being a father. His world kept getting bigger, rather than smaller, and his daughters had a lot to do with that.

Maddie looked nervous, giving truth to Louise's statement that she was there on his daughter's suggestion. Swann poured her a glass of water and passed it over. She drank and nodded her thanks, took off her reading glasses and wiped them on her shirt.

'Mr Swann –'

'Please. Call me Frank.'

'Ok, Frank. Thanks for seeing me. Louise thought it best that I share with you ... get some idea of what you think ... before I go to print.'

'Maddie, I'm working for the US Navy as a liaison, and most likely, this is the last time. I don't owe them anything.'

'That's good, Dad, because ... you tell him, Mads.'

Maddie took a deep breath. 'Well, I started looking at the incidence of rape, assault and murder when the USS *Carl Vinson* was last in port. That didn't go too far. There was a stabbing death of a US sailor by a local boy, here in Fremantle. Some fights, drunk and disorderlies.'

'Yes, I remember the stabbing.'

Maddie opened her notebook, skimmed her shorthand, and flipped a page. 'So then I started looking overseas. Not just at the *Carl Vinson*, but at ports where the Americans dock regularly, or at least on a cycle. Mombasa in Kenya. Ports in Turkey, Egypt, Spain, Japan, the Philippines. I've put in calls and faxes to newspapers in those ports, or in those countries. I've got two faxes back. One from Kenya, one from Japan. In Mombasa, the last four times the US Navy has visited for

R&R, there have been a total of five murders of prostitutes coinciding with the shore leave periods. The journalist, a Mrs Unis Lubembe, said that none of them have resulted in arrests. She feels that the Kenyan government prioritises the money the sailors spend over the safety of its citizens. She said that she started writing a story about the murders but it was shut down. In Japan, according to the journalist over there, this is a historical problem, with dozens of sexual assaults and murders over the past decades in cities near military bases, and only a handful of convictions. The Japanese public are aware of the issue, and it gets a lot of press, resulting in pressure on the Japanese government, but apparently there's little they can do except formally protest. They can't force the NISCOM – the navy's investigative branch – to investigate. I'm still waiting on responses from journalists in the other countries.'

Maddie lit a cigarette and stared at Swann. She was good at her job, waiting for him to ask the obvious question, reading him to see if he already knew the answer.

'Anything involving the *Carl Vinson*? Recently?'

Maddie looked at Louise, who nodded.

'Yes, sad to say. The *Carl Vinson*'s recent shore leave in Mombasa, for a duration of three days, resulted in the murder of a sex worker. Reported in the Kenyan papers, but not officially linked to the US Navy.'

'Was it investigated by the local police?'

'That's what I'm waiting to hear. Mrs Lubembe is looking into it.'

'Please ask her to try and establish whether the murder was done by way of asphyxiation. Strangulation by ligature. If that's the case, then your story is even more important. And I'm sorry, I didn't know about any of this.'

Maddie looked surprised, but Louise didn't.

'Dad, there's something else. Maddie wants to interview some local madams, or prostitutes. Do you think Kerry Bannister would speak to her? She wouldn't answer the door when we went last time.'

'Only one way to find out. I was headed round there anyway, to follow up on something. But tread lightly. They're open for business, but Kerry's brought in new workers from Kalgoorlie, Sydney and elsewhere. Most flew in last night – they won't know anything. Her regular workers are on leave. They're grieving, getting ready for Francine's funeral.'

Maddie's pen was poised on the page. 'Has her body been released?'

'Not yet. Could be a while, I'd think. I'm trying to get that information for Kerry. I'll let you know. Shall we?'

Swann slipped into his boots, swallowed the last of his water. Louise and Maddie rose from their chairs and stepped off the creaking porch.

32.

Pascoe shouldn't have closed his eyes, not even for a moment. There he was, flare gun in hand, in the middle of the street, looking at Mark Hurley entering the restaurant. Pascoe turned away but had to conceal the pistol from two pedestrians walking their sausage dog in the semi-dark. Fortunately, the old couple were preoccupied with the stiff-legged dog, so black and low to the ground that it looked like they were dragging a shadow behind them.

Pascoe had gone close to doing it. He cursed under his breath as he strode to the van door and pulled it open, even though it was understandable for him to have taken his eyes off the target. He'd never killed a man in cold blood before, and Jared Page's death would be followed by his own.

Pascoe stowed the pistol under the newspaper that had his mugshot on the cover. He was out of oxygen but he still had the asthma puffer. He gave himself a couple of good blasts and wheezed in the chemical-tasting air. If Pascoe had an attack now, then he would suffer the death he most feared – slowly and painfully choking out, suffocating while his lungs haemorrhaged and his heart burst. He took another hit off the asthma inhaler and tried to calm his heartbeat.

Nobody in the street had seen the pistol in his hand. Neither had the bodyguards in the restaurant or Jared Page, who was holding court now with a middle-aged man in a suit while Mark Hurley stood and waited, hands at his waist like a chastened schoolboy.

Two sets of people had entered the restaurant while Pascoe had his eyes shut. Pascoe didn't recognise the man in the suit, whose body language said victim or supplicant, alongside another man who did look familiar. Pascoe sifted the face through his memory and came up with the name – Dave Gooch of the CIB branch. Gooch was a detective sergeant in armed rob when Pascoe was arrested those nineteen years ago, one of three arresting officers who'd then stolen most of the takings from the botched robbery, when only Pascoe had made it out of the bank. The bank said one hundred and fifty thousand and the newspapers concurred, but only fifty thousand was recovered and presented as evidence in court.

Pascoe didn't care about that. He'd do the same in their position. What made it hard to stomach was that they'd beaten him for two days, pretending to extract the whereabouts of the missing money. Then they verballed him by presenting Pascoe's unsigned 'confession' at the trial, stating that Pascoe refused to tell the court the whereabouts of the missing money. Pascoe's accomplice Ben Davey had wounded a security guard before being shot dead himself, and Pascoe took the full punishment for the crime. The appearance of holding out on the missing money and Davey's violence meant that Pascoe received the harshest sentence ever handed down to an armed robber. Pascoe hadn't cared about that either. Davey wasn't part of his regular crew, but Pascoe took responsibility for hiring the young hothead. He'd gone to the trouble of unloading Davey's sawn-off before they'd gone in, but somehow Davey reloaded again between leaving the car and entering the bank.

What nobody else knew was that the guard was their inside man. He'd told them where the alarm buttons were and who knew the safe combination and who didn't. Which of the banded notes in the tills contained dye packs and the temperaments of each of the tellers. Pascoe hadn't told his young accomplice about the guard, in case they were caught and the kid spilled. In those days police interrogations always involved beating and torture, something for which the Armed Robbery Squad was famous. And that was Pascoe's big mistake. The guard had overcompensated for his complicity by acting up during the robbery, presumably to protect himself from the suspicions of the armed-rob detectives, thinking that he was safe. The kid had lost his nerve and fired, seriously wounding the guard. Everything changed in that moment. It mightn't mean anything to people outside the trade, but Pascoe had built up a reputation over the course of his lifetime of being a smart and staunch armed robber, something that was blown when the guard went down. The kid fired the shotgun, but Pascoe had organised the robbery. It was on him – the guard's shooting and the kid's death at the hands of the police.

The memory of the slain kid and Detective Sergeant Dave Gooch working Pascoe over with a phonebook and a gloved fist brought on the sense-memories of the beating he took that day. Pascoe's heart fluttered like a small bird in his chest. Every now and then it missed a beat, and he felt a hot charge of shock flood his body. He knew that he should return to Fremantle and get more oxygen, but there was the matter of Mark Hurley.

Pascoe couldn't do the job now, not with the kid in there, newly released on parole. He watched Gooch and Page round on the suited man, smirking and poking him while Hurley stood and waited his turn. Gooch and Page were clearly enjoying themselves. There were no other customers in the restaurant now and their gestures were theatrical. Gooch slapped the table and the suited man flinched. The man clearly didn't know the rules. Pascoe would never flinch around men like Dave Gooch or Jared Page, which would just spur them on. Better to take the slap or the punch than give them the satisfaction. And just like that, it was over. The suited man was forced to shake Page's hand. He stood and was led to the door by Gooch, who ushered him out onto the footpath. Gooch followed him but they went to their cars separately. The suit drove a white Mercedes sedan while Gooch climbed into a silver LTD with mud on its rims.

The two vehicles drove away and Pascoe turned his attention to Hurley, now seated at the table with Page. Hurley was trying hard but whatever Page was saying at him, barely even bothering to meet his eyes, was bad enough news that his shoulders sank and his head bowed. There was a moment when Hurley raised his right hand and shouted something, which made the bodyguards pay attention, but he soon enough returned to his resigned posture while Page talked. Then the meeting was over. Hurley too was forced to shake Page's hand before being waved to the door. The bodyguard turned the open sign, locked the door and dimmed the lights in the room. Page could no longer be seen. Tony Pascoe had missed his chance.

He watched Hurley stride down the footpath opposite, away into the gloom. He turned the ignition and set the course for home. He was just about to pull away when he heard tapping on the passenger window. It was Hurley, who'd doubled back. Pascoe leaned over and cracked the door, but didn't invite Mark in. He kept his eyes straight ahead while

Hurley crouched on the footpath below window level. 'I saw you there, before I went in. I know what you're planning to do. I want to thank you, but –'

'You should get lost,' Pascoe said. 'You never saw me.'

Mark Hurley's voice wasn't as he remembered it. Gone was the humour and enthusiasm. He sounded broken.

'You don't understand, Tone. Things have changed. What that meeting was about. Page has sold my debt. He's sold all the debts owed to him. He's got something else on.'

Pascoe felt his heart tumble again. He saw that his knuckles were white on the wheel. 'Sold it to who?'

'The Nongs. For a fifty-fifty cut.'

'It must be big, whatever he's got on.'

Already, Pascoe was working the angles. He couldn't take on The Nongs, the state's most notorious bikie gang. Not the biggest, but certainly the heaviest. Pascoe had served time with plenty of Nongs over the years. They had it good with the guards and no prisoners messed with them. He could remove their leadership group, but others would take their place. Mark Hurley's debt would stand.

'Whatever it is, it has something to do with that bloke they had there, before me. I could hear everything and they didn't care. They were all over 'im. Page and that copper. That's the reason Page's offloaded his debt-collection goons. They're all going to be working for the guy in the suit, the one they were threatening.'

'The guy have a name?'

'Tremain. They kept calling him that. I dunno who he is, some kind of gold miner.'

'What makes you say that?'

'They were talking about shares in his company. Equal shares. Classic standover. They let 'im keep his naming rights, but that's about it. The copper said, the company stays Lightning Resources, but we come on as directors. Equal share of profits. Like I said, they didn't even care I was listening.'

Pascoe averted his face from the kid, didn't want Hurley to see the struggle for breath. Pascoe's body was warning him with little bolts of shock that every breath might be the last. He took a long while to fill his lungs. When he did, he yanked up the three-on-the-tree gearstick. 'Who are you going to be paying at The Nongs? Who precisely? Where and when?'

'I got to go to the clubhouse, every Thursday at five. Pay the sergeant-at-arms.'

'Yeah, I know him. He going to give you product?'

'Every Thursday, five o'clock. Takes my money and gives me more gear. But you don't need to be –'

'I do, son. And now, it's goodbye again. We never met and we'll never meet again. You keep doing what you need to do. I'll do the same.'

'Sure, Tone. It's just ...'

Pascoe dropped the handbrake, gently lifted the clutch until the engine engaged. 'Now walk off. I can't pull away till you leave.'

Hurley shut the passenger door, tapped the side of the car as he wandered back into the darkness. Pascoe lifted his foot and rolled the van through a turn. The restaurant was empty now, just the glow of fridge lights while the kitchen-workers behind the service counter flitted to their tasks.

33.

Swann could sense Maddie's reluctance in her shortened step and the way her arms became stiff against her ribs, holding the notebook. He couldn't blame her. It was a normal sight for local residents but he could see how the line of sailors snaking out the brothel front door looked sinister from a distance. The men were quiet under the weight of the silence in the suburban street, passing cars illuminating them for a moment before they were once again shrouded in darkness.

Gone was the earlier joviality from the first two days in port. The navy didn't advertise the duration of its stays ahead of time, not even to its own sailors, for fear of providing an opportunity to terrorists. Every sailor on board the ship had already been granted leave. The sailors at the brothel now were on their second night's leave, but many of them had already blown most of their money on their first night out, which explained the difference in attitude. Those men who genuinely wanted the company of women to cheer themselves up would still visit the bars and clubs, but those low on money or who solely wanted sex chose to visit the town's brothels instead.

Swann led the way down the side entrance, turning to make sure that Maddie was alright. He wasn't sure what she expected, but it obviously wasn't the tipping of Dixie cups, or the 'hello, miss' that most of the men gave her as she walked past. Louise was still at home, not wanting to crowd Kerry's small office and not wanting to wait in the lobby with the sailors. Swann would deliver Maddie back home after the interview.

In the lobby, Swann's young apprentice Lee Southern looked up from his newspaper. He wore his regulation jeans, boots and tight blue Bonds tee-shirt. Lee held up the front of the *Daily News* and showed them the picture of Charles Bernier that took up most of the page. The headline in capitals. WANTED, was all it said.

'Your work?' Swann asked Maddie, who was staring at the dark floral wallpaper and antique lamps sporting red bulbs that gave the room a hearth-like warmth.

'Yes. Some of it. I filed it this morning.'

The natural grit in her voice was subdued, but Swann didn't worry about that. Kerry Bannister would read her discomfort and put her at ease.

Swann knocked on Kerry's office door. The rooms along the hall were hushed except for the occasional creak, the running of a tap and the occasional whisper.

'Come in,' came the reply.

Swann opened the door and saw that Kerry was reading the same newspaper, her Dame Edna reading glasses perched on the bridge of her nose, a rollie dangling from her lip. She had a bottle of white cooling in an ice bucket.

Swann made the introductions, adding that Maddie had written the article that Kerry was reading, knowing that this would impress her. Kerry waved Maddie into a seat across the desk, pushing aside the unfinished Bulldogs scarf that she'd been knitting for the past five years, the two needles there as insurance in case things got out of hand. Maddie didn't know that the steel knitting needles were weapons and smiled at the scarf, accepted the offer of a glass of white. Swann could see Kerry sizing up Maddie as the potential writer of her life story, something she'd often talked about as long as she didn't have to write it herself.

Before Kerry started speaking, Swann cleared his throat. 'Kerry, that driver's licence you took off the creep the other night. You still have it?'

'Course I still have it, Swann. Just let me ...'

Kerry rummaged in her desk and drew out a child's pencil case with the letters DANIEL spelled out in cardboard insert letters. She worked open the stiff zipper and poured the lot onto the desk.

'The rogues' gallery. He was a ginger, was he not?'

'He was.'

Wrapped around each licence was a piece of paper beneath an elastic band, listing the date and offence of the man whose identification was confiscated.

'Frank Drury,' she began to recite. 'Tried to do a runner. November sixteen, nineteen seventy-seven, sorted by Daniel ... Thomas Kilpatrick, refused to pay because he couldn't get it up, sorted by Daniel ... Gerald Kimpton, tried to steal Jacinta's knickers, sorted by Jacinta. Here it is. Mr Dennis Cord. February second nineteen eighty-nine. Locked himself in with Francine. Sorted by Frank Swann, and his chainsaw.'

Kerry passed over the licence. Maddie looked at him strangely. 'Sorted by chainsaw? My God.'

'More than subtle intimidation was called for, young lady,' said Kerry. 'Why I called an ex-walloper. Though no blood was spilt.'

'The Francine that he locked himself in with. Was that Francine ... McGregor?' Maddie asked.

Swann nodded. The man's silence and quiet menace had stayed with him, but he didn't want to say that in front of Maddie, not yet at least. He turned to Kerry. 'You didn't give this to Cassidy, any of the other Ds?'

'They didn't ask about it. I didn't think of it, either. As you know, we've been grieving ...'

Kerry waved an arm at a photograph of Francine that Swann hadn't noticed, pinned on the wall beneath a picture of John Gerovich flying for a mark. Stapled to the photo was a single rose, and what looked like a poem. Maddie lifted her notebook, asking permission to write. Kerry nodded, her eyes shining as she looked at the photo; Francine holding a cat next to her face, the cat licking her cheek.

Maddie was busy drawing the photograph and flower.

'Did Francine say anything about the man after I left?' Swann asked. 'Did he ask her any questions?'

Kerry's eyes never left the photo while she sipped on her wine. 'No. Wait on. Yes. Did she have a boyfriend? Just the usual stupid stuff.'

'Take this with me?'

Kerry nodded and Swann pocketed the licence. 'Maddie, I'll be across the road in the pub. Come over when you're done. Otherwise, thanks, Kerry.'

Swann patted Lee Southern on the shoulder as he left. The line of sailors hadn't moved, the same looks of boredom and frustration on the same faces.

The pub was quiet except for some regulars that Swann acknowledged with a nod before taking a stool. He looked at the ice-frosted taps and for the first time in many months felt like a cold beer, although he decided against it. Old Tom wasn't too particular about cleaning the pipes. His draught often carried the odour of rotten eggs.

Tom shuffled out from his office and gave Swann a little smile that showed his teeth; Tom's version of a bear hug and kiss. He nodded to the taps but Swann shook his head.

'Tom, you seen this man before?'

Tom took up the spectacles tied with fifty-pound fishing line around his neck, put them on his nose. He nodded, then waited a beat, then smiled again.

'Ok, Tom. When?'

Tom frowned with the effort of forming words out of the great silence behind his eyes. 'He stay here a long time. Last year. Mr Cord.'

'Any problems with him?'

'No. He was quiet man. Released prisoner. Always pay rent on time. Eat here. Sleep here. Watch footy. Play Rose Tattoo on jukebox.'

'Can you show me the dates he stayed here? Which room?'

Tom nodded, relieved from the task of speaking. Scratched his gut. He went into his office and came back with a ledger book, put the glasses on his nose and held the page close to his face. After he'd flicked through half the ledger he put it down on the counter, pointed a fat finger at a name.

Cord had stayed in the room, like Tom said, for nearly a year. Strange, because Swann didn't remember seeing him in the neighbourhood. He stayed in room four, which Swann knew had a view over the street to the Ada Rose. Swann was just about to shut the ledger when he remembered the other man he'd seen last week, another man with the edge of recent prison time on him, coming out of the shower and walking over to room four. Swann flicked the pages until he found the most recent entries. There it was. Cord. Not Dennis, but Ralph Cord. Swann pointed to the name and Tom leaned over, nodded, and paused until it was clear he'd have to speak.

'Yes. Cord. Not quiet. Also red hair. Many problems. The brother.'

Swann looked at the dates. Ralph Cord had checked out the day Swann had seen him, after a month's stay. The same day that Bernier and Francine went missing. Had the same air of menace as his brother.

34.

The CO's eyes had sharpened when Devon volunteered to work the cocktail party at the racecourse. It was a tradition dating back to the Second World War that senior officers of large USS naval vessels entertained local dignitaries while in port. The public relations exercise was made even more important by the news that one of their servicemen was wanted for murder.

Devon Smith didn't know or care about any of that. He wasn't familiar with the wanted man, Charles Bernier, who worked maintenance on the higher decks. There was, however, plenty of shit talk in the mess and in the berthing room about what the negro sailor had done to the two women. Most sailors talked about the crimes with disgust on their faces. Many of them had sisters, wives and girlfriends, and sex murders were a threat to them all. For others, Devon suspected, it was also the case that the murders didn't assist their getting laid when on leave, not the black ones at least. It was a bad situation for everyone.

Not that Wiggs, the galley CO, picked up on Devon's anxiety about his plan. It was Wiggs who'd made the pronouncement that Devon never leave the scullery. He was a man used to underlings kissing his ass, however, and after a moment of suspicion he took Devon's volunteering for the position of galley-hand as a sign that maybe, just maybe, Midshipman shitkicker Devon Smith was showing a bit of initiative.

Wiggs rode the bus beside the driver as they wound their way along the broad Swan River. It was another hot day and Devon's pale skin was copping a hammering, not that he minded. It was good to see his forearms taking colour and to feel the sun on his eyelids and scalp. It was midmorning and the sun was at ten o'clock above the hills to the east. Devon watched the elastic movement of the traffic as the commuters slowed and sped up, slowed and sped up. Devon looked at Wiggs, a senior officer in his navy whites, joking around with Lenny and Marcus, dressed in their work uniforms, standing above him in the aisle. Their easy familiarity with the white CO was a sham. Devon had heard what they really thought of Wiggs, belittling him every chance they got.

The bus crossed a cement bridge and left the city behind them. The suburbs looked no different to the suburbs at home, except for more trees. He had lived in one particular cinder-block house as a child that had a tall eucalypt in the backyard. He didn't know then that it was an Australian tree – his father wasn't much for naming things. The suburbs they passed through now smelt like that old tree, with its ugly gnarled trunk and white old-man's skin, its green leaves that never fell, even in winter. Devon's father had accidentally set it on fire one afternoon, applying a blowtorch to the skin of a spit-roast pig. The fire didn't spread from the flaming tree because there was nothing near it. It stood there, charred black, for months. Then one day Devon saw the first shoots of green on the higher branches. Within a couple more months the tree was all green again, except that the trunk stayed black.

The thought of his father's spit-roast reminded Devon of the task at hand. One of the meals that would be served at the racetrack was Louisiana barbecue. Twenty pigs had been bought on the first day in port and hung from their snouts in the coldroom. The pigs had been slow-roasted on the six galley spits before being placed into the oven to keep warm. It wasn't how Devon's father cooked pork, over charcoal and hickory kindling, but it sure smelt good. The pigs were placed into huge oven trays where the flesh was pulled apart and the ribs cut out and the rest of the bones removed for stock.

Devon didn't usually take an interest in cooking but in this case it was important. He had lifted the laden trays and gauged their weight. He kept watch and waited for the right moment to take two empty trays and slide them onto a trolley. He covered the trays with loose aluminium foil and then went to meet Mike Scully, as they'd arranged. Mike and Devon exchanged identical trolleys and exited the lift at different floors. Ten minutes later they met in the same lift and once again exchanged trolleys. After Scully had gone, Devon peeled back one corner of the foil on both trays. There they were – the stocks and barrels of six M16s, complete with magazines. He replaced the foil and lifted the trays to test their weight – they were a bit light but he could fix that. Back in the galley he took plenty of the pork and scattered it over the automatic rifles so that they'd smell right. He marked the two trays with crosses and put them with the others. He'd personally loaded them in the side of the bus, placing them deepest in the luggage compartment so that they'd come off last. All the while his heartbeat was rising – it was too late to turn back now. If the trays were discovered, Devon planned to rat on Lenny and Marcus, say that they tried to include him in their plan but that he'd refused. It would be dicey but he relied on the fact that he was white and they were black. He watched them now, leering through the windows at some passing girls dressed in heels and light dresses as the bus turned onto a long flat road toward the river, the racetrack there in the distance.

35.

Swann's best night's sleep in six months ended when the phone rang in the lounge room next door. He ignored it, keeping his eyes shut to prolong the fugue, but the phone kept ringing.

He was alone in the house except for the dog which joined him as he padded down the hall. He answered the phone and sat on the floor, let the dog nudge into him.

'Swann, Steve Webb. Sorry to wake you but we've got a situation down at the wharf. Cassidy is here and demanding entry onto the *Vinson*. There's media. Get down if you can, please.'

'Ok,' was all Swann could manage before hanging up. The dog followed Swann into the kitchen where he took down the makings for his morning injection. He broke an ampoule and drew up the solution into a fresh syringe, planted it in his thigh. It was the time of morning he and the dog normally walked into town, but he didn't want her around angry crowds – the anti-nuclear picket that his daughters attended would be raucous if the media were there. Swann dressed in a collared shirt and dug out some fresh trousers, put on socks and shoes. He took his cap off the hook behind the front door, put on his sunglasses and walked into the glare of another hot day.

The wharf was crowded with punters arriving from Rottnest Island and the anti-nukes picket, fenced at a distance from the passenger terminal used by the *Vinson* for embarking and disembarking personnel. Beside them were many of the same journos and photographers from the Northbridge crime scene yesterday, with the addition of Louise's friend Maddie. She clocked Swann from a distance and watched him come. He pulled down his cap but was relieved to see that she wasn't going to collar him for questions. She gave him a small wave instead and turned toward the sight of Cassidy and two of his detectives, stood at the bottom of the gangplank, berating Steve Webb and four burly uniformed Shore Patrol sailors who were blocking their path.

Swann climbed over the low barrier fence and heard the cameras clicking behind him. One of the Shore Patrol uniforms reached for his sidearm as Swann approached but Webb stayed his hand. Neither Cassidy nor Webb spoke until Swann joined them. The look on Cassidy's face said it all – red from arguing in the hot sun. He held up what Swann recognised to be a magistrate-signed search warrant.

'But as I've explained, Detective Inspector. The USS *Carl Vinson* is sovereign American territory and therefore your search warrant has no legal status.'

Cassidy put a foot onto the gangplank and once again the uniformed officer reached for his sidearm. Once again, Webb signalled for him to stand down.

Finally, Cassidy turned to Swann. 'I caught your mate out. I called him this morning, asked him a simple question –'

'Which I was under no obligation to answer.'

'Asked him a simple question. What brand of cigarettes does Charles Bernier smoke?'

Webb looked to Swann. 'I had to check my interview records with his work crew. He smokes Kools. Menthol Kools. Which I communicated, in good faith –'

'Caught you out, being honest for a change.'

Webb lifted his chin. 'If leading me to believe one thing, and then telling me something else after I've trusted you, is catching me out, then –'

'Not like I've got a choice. Otherwise you wouldn't have told me anything, like you're doing now.'

Swann put his hands up. 'Cassidy. You've only got three men. What do you expect to find on the *Vinson*? What's the warrant for?'

'Charles fucking Bernier.'

Cassidy had no real intention of searching an aircraft carrier that housed over five thousand crew. Which was why he'd called the media. This was all about making Webb hand over Bernier. Swann looked to Webb but his face was unreadable behind the aviator glasses. His jaw was set and his body rigid with determination, but there was nothing else.

'What makes you so sure that Bernier's on the *Vinson*?'

'This morning, we found Jodie Brayshaw's Datsun 120Y parked over there, hundred yards. Fucking ashtray full of Kools menthol butts. Some of them got lipstick on them. Same lipstick Jodie was wearing. Which tells me that Bernier's quit running, hiding, come and handed himself in. To the place and people who don't accept our laws.'

'That's not true, Detective Inspector. He's not here, and even if he handed himself in, we would turn him over once formal charges have been laid. A lawyer would be hired through the consul, I can assure you –'

'You're lying. I'm going to go over there now, and tell the papers, and through them, the people, that you're stonewalling, protecting one of your own. I'm then going to report this to the commissioner, who will report it to the premier, who will put a rocket up your consul, who will report it to your ambassador, who will report it to your state department, who if I have my way, will report it to your war-hero fucking president. This is going to get very hot for you, my Yank friend. So I'll say it once again. Let me board your so-called sovereign fucking territory and search for what I know is there.'

Swann hadn't taken his eyes off Webb's face. Webb was a trained investigator. His stillness could be explained by his reluctance to exhibit signs that might give him away, but Swann felt that Webb was telling the truth. He couldn't say that to Cassidy, who'd accuse him of being a stooge.

'Webb, let the detectives examine the brig,' Swann said quietly. 'As a personal favour, before this gets out of hand.'

Webb's face darkened. It meant backing down, but he nodded.

'Acceptable to you, Cassidy?' Swann asked.

'Yes. As long as we go directly there. Long as nobody from here communicates with anyone in there.'

Webb didn't move, staring hard at Cassidy. Finally, Webb handed his walkie-talkie to Swann. 'You'll be interested to know that Charles Bernier called his mother last night, from a local number. Not collect, unfortunately, which would leave a record. According to her, he sounded agitated. He asked her to wire him money, to the Perth GPO. Not a lot. Five hundred dollars. We've been in contact with her. She told Bernier to hand himself in, but he hung up. She then called us at a number given to her, toll-free. She's going to ring if he calls again. She doesn't know anything about Australia or about what he's been accused of doing, except that he's AWOL. She doesn't want him going to any foreign gaol.'

Webb had spoken to Swann but it was for Cassidy's benefit, whose posture lost some of its shape. Cassidy straightened his tie as Webb stood back and waved them on board.

36.

Pascoe stared at the asbestos fence as though it were a life raft, keeping him afloat. He was alone on the back porch. *Dying.* He'd awoken on the sleep-out bed that the Sannyasins had set up for him, a fresh oxygen bottle on its trolley with the tubes attached to his nose. His breathing was even and the pain in his chest was no more than a dull ache. Then he felt the first convulsion in his lungs, the sharp burn of pain that spread into his belly, his throat. The cough came from somewhere deep and put blood on his lips. He turned his head and hawked onto the concrete, not looking. Stared at the asbestos fence and tried to stimulate his heart, which was struggling. He was accustomed to maintaining his calm but calmness wouldn't cut it now. He had to bully his heart into beating harder so that he didn't pass out. He wanted to be conscious at the end.

Pascoe put his focus on Jared Page, stoked his anger until it was glowing hot. There were men like Page at the beginning of humankind, and they would be there at the end, manipulating and taking.

Pascoe could see clearly what the oxygen starvation was doing to his eyesight, blurring at the edges, leaving the hard focus at the centre of his vision, his anger not working. So easy to close his eyes and drift into the ether, to fall into a coma and move on to the next place, or the no place, he didn't really care. Pascoe found himself thinking of his good friend Des Ryan, next door, bringing a smile to his face despite the pain. Yesterday, while Pascoe was out casing his target, Ryan was busy drafting a letter to the editor of the two daily newspapers, demanding that Tony Pascoe be pardoned. The first letter Ryan had ever written, he told Pascoe upon his return. In the letter he wrote that Pascoe had done the crime, but had also served the time. Surely busting out was a dying man's last desperate attempt to die a free man, and not a convict? Pascoe had admittedly been present when a security guard was shot, but it wasn't Pascoe who'd pulled the trigger, or ordered the man to do it. The guard had lived, anyway, and twenty years was a long sentence. A death sentence, as it turned out.

Ryan had told Pascoe about the letter because he knew what it meant. While Pascoe served his time, Ryan had dropped off the coppers' radar, living the quiet life. Pascoe doubted that the new generation of detectives would have heard of Ryan, let alone bothered to read through the old case files that listed him as one of Tony Pascoe's closest associates. Now, however, he'd gone and stuck his head above the wall.

Pascoe heard the padding of bare feet inside the house. He realised that the pain in his chest had diminished, and so had the convulsions that felt like someone opening and closing their hand inside his lungs, little punches to his heart.

It was Sarani. She took one look at his face and whispered, 'Oh shit.' She opened the oxygen to full, ran inside and returned with a bag valve mask. She took out the tube from Pascoe's nostrils, replaced it with the tube from the valve bag, then fixed the mask over his face. Gently at first, but then more forcefully, Sarani began to pump oxygen into his lungs, the valve bag filling with the beautiful gas that she squeezed from the rubber bellows, forcing it deep, beyond the scarring and constriction that his cancer and emphysema had produced. Slowly, he began to feel better, mirroring the relief on Sarani's face. When he felt good enough to speak, he nodded to her and she removed the mask. He was just about to thank her when she put a finger on his lips. 'Don't speak. Can you hear next door? The police are interviewing Des. They're parked out front.'

Pascoe lifted his head. Where the bed was situated, even if one of the coppers stuck his head over the fence, he or she wouldn't be able to see them.

He had to smile. Ryan had of course been right. He'd told Pascoe about the letter to the editor and insisted that Pascoe sleep next door. He'd gone and asked Sat Prakash and Sarani if that was alright.

'You're all over the radio, too. The talkback. Half of it's about the American sailor wanted for murder. But because of Ryan's letter, some of the radio hosts have been talking about you as well. Every second caller is saying that you should be allowed to die in peace. Plenty of them are saying they'd put you up, if you came knocking.'

That made Pascoe smile, too. He accepted the nostril tubes, drew in a deep breath. He squeezed Sarani's hand, closed his eyes, tried to gather his strength. None of this was how he'd imagined his end days – bunking down with hippies, accepting the kindness of strangers, on the run from the law. It was absurd enough to make an old crim laugh, which made Sarani put a hand on his chest, and another finger on his lips.

37.

Swann sat in the carpark of the Perth Central Police Station and waited. He had worked in this building for twenty years and risen to the rank of superintendent of uniformed police, responsible for several hundred men and women before he turned whistle-blower and put a flame to his career. He didn't miss the institution, although his years of training were ingrained in him – the reason he was there in the carpark, waiting for Cassidy to return.

The brig of the USS *Carl Vinson* had been empty except for three white sailors and one black sailor awaiting charges for minor crimes. Cassidy still didn't trust Webb, and Swann couldn't blame him for that. The location of Jodie Brayshaw's Datsun so close to the aircraft carrier was a convincing piece of evidence, especially the presence of Bernier's brand of cigarettes and Jodie's distinctive purple lipstick in the ashtray. Cassidy had done what Swann would have done – rolled the dice. The problem was that he came up empty, and as a result had lost Webb's trust.

Cassidy had tricked Webb by saying that they'd discovered a makeshift camp in Kings Park, scattered with cigarette butts, in the context of enquiring about the brand Bernier smoked. Cassidy at that point felt sure that Webb had taken Bernier on board the *Vinson*, knowing that each sailor was scrutinised upon returning to ship – there was no way that he might have slipped past.

Cassidy was under a lot of pressure, and it was showing. That was the problem with being a senior detective in the CIB, who'd been promoted on merit and not because of how much money he earned or what he knew about others – Cassidy was tolerated but hardly trusted. And then there was the media pressure, with the two murders leading every radio and television bulletin and monopolising the front page of the dailies. The media was doing its bit to advertise Bernier's image and other pertinent details, but according to Cassidy there was a developing political problem as many weighed up the economic benefits of the Americans in port set against issues of public safety. It was the hottest topic on talkback radio. According to Webb, last night two black American sailors had been assaulted in Fremantle by local youths and kicked to within an inch of their lives. In the meantime, Cassidy had men and women at the airport, the bus and train stations, asking around in the city's pubs, markets and restaurants, undercover police in the parks and nightclubs, uniformed police canvassing Jodie Brayshaw's neighbourhood, and detectives questioning her friends, work colleagues and family. The investigation was large and as a result, thinly spread.

Which was where Swann came in. He had mentioned to Cassidy the Cord brothers renting at the Seaview Hotel, the younger brother being present when Francine and Bernier were staying there. Cassidy's junior detectives were looking to interview Cord, but so far hadn't been able to track him down. The fact that both brothers had lived there straight after gaol wasn't unusual in a hotel that routinely housed parolees, but Cord might have been a witness, and Swann offered to locate him. The elder Cord brother had spent time with Francine the day before she went missing. It wasn't the fact that both brothers were ex-convicts that interested Swann, although it might be significant. It was the quiet menace he'd sensed when observing them. Neither had spoken, but the memory of both men stayed with him, in particular the look in their eyes, lit by something smug, confident – more than the regular hatred of authority.

Swann watched Cassidy grow larger in his wing mirror. On top of everything else, being seen with Frank Swann would do Cassidy no favours among his peers, and he was careful, looking around the carpark for observers. He leaned down and placed a folder in Swann's lap, still warm from the photocopier. He looked harried, but determined. 'Dennis Cord did his time for aggravated sexual assault. It's in there. Found a girl asleep outside the pub up in Seabird. Raped her, and when she awoke, shut her up by bashing her. Ralph Cord just got out after a three-year stretch for aggravated assault. He's ex–Junkyard Dogs.

Kicked out of the club, would you believe, for being too racist. Took issue with another club member who he suspected of being part-Aborigine. Got a tattoo on his forearm of a lynched black, which didn't go down too well. Never handed back his patch.'

'Lovely family. Please tell me there are only two brothers.'

'Only the two.' Cassidy tapped the roof. 'Got to go. The minister's reached into his pocket. We're announcing a hundred thousand reward for information relating to the McGregor and Brayshaw murders. The minister, the commissioner, me. TV tonight.'

'There's a coffee stain on your tie. Might want to change it.'

Cassidy looked down his nose at the stain, shaped like a head on the silver and blue striped tie. 'Smart-arse. Thanks. And by the way, thought you might like to read this, page three.'

Cassidy reached into his jacket and withdrew a folded *Daily News*, dropped it in Swann's lap, turned and left. Swann looked at the picture of the Brayshaw crime scene, over another headshot image of Bernier, appearing every bit the proud new recruit in his pristine whites, a dutiful confidence in his eyes, the black neckerchief tied with a square knot, now marked with a superimposed red arrow.

Swann turned to page three, saw the sketch done by Maddie of Francine and her cat, the rose and poem. Instead of a description of Kerry Bannister, and her brothel, as he expected, the piece started with, 'My guide is Frank Swann, ex-detective and superintendent. Mr Swann grew up in the streets of Fremantle, employed first as a newsboy before graduating to working as a runner for the brothels on Bannister Street, taking orders for sly grog, condoms and cigarettes. Mr Swann takes me to the Ada Rose brothel, where he's a good friend of the proprietor, Ms Kerry Bannister, a formidable woman in her sixties with a sharp sense of humour. The pair met when Frank Swann was a ten-year-old sly-grog runner and she was a prostitute in a brothel called Aphrodite's ...'

Swann folded the paper and tossed it onto the seat beside him. It wasn't a problem, Maddie saying all that, although Swann was going to have to be clear with her about what was, and wasn't, on the record. She had asked him the questions on the walk to the brothel, and he'd answered them, not realising that he was part of the story.

Still, Kerry was going to like the trip down memory lane, despite the sad circumstances, with the piece going into some detail about her history.

Maddie had been respectful and matter-of-fact rather than sensationalist, and Kerry's portrait of Francine McGregor gave a good picture of the complicated person behind the worker in the oldest profession.

38.

Devon Smith heard Lenny's cartoon chuckle inside the kitchen entrance and checked his watch. The last three trips Marcus and Lenny had made with the service trolley had taken forty seconds, thirty-five seconds and fifty seconds. Devon dragged another pork-heavy tray and got it ready to transfer. The pair exited the entrance with their rolling hustler walk now amplified, and Devon saw why. A young white female kitchenhand in the universal check trousers and apron followed behind, pushing a service trolley that was large enough to take two trays, at least.

Bitch.

Now Devon had two sets of potential witnesses to worry about. His heart rate increased and he felt the pressure of blood in his cheeks. His palms were clammy and his mouth was dry. There were only five trays left and two of them were his. He couldn't help glancing again at the parked Ford transit van two spaces down from them, as arranged with the biker chief. Devon looked deeper through the alley but he couldn't see anyone watching. There were no security cameras covering the service alley. Marcus and Lenny pushed the trolley over and Devon lifted the trays one at a time, the two sailors sharing a joke with the young Aussie woman who Devon noticed was glancing at him, his muscular arms taut when he hefted the trays. She was cute, but Devon knew that if he showed the slightest interest then the two sailors would start ragging on him. He had other priorities, and didn't meet her eye, even as Marcus and Lenny began to lead their trolley away. She pushed her trolley closer and waited for him to load the final three trays. Devon loaded the first, making sure that it wasn't marked with his X, then nodded her toward the door.

'You don't want me to take them other two?'

She had a singsong voice and he realised that she was the first woman who'd spoken to him in three months, except for the *Vinson*'s doctor when he'd burned himself that time. The doctor had seen his tattoos and kept her conversation to the minimum.

'Naw, they've spilled a little. I'll clean 'em up and bring 'em in myself.'

'I can do that. We can do it together. Before we put 'em in the oven, to warm with the others.'

Devon tried to be polite, but ten seconds had passed. 'Said I'd do it, lady. You get back inside.'

He watched the hurt expression on her face turn to hatred.

'No worries. Was just trying to help.'

She began to wheel away the trolley and he glanced at his watch. Fifteen seconds. He ran to the transit van and cracked its back door, saw the canvas bag that he hoped contained fifteen thousand dollars, as arranged. Devon ran back to the bus and took the first tray and ferried it to the van, tipping its contents onto the black carpet. Ran back to the bus and did the same with the final tray, the metal clanking of the spilling weapons loud in the alley. He looked at his watch and saw that forty seconds had passed. He heard Lenny's exaggerated laughter, returning. There wasn't time to take the money. He used his knee to push the transit door shut. Rushed to the dumpster across the alley and lifted the lid, pretended that he'd just tipped the trays' contents inside.

Marcus and the young woman were first through the door, followed by Lenny. 'Aw fuck man, what you gone and done now?'

Devon had meat juices down the front of his trousers. 'The fuckin trays tipped over. Lost the whole shittin lot.'

Lenny laughed, because of the presence of the woman, but Marcus was staring at him hard. That street-sense of his. The woman, too, was looking at the trays and the bitumen beside the bus. There weren't any meat juices or pieces of shredded pork on the ground.

'Just let me clean up and I'll join you inside. Won't be a minute.'

Devon closed the dumpster lid, hoped that Marcus wasn't going to stretch out his humiliation by coming over and looking.

'Naw son, Wiggs wants us now. Runnin order and whatnot. Then we got a fifteen-minute break. Sharon here's gonna show me an Marcus round the place. You can clean up then. Them two trays will need washin for a start.'

'Yessir,' Devon replied, letting his sarcasm hang there. He didn't like the look in Marcus's eyes, reading the mismarriage of Devon's voice and his hands that were beginning to tremble at his sides. Devon wiped his palms on his trousers as though they were dirty. He was lucky that Lenny was so excited by the presence of the woman. 'Sharon, you ever heard the expression *dumb-ass Nazi peckerwood* before?'

Devon put his head down and carried the empty trays past Marcus at the door, following the others into the vast industrial kitchen where Wiggs and the *Vinson* chefs and their Australian counterparts were waiting for him. Wiggs looked at the empty trays and said nothing, but didn't bother hiding the contempt in his eyes.

'Now that Gomer Pyle has joined us,' he began, 'the running order is as follows ...'

Devon listened to Wiggs drone on, the jovial self-importance in his voice more grating than usual. Devon thought about asking permission to go to the toilet, but he knew that Wiggs would refuse, and in any case, it was nowhere near the service entrance to the alley. The nerves in Devon's chest and belly were threatening to overwhelm him. His hands were visibly trembling now and a blush had settled across his face and neck. Marcus was still staring at him with a detached curiosity in his eyes, but Lenny was on the verge of chuckling, assuming that Devon was angry as a result of his earlier insult. Finally, Wiggs put down his clipboard and began to shake the hands of the Australians while the American seamen took out cigarettes and combs and made their way toward the alley. Devon followed, sick to his stomach. He saw that the Australian woman was beside him.

'I didn't mean to make you angry,' she said. 'Those guys are jerk-offs. It can't be –'

Devon didn't hear the rest of what she said, just felt the vibration of her voice combine with the roaring of blood in his ears as he walked into the alley and saw that the white Ford van was gone.

39.

There were a few Nongs working on their bikes in the shadows of the clubhouse walls, but one by one they stood and wiped their mitts on oily rags, began to give Swann the slow handclap. Swann had been buzzed in almost as soon as he pulled in front of the clubhouse gates painted with the skull and double piston symbol of The Nongs.

The handclapping continued on his walk to the clubhouse bar and offices, and included a few unlikely bows and doffing of imaginary hats. The Nongs were clapping him because they believed that he'd almost single-handedly destroyed their main rivals, the Junkyard Dogs, in a shootout those five years ago. A detective inspector, Ben Hogan, had been killed in the same shootout, and those Dogs who weren't wiped out in the gunfire were cleaned out by Hogan's colleagues following his funeral. Fitted up and locked away or exiled interstate, never to return. Some had just gone missing. That Swann carried Junkyard Dog buckshot in his body was well known, as reported in the papers at the time. The Nongs had swooped in and taken over most of the Dogs' financial infrastructure: the tattoo parlours, bike shops, hotels, speed labs and grow houses. The Dogs endured as a one-precenter club, but their membership had shrunk to fewer than a dozen men.

The truth was that Swann was so injured by the shotgun blast on the Kwinana Freeway that he'd only played a small part in the shootout, but The Nongs and in particular their president, Gus Riley, didn't need to know that. Riley, like most people in their world, also believed that thirteen years ago Swann had gunned down the head of the CIB, Donald Casey – another false belief that had served Swann well.

The door to the clubhouse bar and offices was opened by Gus Riley himself. His red hair was combed wet and his goatee beard was trimmed.

'Never seen you so cleaned up,' Swann said as he was led into the bar, pointed to a table. Gus Riley read Swann's face, took the comment as genuine, and decided to share. 'Things are looking up, Swanny. I've been wearing lounge suits, meeting with banks. With the opening of the new casino, the Italians are moving out of Northbridge, looking for the next Noah's ark.'

'Which is?'

'*International* operations. Closer ties to the old country, the old families. Instead of laundering money at their gaming tables, they're reinvesting it overseas. Cocaine into Europe, mainly, I hear. Big new market that they're determined to own. Leaves us clear to move into the stripper and nightclub scene in Northbridge. Licence to print money, mate.'

'... and launder it.'

Riley shrugged, took his seat, turned to the young woman at the bar and pointed to the table.

'Not for me,' Swann said.

'Was wondering. You've lost weight. Cancer, or has your liver finally blown up? You used to drink the Jameson like water.'

It was Swann's turn to share. 'Lead poisoning. Those dozens of pellets still in my body, breaking down.'

Riley whistled. 'Didn't know that could happen, Swanny.'

'Me neither. Took a Yank doctor to diagnose it.'

'Makes sense. Now, why you here? I won't ask what you're doing with the Yanks, though I can guess. Hope they catch the nigger bastard.'

It was like that with Riley. Just when you thought you were talking to someone reasonable ...

'I'm here about an ex-Junkyard Dog, name of Ralph Cord. Was kicked out of the Dogs, sent down for assault. Just got out of Fremantle.'

'Yeah, I know *of* Ralph. We looked at him for a while. Why you askin?'

'He was a witness to something, possibly. Cops haven't been able to interview him, so ...'

'... he's not wanted?'

'No, he's not. Is he with you? I heard he refused to hand his patch back to the Dogs. Figured the only way he'd survive three years in Freo Prison is if he was protected.'

'We looked at him, like I say. Gave him protection for a few months, but no affiliation. Just wanted to see how he went. We watched him pretty close. He was a good earner for the Dogs, and we thought –'

'Earning how?'

Riley took a cigar from his denim vest, already guillotined. Put flame to it and huffed, smiling behind the grey smoke. 'Guns and ammo.'

'Alright. So you watched him swim the goldfish bowl. You take him on?'

Riley shook his head. 'Nah. We put him through his paces. He bridged up ok, when threatened. Was staunch with the screws. Did his time like a man.'

'But?'

'Yeah, the but. The guy's no good. A psycho, but not in a good way. Didn't know he was being watched. Kept trying to play one of us against the other, if you know what I mean. Not for any advantage, though, which is a skillset I admire. Just for his own amusement. When we figured him out, we cut him loose.'

Swann thought about that. 'How'd he make it through then? He find new brothers?'

'I'd have to ask.' Riley turned to the young woman wiping glasses. 'Bethany, Darryl here?'

Bethany got the rabbit-in-headlights look.

'Fuck me, Bethany. Go and fuckin look for him.'

Riley turned the cigar on the edge of the table, peeling ash. 'The strippers. They aren't the brightest. We get 'em to do a shift here a week, remind 'em of who they work for. But Darryl, he's your man.'

'She looks like she knows him. Doesn't like him.'

Riley laughed. 'Well, the Dazzler just got out of Freo too. He's makin up for lost time, shall we say.'

'Right.' Swann stood, turned to Bethany, who was nearly at the door. 'Bethany, don't worry about it.'

She paused with her hand on the doorknob. Swann's not the voice of her employer. Riley stood and pushed in his chair.

'It's alright, girl. Back to drying glasses.'

'When Darryl surfaces,' Swann said, 'let me know. I want to –'

The phone behind the bar rang. Bethany rushed to it, relief on her face. She picked up and pointed to Riley, who smiled, the look of a man expecting good news, *more* good news.

Swann took a step to the door, but Riley put up a hand. Swann watched the confidence on his face drain away, replaced by a flush of red anger, rising from his neck to his cheeks. The thing about redheads, Swann thought, watching Riley's face fill with blood – there's always fire with the smoke.

Bethany stood clear as Riley began smashing the receiver on the bar top.

40.

When Tony Pascoe called Lightning Resources using the number listed in the White Pages, he got a surprise when Tremain took the call himself. The man's voice was wary, and his breathing was audible. He sounded a little drunk, at two in the afternoon. Pascoe didn't know anything about Tremain or his company, although Mark Hurley's description was there in Tremain's mouth-breathing and shaky voice. Pascoe didn't waste any time. Without introducing himself, he told Tremain that he could help 'with his problem'. Did Tremain want to meet in person?

There was a long silence. Finally, Tremain's fear got the better of him. 'If this is from Page or Gooch, I don't need to be tested. I just need more time.'

Pascoe laughed. He'd soaked himself with oxygen. His voice was clear and firm. 'No, mate. Page and Gooch are scum. They're the problem, and I'm the solution. Now, do you want to meet?'

Tremain wanted to meet. At his office. Soon as possible.

Pascoe couldn't wear the white overalls. Sarani led him into the room she shared with Sat Prakash. Pascoe didn't know why he expected otherwise, but it was clean and uncluttered, all bare wood and white-painted surfaces, flowers on the dresser. Sarani didn't want him to leave the house after his morning's near miss, but he didn't have a choice. She showed him the clothes in their cupboard, took out a white dinner jacket and put it against him. Pascoe shook his head and she laughed, passed him a clean white shirt and a light grey suit. Sat Prakash was tall and thin, like Pascoe, and the suit wouldn't look too baggy on his old bones.

Pascoe checked his face in the rear-view a final time. There was no blood on his lips but he could taste it in his mouth. He climbed out of the van and slipped into the jacket, looked down at his polished boots. He wasn't kidding anybody, but the clothes fitted well.

Tremain's Subiaco office was on the ground floor, indicated by a cardboard insert in the postboxes by the entrance. Pascoe went inside and found the room at the end of a dingy corridor, knocked twice and entered. Again, he expected a secretary but there was only Tremain, who looked exactly like Pascoe remembered him, berated by Page and Gooch at Page's restaurant those nights ago – short and nervy, hoops of sweat under his armpits, the room smelling of breath mints and cheap deodorant.

Pascoe braced himself for Tremain's once-over. He'd put on his most assertive voice on the phone, and he carried it now in his posture, the look in his eyes. Tremain didn't need to know that minutes ago Pascoe was sucking on an oxygen bottle, coughing into a tissue.

The office was a one-room affair with a window onto a brick-paved courtyard full of dead pot plants and cigarette butts. The furniture was cheap and mismatched. Tremain didn't offer him a chair and so Pascoe continued his act, taking one for himself and carefully crossing his feet at the ankles, shooting his cuffs.

'I'm glad that you could see me. I'm here to help.'

Tremain ran a hand across his scalp. 'Did Frank Swann send you?'

The name was a jolt, knocked Pascoe off balance, but he showed nothing, instead gave Tremain the prison stare. 'Yes. Is that a problem?'

Tremain gulped, fluttered his hands. 'No, not at all. Of course not. I asked him to help, as you know. Are you an ex-copper?'

Pascoe smiled, kept the stare. 'Yes.'

'Then you know about Gooch. I'm assuming that –'

'I know what Gooch is. That's why I'm here. To brass tacks, then.'

'Yes, of course. Of course.'

Pascoe leaned forward, lowered his voice. 'I know all about your problem. I observed you at Page's restaurant, the other night. Laying the groundwork, if you like. I have another client who's being strongarmed by Page. So I'm going to make you an offer. An offer that works for you, me, and my other client. I'll take care of Page, permanently, if you pay my client's debt. It's a significant debt, so I don't expect an answer right away. Although, as you'll appreciate ...'

Pascoe leaned back in his chair, put up his hands.

Tremain looked stricken. 'Permanently? What do you –'

Pascoe shook his head, eyes hard. 'It's a yes or no offer.'

'How much is the debt?'

'Near to two hundred K.'

Tremain put his head in his hands, thought better of it, reached into his pockets for his cigarettes.

'Please don't smoke.'

Pascoe's voice belying the politeness of his words. Tremain pocketed the smokes, kept one in his fingers, unlit.

'What about Gooch?'

'Leave Gooch to me.'

Tremain's eyes started watering, but it wasn't tears. He looked like he hadn't slept in a week. He blinked rapidly, put his face on his sleeve, a moment of respite from the bright day. 'I expect you want cash.'

'Yes. When the job is done.'

'Do I give it to you, or Swann?'

'Keep Swann out of this. Arms-length, you understand.'

'Of course, of course.'

Tremain's voice was very quiet. 'Can I give it to you, in gold?'

Pascoe didn't see that coming, had no ready answer. Gold was no good to him, or Mark Hurley, but he mightn't have a choice. 'If you can convince the man you'll be paying, then I don't care how you pay him.'

'I'm not paying you?'

'Arms-length.'

Tremain was in the bag, and both of them knew it. 'You take half the money, or its substitute to the equal value, to Gus Riley, president of The Nongs Motorcycle Club. Clubhouse is in Bayswater. Say it's a down payment on what Mark Hurley owes. You do that, I get to work.'

Tremain put the cigarette in his mouth, wiped his eyes with the back of his wrist. 'How do I get in contact with you?'

'You don't. Do you have a better number?'

Tremain laughed, but it was bitter, pointed to the cupboard. 'My bed's in there, rolled up. This is my best number.'

Pascoe felt a flush of nausea in his belly, the first stirring of his lungs. He stood, put out his hand. His peripheral vision began to blur as the oxygen leached from his blood, making his feet unsteady. If it happened now, it was all for nothing.

'I'll call you. Be ready. See myself out.'

Pascoe turned to the door, heard the hiss of a lighter. He reached the front garden when the convulsion hit, doubling him over. His lungs wrung themselves out, squeezing his heart. He coughed and spat and struggled to breathe, staggering to the van and the waiting bottle.

41.

Swann called Cassidy's pager from a public phone outside a Northbridge deli, got a call straight back. It was a five-minute walk over the train tracks to Forrest Place, where Cassidy and his men were staking out the GPO. The overhead sun reflected heat off the paving and concrete walls. City workers buzzed about on their lunchbreak, hitting the sandwich stands, cafes and pie shops. Seagulls and ravens perched on the wall beside Cassidy's position near an escalator and lift. He was speaking into his walkie-talkie, making verbal circuits of the plainclothes and undercover detectives he'd placed around the square. The GPO staff had been briefed and there was a female plainclothes behind the counter, pretending to sort mail into the postboxes to the side of the counters.

'Any hits on the reward money?' Swann asked Cassidy.

'Nothing credible. The usual. Three claims of alien abduction. Charles Bernier is a black prince in the Order of the Golden Dawn. Charles Bernier is a CIA operative released under deep cover to murder women and foster terror prior to a US invasion. Or my favourite: Charles Bernier has never been seen in the same room as Tiny Pinder, did we ever wonder why? That kind of thing.'

'Jesus.'

'Yeah. And so you know, I also put a man on Webb, at least when he's on dry land. Webb and his men are apparently still observing the Fremantle streets near the *Vinson*, going to every dosshouse and bar. Tells me that the appearance of the Datsun made an impression, whether he wanted to admit it or not.'

A burst of static. A female voice, tough voice. 'Three black sailors. Two in uniform, one in civvies. No facial scars. Headed down Murray Street toward your position, over.'

Cassidy pursed his lips, showed some teeth. 'Follow at a discreet distance, over.'

The transmitter went silent.

'Have you considered,' Swann said, 'that Bernier has a second girlfriend, that he's holed up with her somewhere?'

'Lives under a rock, does she, this mystery woman? Or doesn't care that Bernier's a two-time strangler?'

'Or doesn't believe the stories. Or she's a captive.'

'We've been covering that. Asking every barman and barmaid from here to Northam which of their regulars have been seen with sailors, now and in the past.'

'You getting many names?'

Cassidy smiled. 'No, not many. Fair point.'

'I can get someone on that. Given time.'

'Do it, long as the Yanks are paying.'

Another burst of static. 'The three sailors have gone up to the mall, via the arcade.'

'Roger that. Fall back.'

Swann thought about returning to Fremantle, where Webb needed his knowledge of the port streets, but he sensed that Cassidy was holding back on something. Swann looked over the square, where white and black street kids lounged about on the old benches, chased one another through the swirling workers and cadged cigarettes off anyone who looked likely. Two mothers with prams and toddlers stood in the shade of the old GPO, chatting while people-watching, both of them noticing Swann and Cassidy at the same time, the only still points in the chaos of the lunchtime rush. The taller of the mothers, hard-faced and thin, gave them a speculative look before reaching for the arm of a boy who was battering his sister with a Tonka truck. The boy quietened under her grip, began to whimper, used gravity to get away from her by flopping like a doll. She tired of his weight and let him go.

'You ready to share the crime scene and autopsy reports on Jodie Brayshaw?' Swann asked.

Cassidy grunted. 'If you think it'll help. There's no doubt about Bernier's role. The neckerchief found on Brayshaw's body had Midshipman Charles Bernier's name sewn into it, which tells us something about his attitude toward concealment. Francine McGregor was strangled with the same neckerchief. Same dimensions to the ligature marks, same bruising from the knot tied at the back of the neck. Both sexually assaulted, possibly during strangulation, when unconscious but not dead. Type A-minus secretor semen found in both women. Brayshaw had a belly full of Sambuca and chicken parma, also presence of amphetamines in her blood. Had a heroin habit, recently dropped. Tracks in discreet places. Constipated. But nothing in her blood.'

'How recent?'

'Coroner reckons the tracks are a few days old.'

'Anything else?'

Cassidy shook his head, looked out over the quietening square, more seagulls now than people.

The radio crackled, two speakers distorting each other.

'One at a time,' Cassidy barked, turning away from the escalator, where a descending group of teenagers were chattering and laughing. 'What's going on?'

'It's Rogers. Thirty APM men just got into the station, off the Bassendean train. Banners and a PA system.'

'McKee, what you got?' Cassidy asked.

'Another group of forty or so just passing over the train tracks, coming from Northbridge. Same thing: banners, placards. Harassing people. Little melee started with some Aboriginal youth. They'll be at the square shortly.'

Cassidy glanced at his watch, gritted his jaw. 'Fuck it. Stay in your positions.'

'What's going on?'

'Nazi goon-squad rally was scheduled for one pm, here in the square. Tried to get their permission aborted, due to the fucking obvious problem of them potentially scaring off a black sailor like Bernier from the area. But got knocked back. The rally was formally organised, legal assembly, all that. Here they come.'

Swann watched the two groups arrive in the square north down Murray street and east from the train station. He recognised the APM leader, Nigel Kinslow, a white nationalist towing service operator who'd been in the news lately, running for state parliament. He'd polled well considering that the Australian Patriotic Movement was a new party, as had his candidates in Wanneroo, Thornlie and other suburbs with a large migrant English population.

'Ah fuck, worst-case scenario.'

Swann looked to where Cassidy was staring. Behind the column of APM men, now marching in a formation three abreast and singing 'Waltzing Matilda', was a large contingent of uniformed police, including three mounted police. The noise of the singing men echoed off the stone walls around them, filling the square as the column arrived in front of the GPO and began to organise their PA and microphone. The APM foot soldiers wore tee-shirts with either the Eureka flag or Celtic cross above khaki dungarees and boots. Some of them were skinheads and others looked like regular workers, with goatee beards and cropped hair and moustaches, mirroring their leader, who took the mic and began a sound check. Some of the younger Nazis began looking for trouble, eyeing the wagging schoolkids. One of them was an Asian boy, who blanched and then bolted as two skinheads began to approach. The square had emptied out on their arrival, but passengers from the train station and shoppers still cut around the edges. Some paused to watch and others hurried by, heads down and not looking.

Kinslow got right to it, harsh voice biting over the cheap PA. He introduced himself and his movement, which he claimed was growing by the day. Said that they were gathered as a show of solidarity with those calling for an end to the American presence in the city. 'Mandingos, raping our white women. But we'll be out in force tonight, patrolling Northbridge in squads of four, in case we're needed. The police aren't up for the job of protecting our white women, lured by the promise of free drinks and the taboo of miscegenation.'

Cassidy's radio sparked to life. 'Boss, you need to get in here. The money order, it's been collected. Just a couple of minutes ago. By a white male. The teller served him because her super told her she was looking for a black male. Said he had an American accent. Crew cut. Dressed in blue jeans and a white polo shirt.'

'Fucking hell, she served him, gave him the money? He show ID?'

'Correct. No requirement to show ID.'

Cassidy looked like his head was ready to burst. Through gritted teeth he hissed, 'All units. You get that description? White male, blue jeans, white polo shirt. Bring him down and wait for instructions. This man is not, I repeat, not to get away.'

Cassidy raised his hands to Swann, clearly embarrassed, began to jog toward the GPO, pushing a skinhead out of his way, stopping only to bark orders at the uniformed police who were gathered at the edges of the crowd. Swann stayed where he was, looking for the white American sailor who'd retrieved Bernier's money. Kinslow kept on his ranting about the safety of white women and the evils of immigration. Swann looked for Bernier's companion where nobody else was looking, amid the seventy or eighty APM men. It was then that he saw a familiar face. Not the white sailor, but a face he struggled to put a name to until the man removed the hand above his eyes, shielding him from the sun. It was Ralph Cord, the ex–Junkyard Dogs bikie, surrounded by his new brothers. The same ratty ginger beard and deep suntan, stringy mullet hair, chanting along with the others in the crowd.

All those years in prison: Cord sensed Swann looking at him, looked right back while he smiled and chanted.

42.

It'd been the longest day of Devon Smith's short life. As soon as he discovered the theft of both the weapons and the money he was called inside to work the kitchen and servery. He tried to fake a headache but Wiggs wasn't buying it, told Devon to scoff some Tylenol and get back to work. Devon, Lenny and Marcus formed a skeleton staff and Wiggs wasn't about to have the cocktail and dinner service compromised by a slacker. Wiggs instead promoted Lenny and Marcus to the line of bain-maries, and moved Devon back into the kitchen, working the tongs, taking out the heavy trays of pork and stuffing the brioche sliders with the meat filling, supervised by the Australian chef serving tarragon chicken vol-au-vents, both of them working silently alongside one another. Devon stuffed five hundred pork buns that were put on oven racks to keep warm before he was allowed a cigarette break and returned to the alley. There was no sign of the van, or its owner. The alley was hot and still. Devon lit a cigarette and walked to the end of the alley, looked out over the swampy lowlands that skirted the river and a vast blacktop area where the invited guests had left their cars.

Devon couldn't see them, but he knew that they were there, watching. It was possible that the bikers had burned him, taking both the guns and their money, but that didn't feel right. Someone had stolen the car and taken the lot. Possibly an opportunist, unaware of what was in the back of the van, although that too seemed unlikely – there were easier places to steal a car than a working alley where men and women came and went. The other option, the most likely, sickened him with its clear betrayal and its probable consequences.

Devon smoked his cigarette and lit another, glanced at his watch. The smart move would be to return with Wiggs and the others to the *Vinson* and stay put. The bikers couldn't do anything to him while he was on the aircraft carrier. He would be safe until he returned home. The senior Nongs biker, Barry Brown, who'd made contact with clubs back home, would get the word out. That might mean that Devon's father would be forced to take over his debt, and there was no way that Devon's father could afford to pay that kind of money. It was true that Devon's father had caused the whole problem by trying to screw the bikers in the original deal, but it was also true that he would find a way to blame Devon, like he always did.

Devon decided to call the bikers and gauge their reaction. If there was murder in the president's voice, then Devon would get back on the bus, call his father to warn him, take his father's ridicule on the chin, try and make amends somehow. The *Vinson*'s next stop was somewhere in South-East Asia. There might be drugs to be had there, that he could smuggle home.

Devon turned at the sound to his left, behind the nearest wall, the cracking of a twig. There was nothing behind the wall but as he turned to the alley, he heard the boots. He felt the blow on his neck and then he was toppling forward, gone into the black.

43.

Cassidy took Ralph Cord to the East Perth lock-up rather than Central. Cord wasn't under arrest and wasn't obliged to accompany them but he'd gone along willingly, a smug curiosity in his eyes.

He sat now with a styrofoam cup of International Roast with three sugars, made for him by Cassidy, eyes glancing across the bare and scuffed walls of the holding room. Cord had passed through this room numerous times during his life. Cassidy sat across from him with Cord's file, dabbing his finger and turning the pages.

If Cord was reminded of the cells behind him, he showed no sign. He accepted a cigarette from Cassidy, leaned toward the flame, smiled at both of them.

'I know you,' he said to Swann, his eyes creasing with mirth. 'Seen you around the neighbourhood, when I was livin at the Seaview.'

Swann shrugged. He was there to observe but not speak, in case Cord tipped them to anything.

Cassidy took a deep breath, sighed. 'You hangin round the Nazis now, Ralph? They must love your ink.'

Cord smirked, held out his forearm. 'Self-tattooed mate. Work of fuckin art. I call it the *low hangin fruit*.'

Cord was there under his own volition, and it made sense to go easy on him, but Swann and Cassidy knew that the old-school crim wouldn't give them anything if they didn't push, knock him off balance.

'You join the Nazis because of the sour grape you copped last year?' Cassidy asked. 'Down there in Freo Prison? Those brothers who raped you must've loved your ink too, what I hear.'

Cord's face lost its colour. His back arched like a startled cat, cigarette hand beginning to tremble. 'Fuck off.'

'I heard the story from Gus Riley,' Cassidy continued. 'He told me that after you got excommunicated from the Junkyard Dogs, he had his blokes look at you while you were inside. Didn't like what he saw, apparently. Left you exposed. Some of our native sons took offence to your work of art, I heard. Held you down and give it to you, and not once, either. Those new mates of yours, Kinslow and the other Nazi fuckwits, they know about you being used as a sperm bank by all the black boys who wanted a turn?'

The hatred in Cord's face made his eyes bulge, which only made his tremble worsen, dropping ash onto the table. 'What the fuck you blokes want?'

'Perhaps that's unfair of me, Ralph. Seeing as how we just met. What about if I told Nigel Kinslow that your brother was incarcerated for the rape of a white woman? Found her unconscious under a tree and thought he'd have a crack?'

'He didn't know she was white. It was dark.'

'We told you back at Forrest Place, Ralph. We want to know what you saw at the Seaview Hotel, last Saturday night. We know that your brother lived there for a year. What were you doing staying there, after he'd already left?'

'Place is cheap. Bar downstairs. Knocking shop across the road. Stayed there before.'

'But you never visited the brothel, Ralph. It was your brother who was there, the night before Francine McGregor went missing.'

'You better speak to him then.'

'Must've been pretty galling, for a bloke with your … recent experience. Seeing a big black man with a pretty white girl, staying just a few doors up.'

'I mind me own business.'

Cassidy laughed. 'Not good enough, Ralph. You give me something, or I'm going to personally call Kinslow, tell him about your last stretch.'

'I heard bangin and crashin. Arguin. The big buck's voice. Her voice. They were fightin. Like I say, I mind me own business.'

'You didn't feel like steppin in, helping her out? Lone white woman going up against what you call a big black buck?'

Cord opened his mouth, disgust in his eyes. Nearly said it, what Cassidy had been leading him toward, until he understood and pulled back, put out his cigarette on the table. 'Her business is her business. I didn't step in. I got to live with that, every day of me life now.'

Cord's attempt to identify with Francine McGregor's situation was a pitiful lie, and all of them knew it. But the moment had passed.

Cassidy put out his own cigarette, nodded toward the door. 'You're free to leave, shitman. But tell your brother I want to talk to him. He doesn't make an appointment to come down and speak to me, I get on the phone to Kinslow. Understand?'

The bleak lizard-light was back in Cord's eyes. He smiled, stood stiffly, pushed his chair to the table.

44.

In the trunk on the drive to what he assumed would be the bikers' clubhouse, Devon Smith thought about what he could say to save his life. They'd already put a bag on his head and kicked him till he fitted the shape of the trunk, his body curled around the spare tyre. The V8 engine sounded like Barry Brown's Holden Monaro. Blood seeped from Devon's ear and he rubbed his face against the bag to soak it up.

Now that Devon had reached the inevitable destination, he was surprisingly calm. It was almost as if the pointlessness of his life had been preparing him for this end; stowed like a piece of luggage ready to be deep-sixed. At the very least it allowed him to think on his next steps.

Devon's one advantage was that he'd spent his life among predatory men. He had imagined that one day he might join their brotherhood, but in this he was mistaken. Such men had always been able to read Devon and know that he was not like them.

There would be no point begging the bikers for mercy. It was a matter of business, after all. There was no surer way to bring on punishment than to beg, and there was no better way for a thug to justify the meting out of cold and lethal violence than in matters of business. It was this latter thing that had always surprised Devon. His father got the trembles and suffered from the night terrors, woke screaming from bad dreams. He could be generous to his friends, however, and sometimes even to Devon. But he was ruthless when it was a matter of business, burning a drug dealer or ripping a fellow thief – just another transaction, just business.

Devon Smith had fucked up again and now he had to make amends or pay the price. He knew that he had to come out fighting. He prepared the words and rehearsed them in his mind, his fists clenching and his neck stiffening as he made the sounds.

The Monaro chugged down streets noisy with afternoon traffic. The men inside the car didn't speak. It seemed that they too were preparing themselves.

Finally the Monaro came to a stop. He heard the clanking of a gate and knew that they were at the clubhouse. Devon started to breathe deeply, trying to ride the wave of fear that was welling up inside him, turn it to anger.

Inside the gates, the Holden spurted over rough concrete and pulled into a hard turn. The doors opened. Nothing was said. He heard the trunk lock open and then he did what he planned to do – kicked the lid and began to curse.

The first punch to his head made him reel like he'd been thrown off a cliff. He tried to snarl out some words and was punched again, in the forehead this time, the back of his head cracking against the trunk lid. Tears welled in his eyes and he was too dizzy to speak and somebody had him by the legs. He was dragged out of the car, hitting his back on the tow bar, cracking his head on the cement floor.

'You fucken cowboys,' he tried to shout but it came out as a whimper. 'Rippin me ...'

When Devon returned to consciousness the hood was gone and he was bound to a chair. A swell of nausea rose inside him; he coughed and drooled over his kitchen uniform, already bloody where his nose and mouth had dripped down his chin.

The head biker, Devon couldn't remember his name, stared at him coolly, blowing onto the end of a lit cigar, the red ember pulsing in the gloom. Barry Brown was drinking a beer while perched on a bar stool, watching Devon with the expression of a chef eyeing a cut of meat. Brown had bloody knuckles where they'd caught on Devon's teeth.

Neither of them spoke. They were going to use silence to break him open. Devon had to act fast.

'Just do what you gotta do,' he spat, surprised by the forcefulness of his voice. 'Don't know why you gotta do it, though, after what you did. Could've just ripped me off and gone your way.'

The head biker glanced at Barry Brown, which gave Devon time to prepare. His next sentence – his life hinged on it. The head biker sized him up, head cocked, amusement in his eyes.

'Oh, you think *we* took the guns, our cash?'

The next sentence. 'Stop fucking with me. I put the guns in the van, got called inside before I had the chance to take my money –'

'*Our* money, motherfucker.'

'... went back outside, the van was gone.'

'Just gone, eh?'

The head biker blew on the cigar, brought the ember to a fierce glow. *I can take a little burning*, Devon told himself. *I can take that.*

But the man didn't burn Devon. Instead, he nodded to Barry Brown, who snapped his fingers. Another biker emerged from the darkness behind the bar, unwinding an extension cord as he approached. Devon couldn't see what he had tucked up under his arm, and when he did – felt his guts churn, heart putter, throat constrict.

The biker passed the electric drill to Barry Brown, who tightened the chuck on the bit, put the chuck key in his pocket, passed the drill to the head biker who triggered it, made it scream.

It was his body that gave Devon up. Despite the terror, the voice in his head was clear, even as his bladder opened into his trousers.

'Good boy,' murmured Barry Brown. 'Quit the actin and let yerself go.'

'I don't know anything,' Devon pleaded.

The head biker got down on one knee. His red hair glinted in the dull light. His eyes were green and calm. Devon waited for him to say it, as he'd heard his father say it. *It's nothing personal, son. Just a matter of business.*

Instead, he placed the drill-bit onto Devon's kneecap. A strange light entered his eyes. He'd done this before, and enjoyed it.

'Who else knew about the guns?' he asked, his voice barely a whisper.

Devon didn't have to think about that. 'Only my boy on the *Vinson*, got me them. But he ain't on shore leave until tonight.'

'You sure about that?'

The phone behind the bar rang loud and clear, breaking the moment. Barry Brown walked over and lifted the receiver, grunted a couple of times. 'Gus. Bloke at the gate wants to make a payment. Wants to make a payment in gold. He's got it on him.'

That made Gus, the head biker, laugh. 'Tell him sure. I like gold. Everybody likes gold. But tell him we'll need to add a ten-percent commission onto his next payment. Buzz him in. He can wait outside. Within earshot.'

The head biker triggered the drill, put it up near Devon's face, the sound filling his ears. Devon began to rock on the chair, throwing his head about. The sound died off. Devon looked at the biker, who was speaking. 'I said, how do you know that he didn't leave the *Vinson* early, organise a crew, take you for the lot?'

Devon had to admit that it was possible, except that he hadn't been specific about the arrangements when he told them to Mike Scully. If life had taught Devon one thing, it was that you never truly knew another person, but he didn't think that Scully would do him like that.

'He didn't know about the plan. It wasn't him.'

Devon felt the memory emerge, sucking the breath out of him. He'd been so high at the time, and it was just a slip.

'What is it, son? Before I give you a permanent limp? Not that you'll ever have to walk on it. You grew up in the outlaw life. You know we can't let you live, right?'

Devon looked at Barry Brown, arms folded and leaning on the bar. He tried for his most apologetic tone. 'Only person I told about our business was Barry's nephew. Skinhead dude. Ant. *Antony*. I was so damn high, man. I'm sorry. I didn't keep my mouth shut.'

The biker leader turned to Barry Brown, who'd stood away from the bar, his fists balled, trying to erase a look of shock. 'You told *Ant* what we were plannin to do?'

'I'm sorry. He's the only person I told.'

It hit Devon with a flash of clarity and perverse pleasure. 'I guess I trusted him because he's your nephew.'

'You little runt. Gimme that drill.'

In two strides Barry Brown had Devon by the throat, crushing his windpipe, drawing back a fist that was grabbed by the biker leader, got it pinned behind him as other bikers moved into the light.

At first it sounded like stones on the roof. Five single crashes that became a series of louder reports and then a single, continuous tock-tock-tocking. No bullets hit the clubhouse. Devon remembered the high-security wall and heavy front gates, designed to withstand an armoured police vehicle, Barry had told him.

Barry and the biker leader crab-walked to the phone, just as it rang.

Barry lifted the receiver, pressed speaker.

'... under attack. Can't see who but it's our white van. They're driving away. They've gone.'

There was a long silence, broken by Devon. 'I know that sound. That's an M16. Burst-fire mode.'

45.

Swann held the glass of Emu Export to the porch light. His first drink in
many months. The lead poisoning had at least got him off the cigarettes,
something his daughters had nagged him about for years. Every other
time he'd tried to quit smoking it was just as bad as coming off the
drink – sleeplessness, cold sweats, nightmares, ridiculous mood swings.
He'd learnt to control his drinking but didn't think that he could do the
same with the tobacco. It was either smoke or not smoke.

Marion touched her glass of moselle to his beer, put her feet over
his knees. It was another hot night and they were on the back porch
watching the moon rise. Because it was hot, Swann had made them
cheese and salad sandwiches for dinner. Marion was tired after a long
day supervising an East Perth health clinic that treated street people.
The dog snored under her chair, and despite the early hour Swann
found himself yawning. Marion had sore feet from being on the move
all day, and Swann took one of her feet and put it in his lap, began to
knead the instep as she liked him to do.

They'd almost had an argument over dinner. On the table between
them was the front page of the *Daily News*, including the article written
by Louise's friend Maddie. She had done solid work. Her article, which
continued onto page three, detailed a long history of sexual assault and
sex murders in ports frequented by the US Navy, across five continents.
She included the names of correspondents in Mombasa, Hamburg,
Okinawa, Yokohama, Subic Bay, Lisbon, Naples, Lima, Manta, Sydney,
who each quoted specific crimes and their links to US sailors. It was a
damning article, and while it didn't explicitly suggest that the US Navy
was culpable in allowing sexual predators to serve under the flag, the
fact that so few of the assaults had resulted in convictions implied that

there were serial rapists and murderers currently in the navy who'd never been brought to justice.

'I know that look,' Swann said when Marion finished reading the article, not meeting his eyes.

She ignored him because it was a stupid thing to say. Marion worked with victims of sexual assault and domestic violence. These were crimes perpetrated by individuals, but often in an institutional setting, which allowed the perpetrators opportunity and cover. Whether it was a church, school, reformatory, prison or branch of the military, she knew the added damage when the needs of the institution to protect itself were prioritised over the needs of the victim.

Swann was angry at himself for feeling defensive. 'I'm helping Webb find an AWOL sailor. A man who if proven guilty will cop it.'

'You don't know that,' she replied. 'Look at how few of those crimes have been solved.'

There was nothing Swann could say, because it was true. They had raised three daughters together. He shared her anger at the evidence that predators were getting away with murder, literally, by hiding behind the uniform. No doubt Webb had seen the article. He would have some explaining to do.

Both of them heard the front gate open. The dog awoke and looked into the darkness, growled. Swann stroked her ears and waited. If it was family or friends they'd know to come down back, but it was the doorbell which rang. The dog barked and bolted inside the house, pausing only to make sure that Swann was following before doubling the volume of its barking.

It was Tremain, the gold miner, standing in a puddle of light beneath the frangipani. For whatever reason, he waited there instead of the porch. Swann looked past him into the shadows. Tremain's was an old trick used to lure someone outside, prior to their being shot. Swann had put those days behind him, but you never knew.

'What do you want?'

'I tried calling you. A dozen messages.'

Tremain hadn't asked Swann to leave the house. Swann stepped onto the porch.

'I gave you free advice,' Swann said. 'Told you not to contact me.'

Tremain reached down to the Gladstone bag at his feet. Swann measured the distance between them, tensed. The bag that Tremain lifted was heavy, and clanked. Swann got ready to move.

'I know,' Tremain complained. 'But your man told me to make the drop. I did as he asked, but that was before the bullets started flying. Got out of there by the skin of my teeth. Never made the delivery. Can't do it, Swann, cut of the cloth and all that. It's not me. Your man didn't leave me a number. I had no choice but to come here.'

Swann listened to the shakiness in Tremain's voice. Nerves, adrenalin, exhaustion – Swann didn't care.

'I don't know what you're talking about, Tremain. You've got to leave.'

Tremain looked close to tears, or collapse. His whole body slumped. 'I know, Frank. I know you got to say that. But your man –'

'What man, Tremain? There's no man.'

Tremain looked at him in the eye for the first time, tried to understand, but wasn't able. Lowered his head again. 'I tried, Swann. Tell him that. But then the bullets started flying. Like a fucking war zone. They let me out before the coppers came. Dozens of them. TRG. An army of coppers. And me, with this bag, like your man told me to do.'

'What's in the bag?'

Tremain put the weight of the bag on his thigh, pulled the zipper. Gold. Ingots and kilo bars. More gold than Swann had ever seen.

'You've been had, Tremain. There's no man. And I don't know anything about coppers or a shootout.'

Tremain appeared to believe him, which only made him more upset. 'You haven't seen it? It's on the news. I was right in the middle of it ...'

Tremain tried to control his breathing, began to lay it out for him: the older man who claimed to work for Swann, the demand that he make payments to The Nongs on someone else's behalf, the machine-gun fire aimed at the clubhouse gates.

Tremain had been taken advantage of again. Not much Swann could do about that – the businessman was a goldfish in a shark-tank. But someone else was out there, using Swann's name to make fraudulent deals. That couldn't stand.

Tremain's description of the old man didn't match, which meant that Swann would have to lay eyes on him.

'Next time he calls, tell him that you tried to make the payment.

What you just told me. But that he needs to do it. That you need to meet him. Then call me.'

Tremain thanked him and withdrew into the shadows. Swann called him back. 'Do you have a lawyer?'

Tremain nodded. 'My cousin. He's a barrister.'

'First thing tomorrow, make a new will. You don't have a wife or kids, right? Make sure that the will specifically states that in the event of your death, all of your assets including the company, mine and lease go toward a charity of your choice.'

'A will?'

'That's what I said. Make it a children's charity, like Telethon. Make sure that the assay results et cetera are all in the documentation, as well as a description of your tormentors. I don't know what you're caught up in now, but if there's nothing to be gained by taking you off the map, then a new will and last testament might keep you alive. Otherwise, your current beneficiaries will just inherit your problems. Certain people might assume that your beneficiaries will be easier to deal with than you are.'

The idea that Tremain might be knocked because of his sudden wealth didn't appear to surprise him. He nodded and backed into the darkness. Swann returned inside and the dog followed him into the lounge room. Swann saw the messages on the answering machine, which he'd muted earlier. He turned the TV on and waited for the picture to emerge out of the static, fiddled with the arms of the antennae until the image was clear. He sat on the couch, let the dog onto his lap, who began to try to lick his face.

When the advertisements for the new Holden Commodore ended, the screen went bleached red and a male voice emerged from the silence.

'That was a gunshot,' was all it said. A strap of text at the bottom of the screen stated 'Possible bikie gang-war erupts in Bayswater'. The grainy home-video image became focussed on a driveway and garden, the picture bouncing as whoever carried the camera went toward the street. 'Definitely a gunshot,' the male voice said again, before what sounded like a jackhammer began and the camera shook as its citizen operator ran to hide behind a parked car. Between gunshots you could hear the sound of heavy breathing and beeping where expletives were dubbed out, the voice of an older man inside the nearest house calling for the cameraman to return inside. The camera focussed on a white van parked up the street, then zoomed closer onto the driver window where a rifle barrel could be seen resting on the wing mirror, recoiling as the bullets fired in a steady stream.

'Oh shit,' said Swann as Marion joined him at the couch. 'That's The Nongs' clubhouse.' Chips of red brickwork spurted into the air as the strafing went across the front wall, then bashed on the fortified steel doors, shredding the bushes either side of the gates. The automatic gunfire continued until either the clip was empty or the combatant became bored. It was then that Swann saw the tattoo. The gunman straightened the barrel over the wing mirror and his left forearm became exposed. It was only a moment, but Ralph Cord's tattoo of a lynched man was so distinctive that there wasn't any doubt, even as the barrel withdrew and the van lurched forward, then sped toward the first corner where it exited the picture.

The live feed that replaced the footage showed dozens of police vehicles and TRG officers down the dark street, lit only by the strobing of the cherry tops and the bright glare inside the forensic tent. Television station vans were parked further down the verge, where local citizens crowded outside the perimeter tape. The young woman doing a piece to camera held her ear and introduced a live cross to a munitions and firearm expert, former SAS Captain Tom Stanley. Stanley said that he'd reviewed the footage and could state categorically that the weapon used was an M16A2 automatic rifle, going on the barrel form and the front sight post, as well as the three-round burst-fire facility demonstrated in the footage. Ejected shells were clearly hitting a spent case deflector, something only incorporated on the latest model. While the weapon resembled the AR-15 semi-automatic rifle distributed by various manufacturers worldwide, the automatic rifle in the footage was, he said gravely, used solely by the US Marine Corps. He had never seen one in civilian hands before, or heard of one being sold on the black market. Manufactured by Colt, it wasn't offered for sale by international arms dealers either, so far as he was aware, giving the US Marine Corps a technical advantage in the field. When asked where an Australian criminal might source such a weapon, the ex-SAS captain took a moment to consider his answer. 'You will only find that weapon on US military bases, or, because it's used by the Marine

Corps, on US Navy vessels that carry marines, such as aircraft carriers and larger battleships.'

Swann couldn't believe what he was hearing. The ex-soldier had been reluctant to say it, but the inference was clear. The use of the M16A2 directly coincided with the USS *Carl Vinson*'s arrival in port. It was no surprise when Swann heard the front gate creak on its hinges. He peered behind the curtains that gave onto the front yard. Webb stood there in his civilian uniform of chinos and polo shirt, baseball cap pulled low. He lifted a finger to Swann in a desultory salute. The sea breeze gusted and flapped at his trousers, revealing a bulge at his ankle where a sidearm was strapped.

Outside, Webb smoked a Camel and stared up at the night sky.

'How many are you missing?' Swann asked.

Webb exhaled a long blue stream. 'Between you and me? Six. We're missing six.'

'Not between you and me. Not anymore. I know who the shooter was. We need to get Cassidy involved.'

Webb nodded. 'Did you know there's a bloke in a car across the road, watching your house? You're under surveillance. Have you checked your place over lately?'

Webb meant bugs – the reason he was standing away from the house.

Swann walked to the front gate, saw the little glow of a cigarette in the Ford Falcon across the street. Opened the gate and heard the Ford growl to life. He watched as Detective Sergeant Dave Gooch pulled from the kerb, flicked his cigarette onto the road, little sparks carried on the wind like fireflies. Instead of heading up the street, however, Gooch swung the wheel, tyres squealing as he turned toward Swann, who had to step back to avoid getting hit. Gooch was only stationary for a second before he reversed back across the road, kept the Ford idling with his lights on high beam. Swann shielded his eyes, made ready to jump away, but Gooch put her in gear and roared up the street.

Webb was at Swann's shoulder. 'What was that about?'

'Nothing. Something else. No idea. All three of those things.'

They watched the Falcon's tail-lights disappear left at the junction.

46.

The Aussie bikers had gone out in their cars, vans and trucks. They left the clubhouse using a secret exit into the backyard of a Chinese man who pretended they weren't there, passing through his side gate while his family sat at dinner. The door that exited the clubhouse was furthest away from the front gate. It was a crawl-through hidden behind empty forty-four-gallon drums, emerging into the Chinaman's back shed.

Barry Brown and another biker named Ted nudged Devon toward the Chinaman's front gate. More bikers followed behind them. Barry looked left and right, then crossed to his Monaro, now parked under a tree across the road. Devon was dumped into the back seat while Barry got under the wheel and two others piled in. Barry started her up and headed down the quiet street, headlights off until they hit a main road. Devon could see the reflection of the distant police cherry tops on the high walls of an apartment building. Ted, the younger biker, who wore coveralls and tennis shoes, took a CB radio handpiece from the glove box and tested it, but didn't speak. The departure of the gang members from the clubhouse had been done with the efficiency of a military operation. Nobody had spoken and everybody knew what to do.

It was only now that Ted broke the radio silence. 'See you turning onto Whatley. You got visuals on Dave, Mick?'

'Roger that,' came the reply.

'Proceed separately to the place. Over.'

'Roger that,' was repeated seven times.

It was only now that Devon felt it was safe to speak. 'I don't know why you got me. I didn't have nothing to do with that, back there.'

Barry Brown was silent for a long while. 'We'll talk when we get there. In the meantime, don't speak shit. The only reason those Nazi morons would shoot us up, is because they know that we have you. You mean something to them. Which means that you knew something about them stealin our money, our guns. You'll get your chance to talk soon enough. You saw that I packed my drill?'

Devon hadn't seen and the thought made him tremble. He could smell the piss on his uniform trousers. For some reason, when the bullets began firing he'd assumed that the attack would clear him of involvement, that he'd be let go. Now he saw that the opposite was true.

'I swear, Mr Brown. I only met them once. I didn't tell them anything except –'

'...except about our deal. Now shut the fuck up. I don't know if anybody's told you this before, but your Kermit-the-Frog Yank voice is hard to take. Only reason you're still alive is because you got some worth to those boneheads. But you open your mouth once more, I'm gonna put my fist down it, hear me?'

Devon nodded, sat deeper into the leather seat, tried to control his shaking hands.

47.

Swann and Webb drove to Cassidy's home in Doubleview. It was an old worker's cottage built on top of the hill with a view over the distant ocean. Sheoaks whispered in the breeze. Cassidy was dressed in a three-piece suit, hair combed in a side part.

The shooting-up of The Nongs' clubhouse was related to the Bernier murders because Cassidy's interview with Ralph Cord had provoked something vengeful in the ex–Junkyard Dogs bikie. The media was taking a bikie-war angle but both Swann and Cassidy knew otherwise – the tattoo in the televised footage belonged to Ralph Cord. The question was where Cord, a former black-market arms dealer, had sourced the semi-automatic weapon. From the back seat, Webb described to Cassidy how six of the weapons were missing. The M16s were kept in a secure area, accessible to a select number of staff, and it wouldn't be long before the culprit or culprits were identified.

Using Webb's mobile phone, Cassidy called Central Police and put out a KALOF, a keep-a-look-out-for bulletin on the Cord brothers relating to an unnamed aggravated assault, describing them as armed and dangerous, without mentioning the American weapons. He didn't want it getting to the media, at least not until he'd spoken to Gus Riley.

Swann took Cassidy's cooperation as a sign of progress, or at least of expedience. A day earlier and Cassidy would have revelled in embarrassing the US Navy. It remained unspoken that Ralph Cord's actions were the unintended consequence of Cassidy's own provocation.

Cassidy and Webb smoked in silence as Swann pulled the Brougham to the kerb, fifty metres from the media circus outside the clubhouse. He was just about to crack the door when he looked in his rear-view mirror. There was Gooch's Falcon, cutting its lights, parking behind a Channel

Seven station wagon. Swann didn't say anything. Gooch had nothing to do with the matter at hand, although he'd need to be dealt with.

Cassidy straightened his suit, shot his cuffs, while Webb dialled the number. Swann took the phone and waited for Riley to answer. Across the road a forensics team inspected the bullet holes in the compound wall while others looked for casings in the suburban street. It appeared as though the media were packing up. Cameras were being removed from tripods, power cords rolled hand-over-arm. Swann recognised the talking heads who chatted and smoked while techs disassembled the hardware. They would wonder why Swann and a homicide detective were visiting Riley.

Riley picked up. His voice was exaggeratedly gruff, his drawl pronounced. It was his media voice, part of the role.

'Riley, it's me. Swann. We need to come in.'

'Been a long day, Frank. I prefer it when we see each other once a year, like family. Tell me what you need to tell me.'

Swann couldn't say that he wanted to get a reading of Riley's face, his body language, when they told him the news. Only way to ascertain whether he knew already.

'It's about what just happened, and why,' Swann said. 'I'm not talking over the phone.'

Cassidy stood beside him and nodded, drew deeply on his cigarette.

Riley was silent for a long while. 'Stand in front of the camera, and wave. I'll buzz you in.'

'I've got Detective Inspector Cassidy with me.'

'Homicide. Why?'

'Tell you in a minute.'

Cassidy put out his cigarette, checked his shoulder holster. Swann hung up and passed the phone to Webb, staring down the street at Gooch, whose car hadn't moved.

The media pack saw Swann and Cassidy and whispers were exchanged, cameras raised onto shoulders. As agreed, Cassidy took the front position and Swann followed in his wake. Being seen with Swann wasn't a good look for Cassidy but he didn't seem to care, showing his badge to the uniformed police at the perimeter and ignoring the shouted media questions until they reached the clubhouse gate.

'Riley's going to mess with us,' said Swann.

Cassidy pressed the buzzer set into the reinforced steel gate-frame. 'Yeah, he is,' Cassidy agreed.

Behind him, Swann could hear the questions addressed to his back, asking why he was there, what was his relationship to the bikie club, and what did he know about a gang war? Finally, the gate clicked open, but only wide enough for them to enter. As soon as Swann was through the gate, it closed with a thud.

Swann led the way toward the bar and offices. The fires in drums and pits were still burning, despite the hot night. Riley was a cautious leader, and he'd made sure to clean house. Swann walked into the bar area where Riley was sitting at a table, smoking a cigar and watching the news on a wall-mounted television. Riley pointed toward it and Swann saw the footage of Cassidy and his entrance to the clubhouse a few moments earlier, the questions loud and unanswered, both of them identified by the breathless Channel Nine presenter.

'You blokes looked pretty cute, standing there holding your dicks.'

Swann nodded. 'We figured you'd have your fun. Cassidy wore his best suit.'

Cassidy played his part, holding out the lapels of his jacket, model-like, at the same time giving Riley a view of the .38 revolver in his holster.

'Very nice, detective. But *you* could've made an effort, Swann. Same old fuckin work jacket. A la mode, Brando in *On the Waterfront*, nineteen fifty-four. Now, what do you want? I know it don't take much to get a homicide cop out of bed when there's cameras involved, but seriously Swann, I thought you were better 'n that.'

Riley would go on all night with his passive-aggressive bullshit given half the chance. As agreed, Swann led the way with the questions.

'Off the record. You got a line on who did the drive-by?'

Riley grinned, aware that he was being read. 'Course not. Otherwise, you think I'd be sitting here?'

'Where's everybody else? Times like this, you blokes come together, unless of course ...'

'You got me there. Swann – one. Riley – zero. Next question.'

'Not a question. I came here earlier and spoke to you about Ralph Cord. You told me some things. Some of those things were put to Cord in a formal interview. He didn't appear to like what he heard. You getting my drift?'

Riley's face darkened for a moment before he regained composure. 'Right. I see. You threw me under the bus.'

'No need to play the victim. You're a big boy. We know where the automatic weapon was sourced, but we don't know how, or why.'

Riley grinned, took a huff of his cigar, blew perfect smoke rings across the table. 'No fuckin clue.'

He was lying, and that was all they needed to know. Somehow, Riley was involved.

'Your turn to throw Cord under a bus. Tell us where he is, might save some of your blokes, some of Cassidy's, getting shot. We both know that once he's in custody, there's nothing to protect him from your men.'

'No fuckin idea.'

'Cassidy just put out a bulletin on him. Means thousands of coppers are looking for him, dozens of detectives, and that's before the media gets involved. I know you need to make a show of exacting revenge, but that's a lot of coppers between you and Cord. Some of your riders might get pulled over in the process. Easier if you tell me now.'

'Haven't you heard, Swanny? We're flush with soldiers right now, heavy riders one and all. We can take a few hits, here and there. And besides, I ain't a dog.'

'You wouldn't be snitching. You'd be sharing a rumour with me, your old sparring partner. You change your mind, let me know.'

Riley stood, bowed. 'That I will. You know the way out. Remember to smile for the cameras. I'll be watching from here.'

In the compound yard, Cassidy moved alongside Swann. 'I've got to bring the TRG into this. Can't have our men and women exposed to either Cord or Riley's men, unprepared.'

'I understand.'

'You think Riley's got a secret exit from the clubhouse?'

'I know he has.' Swann thought of Gooch, out there in his Falcon. 'But there's a problem.'

Cassidy listened while Swann laid it out. They reached the gate, which buzzed, shifted on its hinges. The fierce light of the camera crews hit their faces, made them wince.

48.

Devon Smith kept his mouth shut as the Monaro chugged along. Ted and the two men either side of Devon were practised at their trade, loading sawed-off shotguns like they were stringing fishing line, checking the Glock 9mm pistols that Devon had sold them. Rather than dwelling on the forthcoming violence they preferred to bask in their easy familiarity, the banter that Devon barely understood because of their gruff accents, the constant talking over one another and guffaws of laughter. The Holden became stuffy with the smells of bad breath, armpits and gun oil, and Devon kept quiet because he didn't want to end up in the trunk again. So he grinned like an idiot, and pretended to understand their coarse speech, nodded along to the instrumental metal track. He tried to be invisible in plain sight, despite his handcuffs and the vial of speed that was passed around, not offered to him.

The loose convoy that stretched ahead consisted of pick-up trucks and nondescript sedans. They broached a hill and there was the ocean, glimmering black behind the yellow lights that followed the coastline. Devon looked through the windscreen and saw the port to the south, the giant container cranes and the silos and loading yards. Behind them was the USS *Carl Vinson*, his home and refuge. He had always thought of the *Vinson* as a prison, or a vast floating zoo, but he'd give anything now to be on his rack, reading a *MAD* comic while listening to his walkman. He could just see the radio transmitter towers and satellite dishes on the command deck, but the *Vinson* might as well have been on a different planet.

Devon knew where they were headed, and it wasn't far away. He remembered the big red dog painted on the white corrugated sheet metal wall and the train tracks downhill, the smell of the ocean and the small industrial area. The men began to quieten as the Monaro pulled into the parking lot of a disused factory, a rusted iron scaffold-winch at its centre. The vehicles raised a chalky dust into the night air. Devon waited until the Monaro was empty before he slid across the bench seat and put his boots on the gravel. Still, nobody addressed or even looked at him. It felt like he could start walking and keep walking, right out of the carpark, down to the port and the safety of the *Vinson*. Devon stood, raised his handcuffs to his face, and wiped his eyes of dust.

When he took them away, Barry Brown was there, smiling strangely. 'Those fucken M16s you stole. The media is onto it. You weren't the only one to identify the semi-automatic used on our clubhouse. The telly expert reckons the weapons came off your Yank-boat. You know what that means, right?'

Devon wanted to keep his head up, maintain what little dignity he had left, but the news cruelled him. He knew what it meant. The navy would probably deny that they were the source of the M16s, but behind closed doors they'd be working fast. The stocktake that was done once the *Vinson* returned stateside would be conducted now. The staff responsible for the armoury would be dragged in by the master-at-arms, worked over. Even if Mike Scully didn't talk, they'd find the five grand cash in his locker, put two and two together. The game was up, the fuck-up complete. If Devon returned to the *Vinson*, he'd be looking at a decade behind bars, and not in a federal prison where at least he'd earn a rep, but in a military joint like Leavenworth, fucking Kansas, where the time was hard and lonely.

Barry Brown looked at him, saying nothing. He had a Glock in his hand, placed on his knee. It came to Devon in a flash of clarity.

'What do you need me to do?' he asked.

Barry Brown nodded. 'Good kid. Smart answer. We own you now. Listen up ...'

49.

Swann's knowledge that Gus Riley had a secret exit from the clubhouse paid off. They were parked around the block on a suburban street that backed onto the clubhouse walls, watching the lights in the houses go out. Swann was about to call it a night when Cassidy heard a gate creak and they saw the hunched figure of Gus Riley in worker's overalls and a beanie come onto the street. He walked to an old Holden utility with a ladder strapped to its roof. The ute coughed to life and blasted a cloud of fumes.

Swann started the Brougham but kept his lights off, following at a distance. Riley turned west toward the city, his arm out the driver's window as he adjusted the wing mirror. It was late now and even the main roads were quiet and empty. Swann hung back but could tell from a distance that the ute was equipped with a CB aerial. He pointed Cassidy toward the console and Cassidy turned on the police radio and began flicking through the channels, catching conversations from long-haul truckies; a wife talking to a husband somewhere out in the Gascoyne; a pair of traffic accident ghouls reporting a pile-up on the Great Eastern Highway.

Cassidy flipped the station again and now the conversation was between two young music lovers talking about the latest Cure album, how beautiful Robert Smith's haircut was, and wasn't it a pity that his flying phobia stopped him from touring Australia?

Cassidy changed to a blank bandwidth and turned down the volume, put the mic onto its hook and accepted a Camel from Webb in the back seat. Before they'd moved to the rear of the clubhouse, Cassidy had gone and had a word with Gooch, still parked down the street. When he returned his face was a mixture of bemusement and disgust. Cassidy had told Gooch that Swann had nothing to do with anything Gooch was involved in, and that Gooch was wasting his time. Gooch had told Cassidy to fuck off before calling him a Mick bastard, the kind of insult that reflected their age, but also the ancient division in the force between Mason and Catholic.

Swann assumed that Gooch had dropped the tail, but now when he looked in his rear-vision mirror Gooch was there a few hundred metres back, not even bothering to pretend otherwise, headlights on high beam.

'Gooch's still with us.'

Cassidy looked in the wing mirror and shook his head. 'That prick gets any closer he'll tip off Riley.'

Riley was keeping to the speed limit, just another night-shift worker on the early-morning roads.

'I'll try and lose Gooch,' Swann said. 'Whatever he's mixed up in, Riley might be too. The bloke that Gooch is standing over, Tremain, said he was at the clubhouse making a payment when the drive-by happened.'

'Small fuckin world,' Cassidy snorted. 'Full of stupid fuckin men.'

In the back seat, Webb dialled the *Vinson* again, grunted a few monosyllables, arched his eyebrows in surprise, hung up. 'Think we've got our man. Was on shift this morning, caught just as he was heading out on shore leave. Isn't admitting to it, but he had five grand cash in his locker, can't account for it. They're keeping him in the brig until I get back.'

'I've got to get one of those,' Cassidy said, referring to the mobile phone. 'Sure beats the police radio. They come in a smaller size than that?'

'Nope,' said Webb. 'You Aussies don't have the cell tower infrastructure yet anyway. They have it stateside, although it can be sketchy unless you're downtown. But it'll catch on.'

Cassidy had used Webb's phone to call Central and order a TRG squad to standby. He'd reinforced his earlier bulletin on the Cord brothers as a 'do not approach, suspects are armed and dangerous' warning, adding to the message 'possible responsibility for drive-by shooting at bikie clubhouse'. Cassidy didn't go into details with the despatcher, but the chances were good that it'd be leaked to the media before morning. Cassidy then called the duty commander of the CIB and told him what he knew about the Cords, without mentioning that he was currently on duty with Swann and Webb. Instead, he told the senior detective that he'd received the information from an informer and that he'd update the day-shift commander in the morning.

Webb and Cassidy began to work through the Charles Bernier murders. Due to the discovery of Bernier's neckerchief, Webb had given up on his earlier insistence that the evidence against Charles Bernier was circumstantial. The clincher was his revelation that Bernier's blood type was A-negative, a rare type, and one that matched the seminal fluid in the McGregor and Brayshaw murders.

'Only one way to be more certain,' Webb said. 'There's a new technology, soon to be in play, based on genetics. It's been used on a couple cases back home.'

Cassidy blew smoke out the window. 'I know it's been used to test paternity. I heard about that British case, the serial murderer, two years ago. There's talk of introducing it here, soon as we have the right case. But for it to work now, we'd need a sample from Bernier, and we can't find the bastard.'

'What about the condoms in the room Bernier rented, back at the Seaview?' Swann asked.

Cassidy nodded. 'They're being tested to confirm blood type as we speak; should know by tomorrow.'

The Brougham rose over a hill and the city sprawled beneath them, glittering under a sky of stars. 'Bernier's out there somewhere,' Cassidy said. 'Though it doesn't make sense that he could murder twice and disappear, unless he's got good friends.'

'Which explains the white man at the GPO,' Swann said.

Webb murmured his agreement. 'The two things are different, however. The murders, and then the disappearance. Both require a degree of planning, forethought, except that the murders don't appear to be well planned. There are witnesses and physical evidence. He strangled two women with his own neckerchief, left it there at a crime scene.'

'Perhaps he was interrupted, had to leave it,' said Swann.

'Perhaps,' said Cassidy. 'Either way, Bernier's real planning went into his disappearance. With the help of friends.'

'Who'd help a man responsible for two brutal murders?' Swann asked. 'And what kind of life awaits him, now that he's disappeared? I can see an AWOL sailor being protected, helped to find a new identity, employment, accommodation – but a murderer? His face has been on newspapers across the country. He'll always be looking over his shoulder.'

Webb sat forward in his seat. 'Was the teller at the GPO certain that the while male who cashed in the money order was American?'

Cassidy nodded. 'She was, but it's not hard to mimic such a universally recognised accent. We occasionally get Australian bank robbers imitating an English accent, for example.'

Swann hunched over the wheel, looked in the rear-view mirror at Gooch's Falcon, who was catching them up as they swung onto the Kwinana freeway, passing through the concrete canyon that broke the western end of the CBD.

'I'm gonna try something,' Swann said.

'Do it,' said Cassidy. 'No point tailing Riley if Gooch gives us away.'

Soon as they crossed the narrows Swann turned left off the freeway, gambling that Riley would continue at least until Canning Bridge. Out of the exit, Swann switched off his headlights and put his foot down, saw Gooch's high beams taking the turn. Swann shanked the wheel and cut onto a quiet suburban street. They watched Gooch drive past. Swann returned to the main road and headed toward the freeway. He accelerated to one hundred and fifty and it wasn't long before he recognised the tail-lights of Riley's old ute, turning off the freeway onto Canning Bridge, headed toward Fremantle. There was a crackle on the empty UHF channel and Swann recognised Riley's voice.

'Be there in fifteen. What's the status?'

The answer was garbled with static but there was enough. 'Sending the kid in now.'

'Roger that.'

Canning Highway was empty of traffic and Swann pulled right back, let the distant tail-lights of the ute guide him.

50.

The path from the front gate to the cottage door was only twenty metres of cracked concrete pavers but Devon's feet were heavy with the dread fear of the firearms pointed at his back.

The neighbourhood was quiet as the sky lightened around him. Birds were chirruping in the shrubs on the limestone hillside. The bikers were crouched behind the low wall at the front of the yard and a dumpster on the street. Ahead of him, there was a man either side of the front door with a loaded shotgun, waiting for it to open. It felt like a scene from a wild-west movie, except that Devon's fear told him it was real.

Devon had agreed to be what Barry Brown called the tethered goat, but there was no guarantee that when the front door opened the bikers wouldn't open fire immediately – their rifles, shotguns and Glock pistols would be no match for the M16s unless they used the element of surprise. Devon walked slowly because the shock that was pumping with every beat of his heart made him feel light-headed and faint. He reached the porch and had to put his hand on the railing. He felt sure that the light in the front room of the house flickered as he took the first step. There was music inside, loud and repetitive, an industrial track where the drums sounded like clanking machinery and the singer's voice was a hoarse screech of laughter that seemed directed at Devon. Even if he lived through this moment, even if the bikers let him survive beyond the recapture of their weapons, there was nowhere for him to run. He was broke and would never be able to return to the US.

Devon heard a sound behind him and glanced over his shoulder to see Barry Brown urging him forward with a waved Glock. Devon took the last steps in a dream. He was panting but couldn't get enough air. He watched his right arm raise itself and begin to knock on the heavy

184

front door. He remembered the fire-drums in the backyard that sloped down to the highway, and the red eyes of the men gathered there and the already paranoid atmosphere among the residents of the skinhead house. He wondered whether he would be shot from the front or the back, but his knuckles kept rapping and the noise grew louder. There were no sounds from inside, and the bikers were already moving toward him, stomping up the steps and taking their positions either side of the front door. As instructed, Devon stood back and kicked the door just inside the jamb and above the handle. The door cracked, and he did it again before he heard the lock break. He was immediately shoved aside as the men moved into the dark hall, clearing the front rooms with the precision of trained soldiers before swarming into the lounge area as others entered through the back door.

When it was finished, and the bikers were searching the cupboards and wardrobes, ripping everything onto the floor, Devon walked inside. He was ignored by the bikers as they went about their business, rapping on the floorboards and hoisting a man up into the ceiling crawlspace, hacking into the drywall with a crowbar and gouging into mattresses with knives. Devon stood outside the front bedroom, watching Ted at work, pulling hanks of woollen stuffing onto the floor, raising a little snowstorm above his head, drywall dust floating in the air, coating him with a fine white powder. When Ted turned, he looked like an enraged clown, shoving Devon out of the way as he went across the hall.

The front door was right there, and it was open. Now was the only opportunity that he would get. Devon shuffled backwards, felt the cool breeze on his barbered neck, replaced by the grasping of a giant's hand.

51.

Swann woke with a bad headache. He'd only slept a couple of hours but that was enough for his neck to stiffen. He got up and padded into the kitchen, drank a glass of tap-water. It was midmorning and already the temperature was in the thirties. The honeyeaters had stopped singing and even the wattlebirds were silent in the trees. Only the whirring of cicadas and the chirruping of a mole cricket broke the heat-heavy silence of his neighbourhood. He pulled the blind and went to the kitchen table, began to prepare his daily injection. The phone started ringing and he let it ring, breaking the ampoule of chelate solution before drawing it into a fresh syringe. He tapped out the air as Marion had taught him and stabbed it into his upper thigh, pressed the plunger home.

The phone kept ringing. Swann rolled his neck and kneaded his upper shoulders, worsening the pain in his head. He went into the backyard and turned on the hose, sprayed it over the parched bushes beside the shed.

Last night hadn't ended as they'd hoped. A few kilometres out from Fremantle, the radio crackled again and Gus Riley answered it. Whoever was on the line told him that the operation was a dud. Riley had grunted a reply and pulled to the kerb, executing a U-turn in the middle of the highway, catching Swann off-guard. Webb and Cassidy hid their faces and Swann drove past with his head down. Riley was so occupied with making the turn that he didn't look at them. Swann then used Webb's brick to call Kerry's brothel, got Lee Southern on the line. Lee had inside knowledge of the APM nationalists, having worked as a Kinslow tow-driver for a spell. He told Swann that he didn't think Kinslow would touch the M16s, or let them anywhere near his towing operation in Osborne Park. He was under Federal Police and ASIO surveillance.

Swann finished watering the garden and went inside. For the first morning in many months, he felt like he could eat something. He looked in the fridge and saw the leftovers from Marion's dinner with their three daughters. Tuesday night dinner was a long tradition and Swann had taken over cooking for the past few weeks, but he'd missed it last night, something that he would need to make up for. There was a plate of mashed potato and some slices of corned beef. A few peas and green beans, some cabbage and diced carrot. Swann took it all out and sliced it up and mixed it together with some beaten eggs. He had grown up on bubble-and-squeak, especially on football mornings when his mother plied him with a heaped plate as fuel for the coming game. Swann spooned the mixture onto a heated pan and watched it bubble in the oil.

Swann's mother had died many years ago, but he thought of her every day. He didn't know whether there was an afterlife, and didn't particularly care, but when he was laid up in hospital and didn't know whether he was going to make it, Swann began to hope that there might be a place where the dead remained alive, if only so that he could see his mother again. She was a good woman who endured a hard life with a deal of grace, humour and generosity. He could hear her voice now, telling him to turn off the gas and put the pan under the grill, just like she'd told him a hundred times before.

The phone began to ring again and this time he moved to the corridor so that he could hear the message. The pan began to squeak and squeal under the grill but he could hear Tremain's voice, telling him that the mystery man had called to ask if he'd made the delivery. Swann turned off the grill and headed down the hall. He lifted the receiver and began to speak, wiping away a little bauble of blood on his thigh.

52.

Tony Pascoe climbed out of the van and straightened his jacket, cinching the top button and lifting his trousers over the boot heel-tabs. The borrowed boots now squeaked when he walked.

It was another hot morning. The shade from the jacaranda tree was weak and he could feel the sunlight burning his face, despite the opiate in his bloodstream.

Something had lurched in his chest this morning. The previously dull weight of the tumour now felt like jagged bluestone against his ribs. Sarani had sourced the pethidine after he awoke grey-faced with his fists clenched. He didn't want to get her into trouble, and had tried to hide the pain, but it was like the bluestone rock had been dropped into a pond of what remained of his consciousness. What were previously ripples of discomfort had become waves that crashed inside him, leaving the taste of blood in his mouth.

The Subiaco street was quiet except for the ticking of a front-yard sprinkler and the warbling call of magpies in the branches above him. Pascoe wondered what his friends back inside Fremantle Prison were doing right now. The truth was that he missed them. They say that you can never really know anyone else, but that wasn't true. The closest friendships that Pascoe had ever made were developed in prison. Once the japing and yabbering noise of the younger inmates died away it was possible to hold a decent conversation, either in the cells or out in the yard. Pascoe supposed that it was like being in the military. The prison walls diminished his world, but that only emphasised the importance of his friends. The regular human virtues of loyalty and generosity were cast into sharper relief by the reality of prison life.

Pascoe missed his closest friends, and he knew that they would miss him too. It was strange, but Pascoe felt lucky. If he died a free man in the coming days then that was a personal victory. But if he was recaptured and was healthy enough to be returned to his old cell, among his friends, then that was alright too. It was only the middle-ground that was unacceptable to him. Most of all, Pascoe didn't want to die in hospital, surrounded by strangers.

He didn't have much time left, but thinking about that time helped slow it down and fill it out. He thought now about what might happen next. The businessman, Tremain, hadn't been strong enough to make the payment himself, meaning that Pascoe would have to do it. This exposed him to a degree of scrutiny that wasn't good, but he didn't have a choice.

Pascoe tucked the flare-gun pistol under the driver's seat. His purposeful walk toward Tremain's office was undermined by the squeaking of his boots, something that made him smile. He entered the gate that fronted the office block, passing between overgrown beds of orange-flowered nasturtium and purple morning glory that he hadn't noticed on his earlier visit. The lobby still smelt of stale cigarette smoke. All of the other offices were closed, the thin veneer doors labelled with the names of various trading companies and mining concerns. Tremain's office door was ajar, and Pascoe didn't bother knocking. He pulled the door back and walked inside. Tremain sat behind his desk, an old Gladstone bag placed between the trays laden with invoices and faxes. Tremain watched Pascoe from behind a veil of smoke. He cleared his throat and nodded to the bag, whose weight Pascoe realised was going to be a problem.

Pascoe stepped into the room and heard the door click behind him. He turned to find a tall middle-aged man with ropy arms and a sallow face. His hair was cut short into natural grey-blond spikes. His jeans and collared shirt looked too large for him, as though, like Pascoe, he'd recently lost weight. He wasn't armed, but the look in his eyes and the set of his feet and shoulders was familiar, poised for action. Pascoe knew who he was, and put up his hands in mock surrender.

53.

Devon Smith lit his cigarette. His right hand was cuffed to the kitchen table so that he had to extract the smoke and place it in his mouth and repeat the action with his lighter. There wasn't much else to do except sit there and smoke. He was tired after the night without sleeping, but every time his head began to loll he was overcome with dizziness and then he gasped awake and grabbed for the table.

Ted, the Australian biker, was hidden in the next room. He was supposed to be keeping guard in case the skinheads returned to the North Fremantle bungalow, but Devon could hear the snicker of his breath as he dozed. Devon was placed out in the open, and anybody who climbed over the back fence would see him in their horizontal line of sight, innocently seated at the kitchen table. The same through the kitchen windows, if someone came down the side of the house.

Devon didn't really understand the purpose of his being there, although he wasn't about to question it. He was sick of being clouted on the back of his head. The bikers weren't going to let him go, and the alternative to his current position wasn't going to be pretty. He wondered how the bikers got rid of their enemies. He had seen the Swan River on his bus-ride into the city, but he didn't know how deep it was.

Devon had never looked at a map of Australia and so didn't know whether there were forests or deserts nearby, suitable for dumping someone in a shallow grave, like they did at home. From the temperature in the low-ceilinged kitchen he assumed desert, because the climate here reminded him so much of summer in San Diego, with the desert ringing the city on every side. It certainly wasn't the same heat as he'd experienced in Florida, or over there in Kenya, where the hot air was so full of water it felt like you were breathing steam, just like it did when he washed dishes in the *Vinson* scullery. The thought of the galley gave him a little stab of regret. His shitty life there didn't seem so bad now, with the exception of the sassing he copped from his two workmates. That was one positive, at least, when the inevitable news broke of his theft from the armoury. At least Lenny and Marcus would be forced to respect him now. No more could they accuse him of being dickless and stupid. He had pulled off the theft right under their noses. Who looked stupid now?

The phone began to ring. Next door, he heard Ted come awake as the weight shifted in his creaking chair. The phone rang and rang. As it rang it seemed to get louder. Devon waited for the line to cut out or for the caller to give up, but instead it kept ringing. One minute, two, three. Ted now stood in the bedroom doorway. He looked angry and, like Devon, probably wanted to answer the phone, if only so that the ringing would stop. Ted walked down the hall and looked through the peephole into the front yard. He skirted the lounge and kitchen and peered into the backyard.

Devon didn't know what Ted was supposed to do if the skinheads returned with the M16s. Ted had a Glock and a sawed-off shotgun. For them to be effective he had to be near his target – the reason Devon was there to lure them inside. Not the same with the M16. It could be fired from some distance and even then its bullets would shred the weatherboard siding. Until the caller hung up, Ted had no way of communicating with his fellow bikers, who'd moved to a safe house to make further plans.

The phone kept ringing. Five minutes, six, seven. Ted was starting to swear. Devon lit another cigarette and kept his head down. Even he could feel it. There was something wrong. The ringing phone was clearly a cover for something. Its volume.

Ted got the idea the same time as Devon. Don't answer the phone, but instead turn it down. Ted moved across to the phone the same time the tall skinhead, Barry Brown's nephew, appeared behind him in the bedroom doorway, Glock raised. Three pieces of floorboard were missing where he'd come up through a cellar or crawlspace. Ted had his back turned and Devon went to cry out but didn't make a sound. The bullet caught Ted in the spine and he toppled onto the sink, slid onto the floor. He was alive, but paralysed. The skinhead, Antony, coolly crossed the room and fired a bullet into Ted's face.

54.

Swann recognised the older man as Tony Pascoe. He'd aged plenty since Swann last saw him, painting a yard wall in 4 Division. It was just a moment, Swann on the way to interrogate an old crim in connection to a murder, but Swann had often pondered upon it. Pascoe was something of a legend when Swann was a kid, as both a notorious stick-up man and safe-breaker. Pascoe had the nerve to handle a timed confrontation but also the brains to execute an overnight payroll heist. But there was Pascoe, a few years into his latest stretch, working quietly alongside another man painting whitewash onto the yard wall. The next time Swann visited the division, the wall had already been painted over.

Swann glanced over the old man's scarred knuckles, looking for the bulge of a concealed weapon in his jacket, but it didn't look like he was carrying. Swann too was unarmed, and because of his neck injury was reluctant to get into it, even with an old stager. Swann knew from the newspapers that Pascoe had a terminal illness, and that he was on the run. Whatever he wanted from Tremain, he would be desperate to see it through.

'I know who you are,' said Pascoe. 'Frank Swann. My apologies for trading on your name. Though it was him who brought it up, not me.'

Tony Pascoe surprised Swann by putting out his hand.

Swann ignored it. He turned to Tremain. 'That true?'

Tremain wrung his hands, shrugged. 'I dunno. Can't remember. Does it matter?'

Swann stared evenly at Pascoe, but spoke to Tremain. 'I don't know what's going on between you two, and I don't care. But it ends here. I'm going to take Mr Pascoe outside, have a word. But you've got to do one thing for me, Tremain, in return. You've got to call Detective Sergeant

Gooch and tell him I've got nothing to do with any of this. He's all over me, and I can do without it.'

Swann saw the flare of anger in Pascoe's eyes. Swann had just named him in front of a citizen. It didn't take long for Tremain to understand.

'You're that bank robber, in the papers.'

Pascoe grimaced, little mutter of disgust.

'You hear me, Tremain? You call Gooch. Soon as we leave. I hear that you're using my name again, you're going to cop it. Tell him whatever you want, but make sure you leave me clear.'

Swann heard the courtyard door open. He turned, and there was Gooch, aiming a Browning pistol at Swann's belly. Not his service weapon, but a throwdown.

Swann looked to Tremain, who looked at his feet. 'I'm sorry. I didn't have a choice.'

Gooch smiled cruelly, looking at Frank Swann and Tony Pascoe. 'Oh, this is just too good.'

Gooch kicked the courtyard door closed behind him. He pointed the gun at Pascoe, who was standing next to the front door. 'Get over there beside Tremain.'

Swann saw how it was going to go. The room was sealed against the sound of a gunshot. 'I've wanted to do this for a long time, Swann. This is for Don Casey. For Ben Hogan.'

It didn't matter to Gooch that there were witnesses. Tremain would do what he was told. Pascoe lived by the code.

Gooch moved two steps to his left, which put Swann in the corner. Three metres to cover the speed of a bullet. Gooch raised the Browning, grinning, teeth like a kicked-in fence, cold light in his eyes, just as Pascoe got beside him, stabbed three fingers into the armpit of his gun-hand. Gooch grunted as the nerves in his arm died, tried to switch the gun to his other hand. Swann covered the space, but he wasn't needed. Pascoe grabbed Gooch from behind, a bar chokehold, left hand gripping his forearm as the terrible weight drew against Gooch's windpipe, his carotids. Gooch fired, the bullet passing through Swann's shirt, the arm flailing as bullets sprayed into the wall, the ceiling, the noise deafening until five second passed and Gooch's lights went out. Pascoe held the chokehold a few seconds more, dropped Gooch where he stood. Gooch's head cracked on the floor. The three men stood around him, looking down.

Swann picked up the dropped Browning and aimed it at Pascoe while they waited for Gooch to come around. But he didn't come around. A stirring behind his eyelids, then a terrible gurgling, and then nothing. Pascoe knelt down, felt at Gooch's neck.

'He's dead.'

Swann dropped to his knees, took Gooch's pulse. Tilted back his head, made sure the airway was clear.

'It's too late. Seen this before. I didn't mean to crush his windpipe, break his hyoid. Oh, Christ.'

But Pascoe wasn't talking about regret. Swann looked up and watched the blood rush from the old man's face. Pascoe reached for his own neck, put a hand on the desk, then fell to his knees. Managed to whisper, 'White painter's van out front. Passenger seat. Oxygen bottle.'

Swann angled his head at Tremain, who hadn't moved throughout. His eyes were big and his mouth was open. 'Get moving,' Swann hissed. 'Oxygen bottle, and hurry.'

Tremain hustled out of the room. Swann knelt down. 'If you go under, mouth to mouth work?'

Pascoe was beyond talking. Shook his head, panic in his eyes. Everything put into drawing breath, his chest heaving, little gurgles of air going in but nothing coming out. Swann heard Tremain in the hallway outside, the hiss of oxygen as he opened the cylinder into the mask. Swann took the bottle off Tremain and put the mask over Pascoe's face, held it firm with his hand, began to pump the rubber valve-primer that forced gas into Pascoe's lungs.

55.

The murder of the biker had shocked Devon in a way he hadn't expected. He had grown up around men who considered themselves killers, and who talked endlessly about violence, but he had never seen a life taken.

And this was what it'd felt like.

Despite the muzzle-blast in the darkened room, and the bullet that'd torn into Ted's skull – a transference of fire from the shooter into the shot – what it felt like to Devon was that the skinhead had reached down and snatched something from Ted, who never moved again. The skinhead looked equally shocked at what he'd done. They both stared at the dead biker for nearly a minute, both of them deafened and silent, in reverence for the strangeness of what'd just happened.

And then Devon began to speak. A stream of shit and drivel that came from some deep reservoir of instinct and dread. He spoke, and he laughed, and played the role of the rescued man rather than the man expecting to be executed. The animated light in the skinhead's eyes died away as the adrenalin left him and he was confronted with the babbling fool still handcuffed to the table.

'You're Ant,' said Devon. 'Barry Brown's nephew. Remember me?'

Ant pointed the gun at Devon, nothing in his eyes, then turned away.

Devon didn't know what the plan was, but the other man didn't appear to be in any hurry. He took the biker's Glock from his dead hand and placed it at the waistband of his jeans. He went into the bedroom and put the floorboard pieces back into position, then returned with the shotgun and boxes of shells. He put them beside the front door and returned for Devon, lifting the kitchen table so that the handcuffs slid down the heavy table-leg, freeing him.

Devon didn't shut up the whole time. He could hear his words but he wasn't really listening, saying how he was glad things had gone the way they had. That he would rather the weapons were in the hands of fellow race patriots than the bikers. That he was going to help them. That he was AWOL and planning to stay in Australia, to help with whatever was needed. On and on he went until the skinhead angled his head toward the front door, indicating for Devon to follow.

The skinhead Antony drove the white transit van that Devon had last seen parked in the alley outside the racetrack. Ant was silent until he lit his first cigarette. Reaching for the dash-lighter, Devon saw that the man's hand was shaking.

'You'll get used to it,' Devon lied. 'First one is always the hardest. Was the same for me.'

'Shut the fuck up now,' the man answered.

Devon still wore the cuffs. He didn't know why Ant had done what he'd done, murdering the biker, except that Devon was grateful, even if he was still a captive, still in danger. The skinhead gave off an acrid odour of stale sweat and possibly fear. How long had he waited under the floorboards? Or had he crept under the house after the others had left, when Devon was left alone with Ted?

'That was a sweet move you just pulled, Ant. Where we headed?'

The skinhead tugged hard on his cigarette.

Devon had to try, and keep trying. He was just about to speak when the skinhead glanced at the dashboard clock, leaned over and turned on the radio. It was ten o'clock.

'Shut the fuck up now,' he said. 'I'm not gonna tell you again.'

The radio announcer's plummy voice sounded comical to Devon, but what he said wasn't funny.

'The US Navy has confirmed the theft of six semi-automatic M16 weapons from the USS *Carl Vinson*, thought responsible for yesterday's drive-by shooting at the clubhouse of The Nongs outlaw bikie gang in Bayswater. Following the premier's comments that the perpetrators would face the full brunt of the law, this morning the headquarters of the APM, a white nationalist organisation, were raided by Federal Police and several squads of the Tactical Response Group. So far the weapons have not been retrieved. The APM has been previously linked to arson attacks against Asian businesses, as well as several serious assaults. It is not known why the attack was made against the outlaw motorcycle club. The leader of the

APM, Mr Nigel Kinslow, who ran unsuccessfully as a candidate in the recent state elections, said this morning that the allegations are based on malicious information designed to further damage the reputation of what is a legitimate political force. Working together with local investigators in an effort to recover the stolen weapons, USS Navy Master-at-Arms Steven Webb has released the name of the serviceman believed responsible for the thefts. He is identified as Midshipman Devon Smith of the USS *Carl Vinson*, who has been AWOL since yesterday. Members of the public with any information regarding Midshipman Smith are asked to contact the police. He is described as Caucasian, five foot nine inches with green eyes and distinctive "Nazi-style" tattoos on his upper arms. The theft and supply of the weapons comes on the tail of the inquiry into the murder of two Perth women, with an AWOL American sailor, Midshipman Charles Bernier, the only person of interest in the ongoing investigation. In other news, Prime Minister Bob Hawke has said that –'

The skinhead killed the radio, punched the dash-lighter. 'Hope you caught all that, Yank. First time I've heard you shut your fuckin mouth.'

Devon didn't reply. They'd already crossed the river. It was too late for him to glance behind, to where the *Vinson* lay moored. Whatever happened next, he had a feeling that he'd never see that damn ship again. The skinhead lit his cigarette and took a long hit.

'Can I get some of that?' Devon asked. The skinhead grunted, passed it over to Devon's cuffed hands, punched the dash-lighter again.

Devon sucked greedily on the smoke, tried to make conversation. 'Sure,' he said. 'I get it. I get all of it. Especially now that it's come out. If you –'

All it took was one glance from the Australian, his arms stiff on the wheel, to shut Devon up again.

56.

Tony Pascoe's breathing stabilised and the colour returned to his face. Emergency over, Swann told Tremain to bring him the phone. The businessman looked stunned, shook his head.

'I'm not going to ask you again.'

Tremain reached under the desk and Swann's gun-arm made ready. Tremain stood holding the phone, whose cord had been ripped from the wall, presumably by Gooch as he lay in wait outside.

'Where's the nearest phone?'

Tremain put the handset on the desk, planted his palms flat and took a deep breath. 'The shopping centre. Five-minute drive, end of the street. Outside the deli.'

Swann wanted to bring in Cassidy, the only way he could maintain some control of the situation. Cassidy was no friend, but would play it straight. Swann had done nothing wrong. The death was an accident.

Swann didn't know what Tony Pascoe's involvement was in Tremain's problems and he didn't want to know.

A hand reached for his wrist. Pascoe's grip was surprisingly strong. He pulled the gun toward his face and Swann didn't stop him. 'You may as well shoot me now.'

Swann twisted the gun away, stood above Pascoe, who gripped his ankle.

'Get talking,' Swann said. 'The gunshots could've alerted someone. I might not need to make a call.'

Pascoe nodded. 'And what are they goin to find? You with a pistol, and a dead copper.'

'It is what it is.'

Tremain had picked up on something in Pascoe's voice. He came around the desk, stood behind Pascoe, and looked Swann in the eye. 'Listen to him, Mr Swann. Please. It was an accident.'

'I was here too. That's why we call it in.'

'No.'

Tremain's voice, finally, had gravel in it. 'He was going to shoot you dead. He made me call you. He even dug a grave out there, in the courtyard.'

Swann stepped around Pascoe, looked out through the smudged windows in their blistered frames. Against the far wall of the courtyard was a long-neck shovel, beside a hole that looked deep. Big mound of grey sand piled at its head. Tremain was telling the truth. Swann's fingers clenched on the pistol grip as the anger rose in him.

'He deserved what he got,' Tremain said to Swann's back. 'It was him and Page who've been standing over me. I told you about it. Page does what he does because Gooch protected him. Without Gooch...'

Tremain's voice trailed off. Swann shook his head. 'You think Gooch is the only one Page's kicking up to?'

'Yes, I do. They went to school together. Page told me that. Boasted about it. How he used to make Gooch fight for him, right back to primary school. Gooch won't be missed. I followed him one night. I fantasised about killing him. He lives alone. No wife or kids.'

Swann watched the sun rise through the higher branches of the tuart outside the office wall. Three crows sat in the tree, watching him.

'That's where you're wrong, Tremain. Gooch will be greatly missed. He's a CIB bagman. You know what that means?'

'So he's disappeared, taken some money and run away?'

The growing desperation in Tremain's voice didn't betray the truth of his words. It was a plausible scenario.

'Who knew that Gooch was here this morning? Who knew that he was standing over you?'

Swann assumed that the order to run a play on Tremain had come from higher up in the CIB, but he could be wrong. It could have been Page. It was possible that Gooch wasn't kicking anything back.

'Nobody knew. It was Page who put Gooch onto me. It's Page who wants my lease, my gold.'

Swann listened for sirens, or a helicopter. The sound of TRG boots on the gravel outside. Nothing.

'You know he's right.'

It was Pascoe, standing now, one hand supporting him on the desk. The oxygen mask was off, a thin red spittle on his lips.

Tremain *was* right. Swann could call it in, bring Cassidy to the scene. He would be cleared of any involvement. But he wouldn't be clear. Gooch's colleagues in the CIB, the remnants of the old purple circle, they would believe what they wanted to believe.

Pascoe could be trusted. Tremain was the problem. If he ever talked, then it would be even worse for Swann. Concealing a murder. Disposing of a body. It would mean years in gaol.

Swann was exhausted. He pointed the pistol at Pascoe, indicated for him to move closer to Tremain. 'Start talking,' he said, but his eyes were on Tremain, who was staring back defiantly, eager to prove himself. For the first time in many months, perhaps, Tremain was seeing a way out.

Pascoe spoke in a clear, even voice. The story of breaking out of gaol to execute Jared Page was believable. Tony Pascoe was a dead man walking, and had no reason to lie. He had just saved Swann's life, and it nearly cost him his own.

'I remember you,' said Swann. 'You ran with my stepfather, Brian Hardy, back in the day.'

'He was no friend of mine. We drank together. He was my inside man on the docks. We did some jobs, until I found out he was a dog. Why he was never sent down.'

Swann nodded. His stepfather had boasted that Tony Pascoe was his friend, but when Brian brought Pascoe home with him one night, both of them drunk, Pascoe hadn't been impressed when Brian started ordering Swann's mother around, demanding that she fix them dinner. Pascoe was a wanted man, named as a suspect in an armoured car robbery out on the Great Eastern Highway, another thing that Brian boasted about – how Pascoe was sheltered by the community that he'd grown up in. How he still drank in the local pubs, went to watch the Bulldogs play on Saturday afternoon, right outside the walls of the prison where he spent so much of his life.

But now Tony Pascoe was dying, warily watching Swann, free for the last time.

Tremain pointed to the desk and Swann nodded. Tremain opened the Gladstone bag, heavy with ingots. He said to Pascoe, 'Take it. For what you just did. Pay off your man's debt. Plenty more where that came from.'

Pascoe shrugged, looked at Swann, waiting for his decision. Swann looked down at Gooch's corpse, his arms spread out like he was falling, needing to break his fall. Outside, the three crows in the tuart began to caw. Swann glanced a final time at the grave Gooch had dug for him, nodded to Tremain. 'He needs to be buried. Then his car needs to be driven to the airport, parked there.'

'I can do that,' said Tremain. 'I'll do it right away.'

Swann stared hard at Tremain, saw that he meant what he said, some wire in his voice. He turned the safety on the Browning, stowed the pistol in his jacket.

57.

The skinhead, Antony, pulled to the kerb on a hillside above the port. Devon looked over his shoulder at the *Vinson*, stolid and grey among the multicoloured container ships at berth. He judged that he was a half-hour walk from the docks, most of it downhill. The skinhead snapped his fingers and brought Devon back.

'You got to put this on,' he said. 'Supposed to have worn it since North Freo.'

It was a black canvas sack, covered in burrs of grass seed and grey dust.

'C'mon, Aussie,' Devon said. 'I already told you, I'm on your side here. No need for this. I can be an asset. I got you them guns, didn't I?'

The man's green eyes caught the light, seemed charged with purpose. He took up one of the Glocks, which rested beside the sawed-off in the driver's side door. 'I take you in there without it, it's gonna be me wearin it.'

Devon picked up the sack, opened its mouth. It smelt like fish bait. He did as he was told, pulled it down onto his shoulders, the handcuffs clacking.

The car engaged gears and whirred as it climbed the hill. Devon's ears popped. The van turned into a drive, drove across what sounded like gravel, and then soft dirt, the tyres snaking. A shadow fell across his hands – he could feel the absence of burning sun. The sound of birds squawking and crickets chirruping. The skinhead got out and came around Devon's side, opened the door and guided him. They walked across what Devon realised was rubble. His boots ground over it and his knees were unsteady. Then they were on some wooden stairs, creaking. He could hear muffled voices ahead. A door complained on its hinges and then they were inside a cool room whose floorboards were angled toward the rear wall. Another door opened, and Devon was thrust forward, nearly lost his balance.

'Here he is,' the skinhead said, his voice more assertive than before. 'I had to knock the bloke guarding him. Got his pistol, and a shottie.'

'Yer first kill, Ant. Come an' have a line, son.'

'Yeah, I will.'

Devon couldn't see, but even through the bait-stinking sack he could smell bacon grease and rotten garbage. His stomach rumbled and he realised that he hadn't eaten since yesterday morning.

'Take that thing off 'is head. See what we got here.'

The sack was ripped off and Devon winced under the harsh fluorescent glare. He'd expected some kind of older man to match the voice, which carried a leader's authority, but he got a shock. It was an older man alright, but one so ugly and mean-looking that Devon couldn't hide it.

'Aw fuck, you see his face?' the older man said. 'Nearly shit himself.'

'You do look like a cat's arse, Ralphie,' said another man, entering from the next room. He didn't look much better, in fact they looked like brothers. But where the man sitting at the table was dressed in jeans and a blue wife-beater, tattoos all up his arms and shoulders, his brother wore chinos and boots, a tight black tee, clean arms. Where the seated man's hair was wispy and red, his face cratered with acne scars, the man watching him from the doorway had short combed red hair and a clear complexion. But they both shared those mean blue eyes.

'He give you any trouble, Ant?' said the seated man.

Ant put his nose to the kitchen table and snorted up the line of speed. He shook his head to settle the rush, wiped his nose. 'Nah, they had him cuffed. He's harmless, Ralph. Reckons he's gonna work for us, somethin like that.'

It was a question, and Devon was ready. 'That's right. I got you that Glock. Then I got those M16s. I can get more, you give me the chance. I told you last time that back home in the States I'm in with white power. Grew up with it. I can't go back to the ship. I'm done with that life.'

'You didn't tell me shit, mate. Never seen you before. And don't talk to me about those M16s. The fucken trouble you've caused me. *Us.*'

'He heard the news on the way over,' added Ant.

The man Ralph got up, spat into the sink, sat down again. Wiped his mouth with the back of his hand. 'We do need your help, mate. But not in the way you might think. You got us into this trouble, and you're gonna get us out. You wanna know how this story ends?'

Devon didn't like the way this was headed. The door was open behind him. All he had to do was run, but the reptile eyes of the seated man caught his glance. The man reached for a carving knife on the table, shook his head.

'This is how it ends, mate, at least for you. You shouldn't have killed that bikie fuckhead back there, and with those M16s all over the media, they're soiled goods – more trouble than they're worth. To smooth it over again with The Nongs we're giving 'em back their guns, their money, and you, who just murdered one of their own. No hard feelings, son. It's just business. We're gonna tell 'em you killed their man, then you got away, came to us, fellow Nazis. As a peace offering, we're giving you back. We apologise for shooting up their clubhouse, offer to make amends. They take out their frustrations on you, probably with a blowtorch. You deny everything but they don't believe you. We all live happily ever after, except you. The End.'

Ralph's brother slow-clapped, nodded toward Ant, who was ready with the sack. Devon tried to kick out, turn away from the strong arms, but he was thrown to the ground, his cuffed hands taking the weight, thrust above his head and straining his shoulders. He was wrenched to his feet, the sack placed onto his neck, then frogmarched deeper into the house. He heard a padlock click, felt a wash of cool air. They were putting him in a basement, or a cellar. He was walked two paces forward, then thrown down some steps. His head hit the dirt, dazing him. He heard boot-steps behind him and he was dragged across rough stone. A chain was fed through his handcuffs, a padlock clicked shut. The footsteps disappeared, up the stairs. The doors closed. Devon pulled the sack from his head, but it was no use. The room was darker than any place he'd ever been.

58.

Tony Pascoe followed Frank Swann's Lincoln-green HK Brougham, past the Karrakatta Cemetery and army barracks, turning west at the showgrounds toward the coast. Pascoe followed at a discreet distance, aware that Swann was giving him the opportunity to disappear into the suburbs.

Pascoe thought hard about that.

Gooch was dead. Pascoe hadn't meant to kill the copper, but Gooch had wrenched sideways at a crucial moment, pushing off the desk, exposing his windpipe to the taut sinews inside Pascoe's elbow, crushing it and effectively taking himself out.

Gooch was the first man that Pascoe had killed outside of the war. It didn't feel good, even though Gooch was a bent copper who lived by the sword.

Pascoe told himself this as he watched Swann's Brougham turn left down Salvado Street, past the SAS Barracks toward the Fremantle port. He told himself that he'd intervened to save Swann because after the detective shot him he was going to shoot Pascoe, although this wasn't true. As a detective, Gooch would certainly want the credit for bringing Pascoe back to serve his term.

Pascoe had intervened purely out of instinct. What happened had happened, and now he was free again, albeit his wings had been clipped. Swann had smiled grimly when Pascoe asked for the Browning pistol, shaking his head in response. Outside, Swann had searched Pascoe's van, discovering the adapted flare gun under the driver's seat. He confiscated that, too, saying that despite his bad feelings toward Jared Page, a man who he'd crossed swords with over the years, he didn't want another murder on his conscience.

Now Pascoe was unarmed. Swann could have taken the bag of gold ingots for himself too, but he didn't. Pascoe put the Gladstone bag on the passenger floorpan, covered it with old newspaper.

They were on the coast road, sandy beaches to their right and train tracks to the left, hard sun reflecting off the wide blue ocean that was still as a pond. Ahead was the port, a tanker breaching the twin moles and moving out toward Gage Roads, big as an island beside the tugboats, tinnies and cruisers that skimmed across the water. Behind the gantry cranes was the raised bridge of the Yank vessel, satellite dish turning and catching the light. Behind that was the port city where Pascoe had grown up; his earliest memories of watching his father head off to work with his stevedore-hook hanging off his belt; his mother returning home from the Mills & Wares factory smelling of hot biscuits.

Swann's Brougham indicated to turn right beyond the prison walls, toward the hospital. He raised a hand to signal his goodbye. Pascoe did the same, kept driving.

59.

Webb was waiting for Swann in his driveway, talking into his brick, glancing at his watch.

Swann was still shaken by what had happened at Tremain's office. The first bullet Gooch fired had passed through Swann's shirt, two inches from his ribcage, six inches from his heart. It'd left a finger-sized circular hole, front and back. If the old man, Pascoe, hadn't intervened then Swann would already be in the sand, six feet under. He could feel its weight on his chest, taste it on his tongue. Instead, it was Gooch in the sand, buried by Tremain.

Swann pulled into the drive, saw the dog rise groggily to her feet in the shade, begin to wag her tail. All Swann felt like doing was holding onto Marion, taking to their bed under the ceiling fan.

Swann took off his sunglasses and folded them, climbed from the car. He had to pretend like nothing had happened. Another secret to bury deep, like all the others. 'Any news?' he asked.

Webb nodded. 'That was the CO. We're leaving port tomorrow eve, latest the morning after.'

Webb's voice was apologetic. He knew what it looked like.

'Your man Cassidy called earlier,' said Webb. 'Overnight, there have been a series of what look like mischievous, even malicious, tips from the public about Bernier. I say public, but they've established that they were made from the same public phone box, here in Fremantle, by the same man. Even so, they need to be followed up. Sightings of Bernier in nine suburbs north of the river and east at the hills.'

Crank calls, thought Swann, pointing to the shade on the front porch. Marion wasn't home yet and the house was locked. He didn't bother opening up, certain that they'd be heading out soon. At the very least

Webb could be his alibi for the next few hours. Swann took a seat and patted the dog, ran his fingers through her silky ears, let Webb finish his run-down.

Webb put the brick on his lap, lit another Camel. 'Your Federal Police have been helpful. Set up a personal liaison officer for me. They've done a title search on the Cord brothers, come up with nothing. Last addresses have been raided. They've had eyes and ears on the organisation the Cords belong to for months. There has been plenty of telephone traffic about the rifles since the news broke in the media. Lots of threats against some of their persons. Putting their own people out on the street. Only communication with the biker club – basically an apology. The Federals suspect that the Cords are operating on their own.'

'Increases the likelihood of them handing the weapons back,' said Swann. 'Too hot, even for Ralph Cord.'

'But if the APM, the bikers and State and Federal Police are looking for the Cord brothers and they still haven't been found, it tells me that they're holed up, not moving. We need to find that place. Any ideas?'

'One. One idea. Don't know what to do if it fails. You have a spare packet of American cigarettes?'

Webb nodded toward his briefcase. 'Yes, several. Why?'

'We're going to visit someone.'

The look on Webb's face told Swann that he was shocked by the condition of the prison. The sun was fading as they walked toward the cell blocks. Swann's friendship with veteran turnkey Tony McIlroy, who lived up the street from Swann in an old limestone cottage, had gotten them into the prison outside visiting hours.

Lee Southern's father, Daniel, had been alerted to their arrival. Swann could see him outside 3 Division, chatting with a screw and watching them come. The limestone walls built by convicts loomed above them, casting shadows over the paths framed by limestone rocks.

As they got closer to the cell block, the sound and smell of caged men grew stronger. The stench of shit buckets, foot odour and stale sweat. Radios blaring from open windows that provided the only circulation in the building. Cage doors rattled, men shouted. They all lived with a sixteen-hour lockdown, and yard time was over.

'Place is fucking medieval. No offence.'

Swann didn't disagree. He glanced at the nearest tower where the guard on duty cradled a rifle, watching them. As senior warder, Tony McIlroy was part of the officer cartel that administered overtime, and ghost-shifts to those guards who played the game. He was a good friend to have, but Swann was glad that he wasn't under McIlroy's watch. Part of playing the game meant meting out punishment when it was ordered, and looking the other way when something more than punishment was required.

'Is that our man?' Webb asked.

Clearly he wasn't impressed by Daniel Southern, wearing tight stubbies and thongs, his bare torso lathered with sweat. Swann had given Webb the bare bones. He had already met Lee Southern at Kerry's brothel and at the gym. Lee's father was in for a short stretch this time, for dope possession. He was a Vietnam veteran and the ex-leader of a paramilitary survivalist group out of Geraldton, who made their money from dope plantations and gun-running. This was also the first time that Swann had met Lee Southern's father. Lee had told him that his dad had changed, and Swann hoped this was true, if only for the kid's benefit. Lee saw his father once a week, on Friday afternoons, and never missed his appointment. He often returned to the boxing gym directly from the prison, and his mood was always good.

'Give one packet of smokes to the guard. We're talking to Daniel Southern outside, so there's no perception of collaboration or snitching. It's a big favour.'

Swann and Webb shook hands with the guard, a short, sturdy middle-aged man with tattoos on his knuckles and a grey goatee beard, and then with Daniel, who paid close attention to Swann. Webb passed them both a packet of Camels, then offered them a cigarette from his own packet. The guard held his out to Daniel Southern to light, then stepped away to give them privacy.

'Thanks for seeing us,' Swann said, meeting Southern's scrutiny with the same measured stare. 'It won't take long.'

'Take your time, mate. My cell's on the eastern side. I haven't seen a sunset in six months. Lee's told me a lot about you.'

It was a question, and Swann nodded. 'He's a good kid. A real good kid.'

Swann's compliment carried a subtle proprietorial tone, wanting to see Lee's father's response, who just shrugged, played along. 'No thanks to me. It's good you're giving him work. Good that he's keeping up his training, at your gym.'

'He pretty much runs the place. The local kids look up to him.'

Lee's reading of his father was correct. Swann didn't know what Daniel Southern was like before, except by reputation, but the news that Lee was making a contribution clearly made him proud.

'What did you want to see me about? Mullins there just told me that it wasn't about Lee, so not to worry.'

'No, it's not. Got a question about a bloke who just got out. Whose sentence overlapped with yours, shared the same division. Ralph Cord.'

Southern's lip curled. 'Yeah, what about him? I don't keep the same company I used to. No interest in a mutt like him. I've been participating in a painting class. Most of the class is Aboriginal. He didn't like that.'

'We're looking for him. You've probably heard the news. So are half the coppers in the state.'

'What's that got to do with me?'

'He's in the wind. No fixed address. Holed up somewhere. Just wondered if he talked about a place. Off the record.'

Daniel Southern thought about it, glanced at Mullins, his warder. Sharing information about another prisoner, even to a civilian like Swann, wasn't a good look.

'We weren't on speakin terms, if you know what I mean. Not after he found out I was part-black.'

'He ever get any visitors?'

'Yeah, he did. An old sheila, every Friday, same time as me and Lee's visit. She always had money put on his gratuities. I think she was his aunt. Remember him telling the screw who escorted us down there. Boasted about putting in orders for big dollars on his grats. Said that she lived up on the hill behind the prison somewhere. As a kid he used to look through the scope of his uncle's rifle, see the little men working the prison gardens, the screws at their business. I remember it because it was an odd thing to say. I remember thinking, who fuckin cares? Same thing the screw probably thought. But that was Cord for you. Always runnin his mouth, even when he had nothing to say.'

'He say what her name was, or what street she lived on?'

'Nah, he didn't care about anything but the grats money, my impression.'

Swann looked to Webb, who'd been listening closely. It was good information, and likely something that the Feds had missed. They could check the visitors' book on the way out.

Swann put out his hand. 'Thanks. See you when your time's up.'

Southern looked sceptical, but nodded. 'Keep an eye out for my boy. Make sure he finishes school.'

'Will do.'

Swann nodded his thanks to the guard, and they turned toward the main entrance where the sun laid golden fingers upon the highest walls. He glanced over his shoulder and saw that Mullins and Southern were sharing another cigarette, watching the sunset come down, the light in the compound softening; mauve and purple tracers illuminating the white cell block walls.

60.

The cellar was so dark that Devon would make out what he thought was a solid shape in the blackness only to reach out and find that it was more nothing. He had two metres of chain he could work with, crawling on his hands and knees, patting the floor of smooth caprock and compacted limestone. Empty bottles and sardine cans. Spent plastic cartridges from a shotgun. A box full of old newspapers.

Devon took one of the bottles back with him to the floor-bolt, placed it there for later. He planned to break it and use it as a knife, if needed. Then he went back to searching, quiet as possible, trying to listen to the conversations above him. No light came through the floorboards but he could hear muffled words. He was distracted by the smell of something rotten every time he reached the end of his chain, away against what he thought was a wall. It smelt like something dead that'd been there a long time. Mummified rat carcass or something. He couldn't reach whatever it was and didn't really want to.

It was so dark that he became disoriented, had to retreat to the floor-bolt fixed into a concrete block, try and work out which direction were the steps and the door that he'd entered, which direction was the pile of bottles and the bad smell. He worked out that if he completed circles around the concrete block holding the leash at different lengths, then he could at least cover the area within the circle. He did so until the chain was at its fullest length, crawling around the block like a hooked fish until he identified the bad smell again. Within the circle he retrieved an old wrench, a couple of torch batteries, three rusty nails and a heavy paper bag containing what he thought might be cement, although it tasted like lime. There was nothing for him to stand on. There were no walls that he could dig into. There were the newspapers that he could set alight, but they'd taken his cigarettes and zippo.

Devon sat on the concrete block and tried to focus on the voices he could hear above him. The voice of the ugly man, Ralph, was loudest, because he appeared to be arguing with someone whose responses couldn't be heard. It was most likely a telephone conversation, because the others had gone quiet. Devon followed the sound of boot-steps as one man moved through different rooms, but most of the sounds came from directly above him, which he assumed to be the kitchen. Devon stood on the concrete block so that he could hear better, but found that in the complete darkness it was hard for him to keep his balance. He spread his feet further, putting his hands out in case he fell. It was so dark that if it weren't for gravity he wouldn't know which way was up, down or sideways. He was groggy from landing face-first on the cellar floor, and he'd torn the ligaments in his left shoulder. He tried to raise his cuffed wrists above shoulder-height but the pain was terrible.

The man who'd been walking through the house returned to the kitchen. When the man finished dragging a seat, it was easier for Devon to hear. It was their leader, Ralph, describing the telephone conversation.

'... Course I told him. He said, why'd he buy back something he's already paid for? It was worth a try, I guess. He wanted to come here, collect both the guns and the Yank. You heard my reaction to that. I know these pricks. They'll wipe us out. So I told him that I'd leave them somewhere, call and tell 'im where, but he reckons that's too unsafe. And that the pigs are watchin him like he's got forty-inch tits. I suggested a middleman. Someone he trusts. Give 'im the guns and the cash, the Yank...'

There was more scraping of chairs and Devon missed what came next, but Ralph's response was clear.

'Yeah, he bought it. I told 'im the Yank turned up here, told us what he'd done to Ted Mangles, in detail. Knowing the ... delicacy of our negotiations, I immediately put 'im in custody. A peace offerin. They'd only just found the dead fucker, you could hear 'em in the background, buzzin round like little bees. Riley swallowed it alright.'

Even through the floorboards, Devon recognised the voice of Ant, who'd shot the biker. He'd been ruthless and efficient during the shooting, but there was something else in his voice now. Devon could guess the reason behind his questions. Ant would want everything nailed down. If word ever leaked that he'd been the shooter, rather than Devon, he was looking at a slow and horrible death.

'... never you mind, Antony. I've got to call back later, to find out where we make the drop. Two-man team. Me and my brother. We hand it all over, our problems go away. Then we return to Plan A.'

Devon didn't know what Plan A was, and he didn't care. He had to find a way to escape before he was handed over to the biker leader, Gus Riley. Devon knew that he wouldn't be believed, even under torture. The bikers would assume that he'd shot Ted and made his escape, went looking for the only people who'd take him in, his fellow travellers in the white power movement. They would assume that Devon had somehow got Ted's gun off him. They had no reason to believe otherwise.

It was then that Devon heard the sound. Earlier, he thought he heard a grunt, but when it was followed by silence he'd assumed that it came from above. But now he heard it clearly – ragged breathing, rapid and urgent – the sound of someone coming awake to find that the nightmare was real.

'Who there?' came the voice.

An American voice.

Black voice.

Plan A.

Devon got down off the concrete block, peered into the darkness, prepared his voice to speak.

61.

The boxing gym was crowded. A few old boys from the docks were sparring in the ring, beer guts and padded arms belying their fitness and desire for the contest. A couple of Noongar kids in their high-school uniforms took turns on the speedball, looking shyly around when they mucked up the rhythm. A mixed group of boys, girls, men and women stretched on the mats near the floor-to-ceiling mirrors, preparing for the one-hour boxing class taken today by Lee Southern and Blake Tracker, who were chatting while putting on their wraps. Blake was taller than Lee and his skin was darker, but they were wiry and lean, and looked like brothers.

Lee Southern glanced up and Swann nodded him toward the door. Lee elbowed Blake and they collected their trail of wraps and stepped through a group stripping down, putting watches and wallets in hats and bags.

'Gerry coming in?' Swann asked Blake.

'Don't think so. He was in last night. Asked me to take the class.'

'Think you could call him? I need you two tonight, couple of hours at most.'

Blake Tracker shrugged, but his face expressed reluctance. 'He's goin fishin. That black bream spot over in Bicton, near the baths.'

'What about you two? Can you help?'

Blake nodded. 'Sure.'

Lee began unwinding the wrap on his left hand. 'No probs. Though I'm on shift at Kerry's place later.'

Swann walked over to the makeshift boxing ring. Craig Little took his eyes off his sparring mates and watched Swann come. Craig was a big man, a maritime union rep and ex-boxer. He was thirty kilos overweight but could spar fifteen rounds and barely break a sweat. He had the face

215

of a thug but Swann knew him as a generous and decent man. Little and his union mates had donated half of the gym's equipment. Swann spoke to him for a couple of minutes until the round-buzzer sounded and the two sparring men joined them. They agreed to leave off training and run the night class. Swann thanked them and when he returned to the door, Blake and Lee were ready to go.

Swann parked the Brougham under a streetlight and spread the map on the bonnet. The Fremantle Doctor was strong from the south and he had to place both hands on the map. In the car, he'd run through what Lee's father had told him, and what they'd discovered in the Fremantle Gaol visitors' book for the months September 1988 – February 1989. Ralph Cord's only visitor during that time was a woman named Rose Cord. She was so well-known to the guards on the Friday day shift that she didn't leave an address or show ID. Swann had asked Tony McIlroy to see if he could retrieve the visitors' books for the first months of Cord's stretch, back in July 1986. This was important because there was no Rose Cord listed in the White Pages, which meant that Cord was possibly her maiden name. Births, Deaths & Marriages was closed for the day and wouldn't be accessible until tomorrow morning – the same time Tony McIlroy hoped to retrieve the earlier visitors' books from the locked cabinet in the prison superintendent's office. In the meantime, Swann decided to hit the streets and knock on doors.

He finished pointing out to Lee and Blake the streets that they planned to cover. Webb talked on his brick to the Federal Police liaison, filling them in on what they'd learned. Swann went and popped the boot of the Brougham, took out his .38 S&W snubnose, checking the cylinder before flicking it closed. Webb had a pistol on his ankle.

Swann decided that Webb and Blake should cover the street nearest the prison, while Swann and Lee would canvass the streets higher up the hillside. The pistol and revolver was insurance in case they knocked on the wrong door, and were recognised.

Webb finished his call. 'All their surveillance teams are on three different APM houses in the northern part of the city, and a small ranch on the other side of the range which they've been watching for some time. Live training exercises have occurred there and the idiots have built army-style obstacle courses and whatnot. They can't spare any personnel.

They also suggest not telling the local detectives what we're doing, due to leaks. Apparently your biker friend has put a fifty-thousand dollar price on information leading to the capture of Cord and his gang, something my liaison believes will be too enticing to pass up for some of the locals.'

Swann talked them through the spiel. They were to work opposite sides of the street and knock on every third door and say that they were locals who lived on the other side of Hampton Road, giving Swann's address if asked. They had found a purse with no identification except a library card. A few days ago an old lady had doorknocked the street asking if anyone had seen her purse. The old lady's name was Rose, and she said that she lived across from Hampton Road. Did they know a Rose, an old lady who lived nearby? If a house was identified then they were to meet at the end of the next block and take a close look together. If necessary, call in the Feds.

They split up, and Swann and Lee climbed the hill until they reached Swanbourne Street. It was one of the longest streets in Fremantle and straddled the ridgeline of the limestone hill that peaked at the war memorial before descending south. The view from its highest point covered both the Fremantle Gaol and beyond to Gage Roads and across Cockburn Sound. If Ralph Cord's reminiscence of sighting his uncle's rifle into the Fremantle Gaol yards was correct, it was unlikely from Swanbourne Street, due to the distance, but there were several positions where the line of sight allowed for a view inside the prison. Swann and Lee leapfrogged their doorknocking, coming up empty by the time they reached the intersection of Stevens Street, where they waited for Webb and Blake Tracker to complete the same length of Bellevue Terrace. If neither party had any luck, the plan was to retrace their steps together along Solomon Street, which was between the two.

Swann and Lee walked down the hill to the corner of Stevens and Solomon. Lee smoked a cigarette under the streetlight, looking down over the city. Blake and Webb should have reached the rendezvous point by now. Swann was thinking about heading down to Bellevue Terrace when he heard the throaty chuckle of a muscle car coming over the ridge behind them. He guessed correctly that it was a Monaro, the Holden turning down from the top of the hill, its headlights off. Swann nodded to Lee Southern. It was too late for Lee to hide himself but Swann stepped into a driveway, hid himself behind a bougainvillea that broke over the driveway wall. He heard the car approach and peered around the corner. The Monaro slowed while the driver, who Swann recognised as Barry Brown, took a good long look at Swann's comrade. It occurred to Swann that Lee looked like a skinhead with his tight jeans, boots and cropped head. Swann took out his revolver and let it hang beside his thigh. When the Monaro pulled to a stop, Swann moved out of the shadows. Four car doors opened. Swann covered the distance quickly, cocking the .38. Barry Brown saw him coming and put up a hand. The three other men, who Swann didn't recognise, paused beside the open car doors. Two of them carried baseball bats, the other a claw hammer.

'He's with me,' Swann said.

Barry Brown rested his sawn-off shotgun on the doorsill. His pupils were dilated and his jaw was clenched as he looked Lee over. Suspicion in his eyes and in his voice. 'You sure about that, Swann? I never seen him before. I know why you're here and who you're workin for. You haven't cut any deals with these bonehead fucks have you?'

At that range, one blast from Brown's shotgun and Lee Southern would be atomised from his boots to his neck. Swann uncocked the .38 and returned it to the back of his belt. Barry Brown nodded and drew the shotgun inside the car.

'We'll be on our way then,' Swann said. Lee Southern finished his cigarette and ground it beneath his toe. The kid hadn't flinched or panicked in the slightest.

'Tell Riley I'll be calling him,' Swann said. 'Don't want any crossed wires on this one.'

Barry Brown smiled. 'You do that. He's been trying to get hold of you. Has an offer.'

Swann heard footsteps behind him and turned. Blake Tracker and Webb rounded the corner off Bellevue. Webb knelt and reached for his ankle. Swann shook his head.

When the bikies were gone, the twin-barred tail-lights of the Monaro crossing Hampton Road toward the hospital, Swann began to speak. 'The leak. Someone from the prison, most likely. Told Riley what we were looking for in the visitors' books. Either a guard or another prisoner.'

Lee shook his head. 'It'll be one of the screws. My father wouldn't disclose anything you said to another crim. Not if he knew I'm involved.'

Swann nodded. 'Either way, we need to get Cord's auntie's address, before Riley's men. Webb, can I use your brick? You three make a start on Solomon Street. Every second house. I'll catch up.'

Swann dialled The Nongs' clubhouse as the three men turned down Solomon and began to canvass. Riley picked up on the third ring.

'Not on this number,' he replied. 'Try this one, and give me two minutes.'

Swann memorised the number, hung up and waited. After a couple of minutes he dialled the number. Riley sounded harried.

'Glad you called, Swann. I need you.'

'I just ran into Barry Brown. He says you have an offer for me.'

Riley was silent, meaning he was weighing up whether to share. 'Yeah, I got the tip from a screw. Said you'd been looking through the old visitors' books, for an auntie Cord who lived near the prison.'

'What of it?'

Riley chuckled. Swann heard the hissing of a lighter, Riley drawing a cigar to life. 'I also heard that the Feds have put a tap on our phone. Legitimised because of the APM involvement. I can do without it.'

'Nothing I can do about that, Riley.'

'Maybe, maybe not. Just wanted to ask whether you'd be interested in me returning those Yank weapons to you, should I come across them in the course of my enquiries.'

'Of course I would. What do you want in return?'

'You won't see it in the media, but we're having our own funeral, Viking-style, out in the desert next week. A fallen comrade, Ted Mangles, killed in the line of duty.'

'My condolences. But get to the point.'

Riley described Ted's execution at the hands of one of Cord's men. He described the Yank sailor, Devon Smith, the one responsible for selling the M16s to the APM, taken captive. After raiding an APM house, Riley's men had left the sailor there, setting up a hidden surveillance camera that captured what happened next. Riley told Swann about the call from Cord – the offer of turning over the weapons and the sailor, who they'd blamed for Ted's murder, to a trusted intermediary.

'So this Devon Smith, the sailor. You don't have an interest in him, or the weapons? You'll return them both?'

Riley laughed. 'Too right. Call it a civic duty, Swann.'

'You mean, it'll get the Fed surveillance off you. Who's choosing the intermediary? You or Cord?'

'Leave that to me, Swann. None of your business. I'll contact you once it's done.'

Swann thought about that. It wasn't good enough. Too many things that could go wrong. A shootout between Riley's thugs and Cord's gang, for one thing, with the US sailor in the crossfire. Swann didn't like it, but he'd have to trust Riley until he thought of something better.

'I'll run it by the Yanks. When is this handover organised for?'

'Soon as possible, Swann, unless we find them first.'

Swann hung up and looked over the black ocean, marker buoys winking out in Gage Roads, the smaller lights of fishing vessels beyond Rottnest and Carnac islands. The sea breeze had dropped and a cold easterly had begun blowing off the desert. It was going to be another hot day. Swann began to trudge up the hill after the others. His legs felt heavy and his hips ached. He was winded by the time he reached the war memorial, where Webb, Lee and Blake were waiting on him. No luck. Many of the street's residents were asleep. Some of those who were awake hadn't answered their doors. Those who had come to the door didn't know anything about an old lady. It was too late to canvass the streets further south.

Swann thanked Blake and Lee. He offered to drive them home but Lee needed to get to Kerry's brothel, to work the door. As they walked to his car, Swann told Webb about Riley's offer. Webb had the same misgivings, although there was nothing they could do. First thing in the morning they needed to get the records from the prison, before Riley's bikies, and if that turned a blank then get a marriage certificate for a Rose Cord from Births, Deaths & Marriages, followed by a title deed search from Landgate. Swann drove Webb to the port, refusing his offer of a nightcap aboard the *Vinson*.

One message on the answering machine. Swann could hear Marion out on the back deck, listening to early Stones while waiting for him.

Swann pressed the button. There was something about Tremain's voice, a tentativeness and strain that told Swann he wasn't alone. 'Swann. This is Paul Tremain. I've got some bad news. Jared Page was here a few minutes ago, with two of his men. He's looking for Gooch. Gooch had told him that he was coming to check on me. I told Page that Gooch was never here. Page then mentioned you. Your role in all this. Said that Gooch had been following you, but that you hadn't taken Gooch's advice and kept –'

The tape ended. Swann was glad that he hadn't been around when Tremain had called. Page had been listening when the call was made, to try and gauge Swann's response.

Gooch was gone, but Page was going to be a problem.

Swann thought about calling Paul Tremain, but that wasn't smart. He didn't want to leave any kind of record. Page may or may not have found Gooch's body, but either way Page couldn't kill Tremain. He needed him alive, at least until he signed over the Lightning Resources lease.

Tremain wasn't built for any of this. Swann had to hope that his instinct for survival had kept his mouth shut. If Gooch's colleagues in the CIB were alerted to his disappearance by Page, then they would search Tremain's office, find the body in the patio yard.

Swann considered giving the flare gun back to the old bank robber, so that he could kill Page as planned, but that wasn't a smart play either.

Swann would have to think on it. Something would have to be done.

62.

Devon Smith had never heard a man weep so raw and powerful. He hadn't mentioned it out of malice, or because Charles Bernier was black, but because he was shocked to find that the midshipman didn't know anything. Soon as Bernier identified himself, Devon had blurted, 'But you're that rapist, murderer.'

Devon couldn't see Bernier and didn't realise that he too was chained. He assumed that Bernier was hiding out. Like the newspapers said he was.

'Man, what you talkin about? I'm a prisoner. I got grabbed my first night shore leave. Been tied up here ever since.'

'You don't know anything about sex murders?'

'I tole you. I don't know nothing about any murders. I been here the whole time. The *Vinson* still in port?'

'Yeah, it is.'

Bernier whistled his relief. 'Tell me about the murders. What they got to do with me?'

Devon described the two murders. What the newspapers were saying about Bernier. A witness statement. The black neckerchief, with Bernier's name sewn into it.

Bernier was silent for near a minute. Devon thought that he was considering the evidence against him, but that wasn't it.

'The prostitute you mentioned. You remember her name?'

'Nope. Just that you were shacked up with her, in a hotel across from a brothel.'

'Franny? Francine?'

'Yeah, that's it.'

That was when the weeping started. Devon had never heard sounds like that come from another man. Deep and long, like a dying steer. At first, Devon was angry with the other man. He wanted to know more about where they were both at. How they might work together, to escape. But when the man kept wailing Devon couldn't help it – his chest started to constrict and tears began to well in his own eyes. 'Shutup, shutup, shutup,' he said to himself, over and again. It felt like the man wasn't just crying for his lost whore, or for the shittiness of his situation, but also for Devon's wasted life, all the stupid lies he'd told himself to get where he was at – helpless and chained to a concrete block on the wrong side of the world – a death sentence hanging over him, soon to be executed.

63.

Swann couldn't sleep. Rather than risk waking Marion, he went into the kitchen and poured a glass of water, then took his revolver and medicine box onto the front veranda. Under the moonlight he fixed himself a syringe of the chelate solution and felt around for the bruises caused by his earlier injections before stabbing it into his thigh. He barely felt the needle, he was so tired.

Swann hadn't been able to sleep because he was expecting a visit from Jared Page and his goons. If what Tremain said about Gooch was true, and that he'd been Page's sole fixer in the CIB, then Page would be feeling vulnerable and unprotected.

It happened just before dawn. A tan Fairlane entered from the bottom of Swann's street in low gear, headlights off. Swann lifted the revolver and placed it on his lap. The Fairlane slowed, pulled closer to Swann's verge. Two men in the back seat stared at him, the driver looking ahead. Swann lifted the revolver and waved as the Fairlane accelerated up the hill.

Swann waited for his heartbeat to settle. He realised that he'd been holding his breath. That there were three of Page's men in the Fairlane told him the visit was about more than reconnaissance. Swann put the revolver back under its pillow, sat back in his chair. He listened as wattlebirds and honeyeaters sang their tentative first notes, soon answered as the sky began to blue. Next door, Salvatore began to water his roses. A milk truck trundled down South Terrace, commercial radio blaring. A newspaper boy on a tricked-up Malvern Star rode past one-handed, tossing a paper into Sal's yard.

Swann closed his eyes to lessen the burn. If he was lucky, he'd doze for a few minutes before he returned inside and made Marion some scrambled eggs.

The situation with Gooch and Page was not of Swann's making, but that didn't make it any easier. Page's men had come to Swann's home, and they would come again.

Swann heard the front gate open. He must have slept for a few minutes. He hadn't noticed the van park in the street, but there it was, nestled under the branches of the bottlebrush. Tony Pascoe stood with one hand on the gate, watching for Swann's reaction. Swann waved him in, looking around to see if Sal was still in his garden.

Pascoe walked calmly down the drive. Apart from the oxygen tank in a small backpack and the tubes running into his nostrils, you would never think that Pascoe was knocking on death's door. He was thin but didn't look frail. His skin was pasty but his eyes were clear and steely-blue.

Swann waved Pascoe into the rattan chair opposite him, protected from the street by the frangipani.

'We need to talk,' Swann said. 'What you did yesterday – it's already come back on me.'

Pascoe nodded. 'I can help with that.'

'I don't want your help. As it stands, you're a liability. I want you to leave the city, or hand yourself in.'

'Not going to happen. I came here to speak with you. Can we speak? You got sleeping people in there. Don't want to wake anyone.'

'One sleeping person. My wife.'

'I thought you had three daughters?'

Swann didn't like that. How did Pascoe know about his family, his children? He read Pascoe's face for the veiled threat, but couldn't see it.

'My daughters. They've grown up, left home. What do you want? I get a sniff that you want to blackmail me over what happened yesterday, I'm going to put my foot through your chest.'

Pascoe looked away, watched a magpie drinking from the birdbath by the drive.

'Nothing like that. Came to get my pistol back. I need it. You know why.'

Pascoe's homemade pistol, ingeniously fashioned out of a flare gun, was still in the boot of Swann's car, along with Gooch's throwdown. Again Swann considered giving it back to the old man, to make Page go away. But he wasn't going to do that. Later in the day, he'd take them to the Fremantle Traffic Bridge and toss them into the churning tidewater.

'It's gone,' Swann lied. 'Never to be found.'

Pascoe looked down at his clenched hands, took control of himself. 'That's a pity. But you know what I need to do. I'm taking Page out, as the saying goes – if it's the last thing I ever do. Which it will be. It's something you want too. Why you got a revolver under that pillow.'

'I can't let you do that. Not after what happened to Gooch. Soon there'll be questions asked. Why Gooch hasn't showed up for work. I can't have your vendetta with Page linked to Gooch.'

Despite himself, the volume of Swann's voice had increased. He knew that Marion would be awake now, and listening. He leaned forward, close enough to smell Pascoe's breath, sense the decay eating him from within.

Swann was just about to speak when Pascoe glanced over his shoulder. Marion came to the screen door, opened it.

Pascoe ignored her. 'There's something else. The other reason I came here. To say goodbye.'

'Why would you do that?'

Pascoe was struggling with something. He wouldn't meet Swann's eye, looked instead at his hands. 'I wasn't going to, but our paths crossed. Frank. I'm your father.'

64.

The negro had ceased his crying but the pain was still heavy in his voice. He talked softly and carefully, like a child's impersonation of a man. He called the men who'd kidnapped him devils. He said that he never saw their faces; he wore a stinking hood the whole time. One minute he was returning to his hotel room, climbing the rear steps to the building late at night, his girl behind him, when *wham*, he took a baseball bat to the face from someone staked out around the corner. That was the last thing he remembered. He woke up here, where he'd been ever since. They stripped off all his clothes, chained him to the brick footing. Left him a bottle of water and a loaf of bread every morning. Let him out, once, to call his mother. Made him read from a script they'd written.

'You'll see,' said Bernier. 'When they open that hatch to bring us some water. Why they're devils, and this place is hell. You probably notice the smell, right?'

The stink was hot in Devon's nostrils. Not knowing made it worse. He had to ask.

'It's a ole dead woman,' Bernier replied, 'that's what it is. Her head stove in. Been dead a long time, too. One of them devils even got a name for her. Calls her Rose. "Mornin auntie Rose," he says to her, every time he brings me my water. Won't tell me nothin though, or show his face. Just tosses me the bread an water like I'm a dog on the chain.'

Devon knew what the men were going to do with him, but he had no idea what the plans were for Charles Bernier. Why they'd kidnapped him and killed his woman. It was still dark in the cellar but outside the house he could hear traffic, and birdsong.

'Can you reach any walls?' he asked.

'Nope, I only got six foot of chain. I tried to dig round the base of the concrete pillar here. Found an old tin can and dug up some sand, but then I hit rock, more concrete. I had to give up. You?'

'Same. We got to think on a plan. Your voice sounds close. Can you come toward me? Maybe if we can reach each other, we can work together to break the chains.'

Devon heard the clanking of a chain.

'Keep talking,' the voice said. 'So damn dark.'

'You do the same.' Devon encouraged his fellow American closer, listened to the sonar of his grunting and ragged breathing, his repeated 'I'm comin' until he heard the chain clank. Behind him, Devon's own chain reached its limit.

'You sound close,' Devon said. 'Can you reach me?'

Devon held out his hands, waving them into the blackness. He felt a touch, and both of them said 'me' at the same time. Devon returned his hand to the place and he felt Bernier's fingers, then his hand. Their hands clasped, and held.

'What you here for man?' Bernier whispered. 'Why'd they grab you up too?'

Devon thought about his answer. It was good to hear an American voice. Might be the last one he ever heard. 'I dunno,' he lied. 'They just snatched me up.'

'Devils,' Bernier hissed. 'Thought they got me cos of my white girl.'

Devon didn't have the heart to tell Bernier that what he suspected was probably true. Or that a couple days ago Devon would've approved of their actions. He was all mixed up now. Nothing about the past days made sense. The bikers and the skinheads treated him no better than the black man next to him. They were all about the colour of money.

Both men heard footsteps on the board above them, the padlock popping. The twin-trapdoors opened with a horror-show creak, letting in a flood of dusty light. Devon looked across at Bernier, naked, afraid, the whites of his eyes big and round, his face and hair covered in pale dust. Devon went to let go the man's hand, but Bernier held on tight. Devon couldn't see behind him. He glanced over toward the smell and saw the dead old woman, still in a floral dress and sandals. Her face covered in congealed blood. Someone had tossed some quicklime over her chest and head, but no attempt had been made to bury her. Footsteps on the stairs, and then a burst of cruel laughter.

'Good morning, Auntie Rose. What … what the? Would ya look at these faggots?'

Two more sets of feet on the stairs. 'Prayin won't do you no good, poofters. Time to clean house. Nigger, don't you look at my face. You look at my face, it's the last thing you'll ever see.'

Bernier dropped his eyes and his hand, knelt like a penitent. Two men walked past Devon, put a hood on Bernier's head. He was handcuffed like Devon, which made it easier for the men to lift him to his feet. The chain behind him was unlocked, and he was taken away. When Bernier was gone up the stairs Devon was grabbed by the ear, got up onto his feet. They didn't use the hood, which wasn't a good sign. Devon was pushed and prodded toward the stairs. He thought about kicking backwards, rushing toward whatever happened next, but his body didn't believe the pictures he made. His feet shuffled on, his head bowed.

At the top of the stairs, Devon heard the sound of the shower, heard Bernier cussing. He was a big man. If he started something then maybe Devon could summon the courage. But the cussing continued until the water stopped. Devon was stood with his face in the corner of the kitchen. Beneath him was the bin overflowing with rubbish. He listened to Bernier being led into the kitchen. Heard a chair creak.

'Get the Yank's clothes,' the man behind him said. It was the ugly man they called Ralph. 'And bring the rifles. All of 'em. We need to get this shit happening.'

The skinhead Ant returned with a canvas bag heavy with iron. Under his arms was a plastic shopping bag full of the midshipman's uniform. Devon recognised the Dixie cup hat and felt a surge of sadness, watching it go past.

'Get dressed, negro. Slow and easy. This pistol is ready to rock and roll, you move an inch sideways.'

'Ah, Jesus. These rifles are covered in fuckin meat, somethin.'

It was Ralph's brother, the oddly neat one. 'Thought I told you, Ant, to wash these down?'

'Don't matter,' said Ralph, at Devon's ear. 'Little parting gift to Riley. Sure he'll appreciate it.'

Devon was turned away from the wall. Bernier had been uncuffed and had put on his bell-bottoms and white tee, his heavy cotton smock, while the kid, Ant, held the Glock on him. The handcuffs were put back on

Bernier, and he was pushed down into his seat. The whole time he never took his eyes off Devon, who was white, could maybe say something. But Devon couldn't think on what to say.

'Ant, give sailor-boy here the Glock.'

The ugly man pushed Devon forward. Devon felt the cold eye of the second Glock thrust against the back of his neck. 'You told us you hate blacks, mate. Now's your chance to prove it. Prove to us what you said, we might let you stay with us. We'll help you get away somewhere.'

Devon had heard their plans, and they didn't include letting him go, but Ant grabbed him by the cuffs and fitted the Glock into his hands. Devon felt his finger on the trigger as Ant stepped sideways, and the ugly man pressed the pistol deeper into Devon's neck. If he could just turn, get off a shot. Drop, roll, fire, like they did in the movies.

But he just stood there. It was Bernier, looking at him, anger in his eyes, and something else, too. Bitter disappointment.

'Go on, sailor-boy. You told Ant you bagged a nigger back home. You do it, or I'm gonna do it. A fucken waste, it must be said. Big reward on him that we won't get to claim. Cos of all this bullshit with the guns.'

Bernier straightened his shoulders as Devon's hands rose. 'What's he talkin about, man?' he asked, and this time his voice was deep and true.

Ralph put a hand on Devon's wrist. 'What's he talkin about? Lookit this.' Ralph peeled back Devon's shirt, exposing the 88 tattoo on his bicep. A sneer passed across Bernier's face, then a mutter of disgust.

'That's right, negro. You shouldn't've raped those two white women. Shouldn't have strangled 'em with those big negro hands of yours. Shouldn't have broke into this house, got yourself shot. We won't get the reward for it, but it's gonna make good press for us, for me. We already got everyone thinkin about the evils of black men rootin our women. Those whores we done in had it comin. Puttin it all on you, we rid ourselves of a scourge on our city. You broke in here, you messed with the wrong white boys.'

Ant took his hand off Devon's wrist. Devon was free to fire the weapon into Bernier's chest. He felt his finger tighten on the trigger. Bernier staring at him, all the fear gone now. Proud and fierce.

But the longer Bernier stared at him, the weaker Devon got, until he wasn't strong enough to hold up the Glock. He dropped his hands, felt the hammer blow from behind, darkness.

65.

'You bastard. You come into my life now, needing help?'

Tony Pascoe shook his head. His eyes were rimmed with tears that didn't fall. Whatever fantasy he had of meeting Swann wasn't going as planned. 'I never asked for your help. You cut into my action. Put me in this position.'

Swann had long ago given up on learning about his father. His mother refused to tell him. There were rumours. An American sailor. A union heavy named Bert who went into politics. Plenty of others that his mother denied. As a boy working his newspaper stand, Swann looked into the faces of men in the street, hoping for a resemblance or a flash of recognition. He had fought for his stepfather, Brian, in back alleys and outside pubs, against larger and older opponents, hoping that one day his father would step out of the crowd and intervene.

But it never happened.

Swann and his mother were stuck with Brian, a hopeless gambler who was also a mean drunk. Swann remembered the time Pascoe had been in their kitchen, when Brian started getting surly with his mother. How Pascoe had stopped it with a few harsh words. But that was just one night, and there were thousands of others where he wasn't around.

Now it dawned on Swann. 'Brian. The bashing he copped. You were out then.'

Pascoe met his eyes, giving him the warning not to dig deeper.

'What have you got to lose? What does it matter now?'

Swann felt Marion's hand on his shoulder. Gentle squeeze. Despite the fire in his eyes, Pascoe didn't look good. He nodded. 'Yeah it was me. It won't come as any consolation, but every time I heard he knocked your mother around, I went after him. That night he was ready for me. Pulled a revolver. In the process of getting it off him, he hit his head. I didn't mean for it to finish him off.'

Brian had ended up in hospital in an induced coma that he never woke up from. His liver packed it in from all the booze. His kidneys followed. His heart gave out. He died. He was forty-one years old.

'He wasn't missed. You did my mother a favour.'

Swann didn't say it, that Pascoe had done Swann a favour as well. Swann was sixteen at the time and boiling with fantasies of killing his stepfather. He'd beaten him up aged fifteen, but that didn't stop the drinking, the stealing off his mother, the psychological and physical abuse when Swann wasn't around. It was a matter of time.

'I'm sorry, son. For everything.'

'Don't call me that. You haven't earned the right.'

But the truth was that he'd never heard the word, addressed to him, the word that he'd yearned to hear. He felt it even as he pushed it away.

There were boot-steps on the footpath. Swann caught sight of Tony McIlroy's prison guard uniform the moment it passed along the fence-line. Without thinking Swann stood and blocked McIlroy's view of Pascoe, waved. Marion stepped beside him until McIlroy was at the front gate, and Pascoe was out of view.

Now was the perfect time to hand Pascoe over. McIlroy was his gaoler. As the watch commander, he'd be wearing heat for the escape. But Swann stepped off the veranda, onto the bricks. McIlroy held up a slip of paper.

'Just got a call from the superintendent, found my note. You were right. Cord was Rose McCartin's maiden name. Her first visits she showed her driver's licence. Here's the address you wanted. Solomon Street.'

Swann took the slip of paper, thanked McIlroy and asked him to pass on thanks to the super. Didn't mention the leak to Riley's bikies.

'I'll be off then. Is there something else, Frank? You look worried.'

Now was the time, but Swann let it pass. 'Just tired. Stay safe.'

'Always.'

Every workday morning, McIlroy walked fifteen minutes to Fremantle Gaol in his uniform, as he'd done for two decades, through the same streets where plenty of his ex-inmates lived, or had family.

A taxi turned into the block, pulled to the kerb. It was Webb, wearing chinos and a denim shirt. He paid the driver and walked toward them.

Swann shook McIlroy's hand and watched him leave, his khaki uniform already striped with sweat.

Webb nodded to the slip of paper in Swann's hand. 'Are we on?' he asked.

Swann was still dressed in yesterday's clothes. All he needed was his revolver.

'Yes. We are.'

It was a two-minute drive to the Rose Cord house on the rise of Solomon Street. The house was an odd number, which put her backyard on the western side of the street. It was coming together. The backyards on the western side of the street sloped to give a view over the prison walls. Swann parked the Brougham downhill of the house. Webb put his briefcase in the boot after removing his pistol.

Webb had just finished talking with his Federal Police liaison. It looked like they hadn't taken his information conveyed last night seriously. They weren't ready to despatch a team as Swann had hoped. They didn't want Webb to notify the locals either. When Webb suggested that he and Swann scout the premises for signs of occupation, they agreed immediately, told Webb to stay in touch. The liaison officer's voice was tired. He'd been up all night in the station monitoring the surveillance teams spread around the city.

Swann entered the grassed driveway. The house was an old weatherboard affair built onto limestone foundations. The paint on the weatherboards had blistered under the ferocity of the sun and some had warped and slid where the nails had rusted through. The old tin roof was rusted. The red-brick chimney was perched on a dangerous angle. The jarrah-board steps leading to the front veranda were silvered and buckled. There were a few dead pot plants beside the front door but no other signs that it was used.

The veranda would creak loudly under foot. Swann nodded toward the side of the house where the grass drive gave onto a limestone rubble path. There was no gate separating the front yard from the back, and so a dog was unlikely. Swann led the way, stopping under the first window. He tapped his nose and Webb nodded. There was a strong smell of diesel exhaust in the morning air and no other driveways nearby. A vehicle had recently left the property. Swann continued to the back wall. He peered around the corner into the empty yard, strewn with rubbish. There were cartons filled with empty stubbies and beer-cans. Some empty bottles of Bundaberg. A punching bag hanging from an ancient blue gum and a drum-fire stuffed with jarrah fence pickets. Didn't look to Swann like the old lady was living alone.

It was then that they heard the voices. Two voices, both male. One of them American. Swann cocked his revolver and Webb nodded him toward the back door. Five steps from the concrete-slab pavers to the stairs. Swann assumed that the American was the gun-trader, the kid Devon Smith, but something in Webb's eyes told him different.

Swann went to the door and listened. Still only the two voices, in the room nearest the steps. Swann was a metre from the two men. Webb took up his position at the base of the steps. Swann peered through the crack in the back door where it met the jamb. The old screen door was warped. The American spoke.

'You don't got to do this, man. You can let me walk. I know we ain't far from the port. I can just walk there. Those brothers won't never know that you let me leave. Nobody will ever know.'

The other man laughed. 'You don't get it, negro. We're owed the credit for taking you out. You got to die, here, now. Get ready.'

Webb was too distant to hear the words but his face told Swann that he recognised the accent. The American was Charles Bernier. Swann nodded to the side and Webb scooted away. Swann counted to five before he heard the loud knocking on the front door.

'One word, negro, one noise – I'll shoot you in the balls first.'

Webb kept knocking. 'Open up, police.'

The Australian whispered, 'You're goin down into the cellar. Quiet now. Stand up.'

Webb kept knocking. 'Open up. Police. Or we're coming in.'

Swann didn't see what happened next but Bernier burst through the back door, rolling down the steps. When his pursuer kicked the door and stepped across the threshold, Swann grabbed his ankle, the man's momentum toppling him over. Swann was straight on his back, the revolver at his ear.

'Drop it. You're done.'

Charles Bernier backed away. His eyes were fierce, his cuffed fists raised like a club. He got a shock when Webb sprinted round the corner, his pistol raised.

'It's alright, son. I'm American. US Navy Master-at-Arms. But you got to lie down. You're under arrest.'

Bernier looked ready to put down his head and charge.

'Webb, no. You didn't hear what I just heard. Call Cassidy, right away. Bring back your cuffs.'

The skinhead beneath Swann's knee began to struggle. Before Swann could stop him, Bernier was across the yard, kicked the man in the head, stamped on his neck, knocking him out cold.

66.

Swann and Webb were parked in the street beneath the shaded arms of a Moreton Bay fig. The Federal Police had given Webb a walkie-talkie as a courtesy, and it crackled between bursts of communication from the officers staked either side of Page's restaurant and the mobile command post. The command post was stationed inside a Main Roads van. It had eyes on the Big Salty restaurant, twenty metres down the street from where Swann's Brougham also had a clear view of the darkened glass windows. Two police officers in Main Roads uniforms were sketching out a dig site with spray-paint and witches hats. It wasn't subtle, but the street was narrow and there was nowhere to hide. In the commandeered video store beside Page's restaurant, a squad of TRG officers waited for the signal, armed with shotguns and tear gas. Jared Page and his two goons had entered the restaurant five minutes earlier in preparation for the handover. The Cord brothers and their offsiders were due any minute.

Swann had called Riley from the backyard of Rose Cord's house while they waited for Cassidy to arrive. Webb had cuffed the skinhead who wouldn't give his name, and sat him in the dirt. Charles Bernier sat on the back steps and chain-smoked until he was sick, had to lie down in the shade of the blue gum to recover.

It hadn't taken much to convince Gus Riley to frame-up Jared Page, real-estate developer and social-page celebrity, which surprised Swann. By the sound of it, Page sent plenty of business Riley's way. But he was also a competitor and, according to Riley, someone who treated the bikie outlaws like hired help. The deciding factor, however, was Swann's threat to inform the Federal Police that the original buyers for the guns were The Nongs, and Riley in particular. Swann didn't know this for sure – it was a gamble, but Swann meant every word of it, and Riley went very quiet. When he spoke again, his voice was even. Riley's only concern was that if he asked Page to act as intermediary in the handover of the stolen M16s, then he'd cop the suspicion of being the informer. Swann assured Riley that the suspicion could be explained away. It would be simple to claim that the Federal Police already had eyes on the Cord brothers, and had followed them to the restaurant.

Riley's only caveat on the arrangement, and one which confirmed his involvement in the weapons deal, was the matter of fifteen thousand in cash that he said the Cords had stolen. Swann thought about that, before suggesting to Riley that he say the money was payment for Page's service. Swann was relying on Jared Page's ego, assuming that he'd agree to act as intermediary and peacemaker. If Page took the money then he wouldn't be able to say, later in court, that he intended to turn the weapons over to the authorities, that he was doing a public service. It was the price of staying off the Feds' radar, Swann told Riley, and he took it on the chin.

When Swann called back five minutes later, Riley told him that it was on for midday at Page's restaurant. He was expecting a call from the Cord brothers and would relay the same news to them. Swann passed the information to Webb, who instructed the Federal Police. Page's restaurant didn't ordinarily open until evening, and this gave the police time to get inside the restaurant via a back door and wire it with cameras and sound.

As soon as Swann hung up the call to Riley, Cassidy arrived at Rose Cord's home in his white Commodore. The skinhead immediately began complaining, repeating that the cuffs should be on Bernier and that he was a hero who'd caught Bernier trying to steal food from the kitchen. Webb had to restrain Bernier from repeating his assault.

Webb held Bernier back until the skinhead finished his story.

'Man,' said Bernier. 'That's bullshit. They had me locked in the damn cellar under there. You can go check it out your own selves. There's a dead old woman down there too. Been there so long she looks like some kinda mummy. They call her Auntie Rose.'

Swann exchanged a glance with Webb, caught by the skinhead, who tried to stand. 'I didn't have nothin to do with that.'

'Who did then, son?' Swann asked.

The skinhead spat and sat back down, but something changed in his eyes. Swann knew that look. He recognised it from all the interrogation rooms he'd worked over the years – the skinhead weighing up whether it was worth staying silent, a doubt that Cassidy would certainly exploit.

Cassidy got out of the car and scanned the scene. 'Get in the car, Mr Bernier. I've got some questions I want to run by you, back at the station.'

'Is he under arrest?' Webb asked.

'No, he isn't.' Cassidy took out a piece of waxy paper, passed it to Webb. 'Got this fax first thing this morning. It's from the lab that tested Bernier's seed, left in the Seaview Hotel room. Mr Bernier's blood type is A-negative, like the swabs taken from our murder victims …'

'… but he's a non-secretor,' Webb finished. 'It can't have been him.'

Webb turned to Bernier, who was looking at them like they were stupid. 'Please go with the detective here. Tell the full story to the best of your recollection. When the detective has finished, I'll arrange for you to be picked up. Taken back to the *Vinson*. You can brief me there.'

Webb turned to Cassidy. 'Please make sure that Midshipman Bernier is fed on the way. He's been mistreated.'

Cassidy frogmarched the skinhead over to the car, put him in the back seat, motioned for Bernier to take the front. Cassidy stood beside the wheel and spoke into the radio handpiece, called in a forensics unit and two more homicide detectives, told them not to trample the scene and to wait for his return. Cassidy ended the call and began to climb inside the car, thought better of it and stood again, looked Swann in the eye. 'You haven't seen Detective Sergeant Gooch, have you, Swann? I've been told that he hasn't shown for work. That he isn't at his home, either. Car's missing.'

Cassidy had waited until precisely that moment, including staging climbing inside the car, to catch Swann off-guard. Cassidy's owl eyes were steady and unblinking. Swann met them, shook his head. 'He was tailing me, as you know. I lost the tail when I was with you, haven't seen him since. Gooch is a bagman. Maybe he ran off with the bag.'

Cassidy held his stare, then lifted his chin, a goodbye.

The walkie-talkie crackled. 'Suspects just arrived head of street, northern end, proceeding south in white Ford van, registration 7EH 133.'

'Roger that,' came the reply. The two officers dressed as road workers began to use the jackhammer, following the spray-painted line, eyes down. Swann and Webb sat low in their seats, watched the van pass and drive onto the footpath directly in front of the restaurant. The command vehicle and the officers stationed either side maintained radio silence as Ralph Cord and his brother went to the back of the van, opened the swing doors. Ralph Cord picked up a heavy canvas bag and slung it over his shoulder. His brother reached in and drew out another man, whose hands were cuffed. Webb flinched beside Swann.

'That's Midshipman Devon Smith.' Swann nodded toward the walkie-talkie. Webb picked it up and relayed the message that the cuffed man was the American citizen named Devon Smith, not a member of Cord's party.

There was no response from the command vehicle until the radio crackled. 'Have visual on rear of the van. No other occupants. Repeat. No other occupants.'

The Cord brothers went inside, Ralph's brother prodding Smith through the doors, a pistol at his back. Through the tinted glass Swann could see shadowy shapes patting them down. The radio crackled again. Webb's liaison had placed the walkie-talkie next to the monitoring receiver of the bugs inside. Swann recognised Page's voice, strong, commanding. 'Where's the money?'

'What money?'

'The fifteen K that's been promised to me, for setting this up.'

'Fair play, Mr Page. Worth a try, mate.'

Swann was glad that all of the officers were stood down. None had begun creeping toward the restaurant. The front door of the restaurant opened and Ralph Cord returned to the passenger door of the van, leaned under the seat and took out a small paper bag, returned inside, was patted down again.

'They're all there,' one of the Cord brothers said. 'Six Yank rifles. More trouble than they're worth. Same goes for this fuckhead. Your responsibility now.'

'Go. Go. Go.'

From the video store, the TRG team began to exit, running to the restaurant door. Three smashes with a battering ram and they were inside, out of Swann's vision but the shouting loud and insistent. No shots fired in the seconds that followed, meaning all had complied and were on the floor.

Webb punched Swann on the arm, held out a closed fist. 'Bump fists with me, Sheriff.'

Swann and Webb waited until Page and his men, the Cord brothers and Devon Smith were led away, placed in an armoured police vehicle, its windows painted black. Swann reached onto the seat and picked up the brick. Webb nodded.

Swann dialled the *Daily News*, asked to be put through to Maddie, a cadet journalist. He couldn't remember her second name but she was quickly on the line. Swann introduced himself, wondered if she'd be interested in an exclusive story. He checked the dash clock. It was ten past midday, plenty of time for her to file before the two o'clock deadline. He ran her through it, the arrest at the Fremantle home and the raid on Jared Page's restaurant. Gave her Cassidy's name for confirmation, said to say that Swann was the source before hanging up.

'That was nice of you,' said Webb.

Swann nodded, but it wasn't entirely true. In this town, you were never sure. Swann didn't know if Page was a registered informer, didn't want him squealing out of it. Putting him on the front page of the evening paper would make that impossible. Swann needed Page locked up for a very long time – long enough for his business empire to crumble, for his problems with Swann to be made insignificant.

The command vehicle was getting ready to depart. Webb picked up his briefcase and brick. 'Better go with them. See what charges will be laid against Midshipman Smith. Hope they throw the book.'

Swann watched Webb approach the Main Roads van, knock on the rear doors, disappear inside.

67.

Tony Pascoe had moved into Louise's old room but they ate lunch on the back deck, where no prying eyes could see. The mood was sombre because of Francine McGregor's funeral later in the afternoon. Swann's black suit was airing in the sunshine beneath the old tuart tree. He was going to meet Louise's friend Maddie before the cremation. Maddie wanted to cover the service as a bookend for her articles on the murders and the arrest of the Cord brothers. She also wanted to thank Swann. She didn't say why specifically, although Louise had confided that because of her articles, Maddie had been promoted from cadet reporter to a staff position.

After the arrests, Swann had withdrawn from the picture. Maddie still had Cassidy as her primary source, however, and she made sure to give Cassidy all the credit for the arrests. The younger skinhead that Swann and Webb detained at the Solomon Street house had flipped in the interrogation room. He wanted protection because of something that he'd done, and this had been granted, once it became clear that he knew everything about the Cords' plan to kidnap Bernier and set him up for the two murders.

The barbecue smoked and sizzled. All of Marion and Swann's daughters were there, and their two grandchildren, Jock and Neve. That morning Swann had cashed his money order from the US Navy, payment for his services, and he'd splashed out. It was a generous amount, and Swann paid Blake and Lee, then bought crayfish from Salvatore's cousin over the back fence, and prawns and a whole red emperor which he baked in foil on the barbecue. Tony Pascoe was a vegetarian, so couldn't eat any of it, but Marion and his three daughters would ensure that it wasn't wasted.

Paul Tremain had visited half an hour ago, leaving Swann a felt bag heavy with gold ore taken directly from his mine site. Swann had been paid in kind before, but never in gold, which still had crusts of quartz and rich red dirt over the ore. Tremain had heard of Jared Page's arrest, and assumed that Swann was involved. Swann wasn't glad to see him, not even after he'd given him the gold, but Tremain understood. He'd taken Swann's advice, he said, and had brought in an unnamed senior public servant from the Department of Mines as a silent partner of the Lightning Resources mine, to run protection and ensure that he got a straight road. Swann warned Tremain that once the mine was producing, he needed to buy the building that his office was housed in, and to never sell it, so that Gooch's grave wouldn't be disturbed. He then told Tremain that he never wanted to see him again. He didn't stay to watch him leave.

Tony Pascoe sat alongside his grand-daughters and drank his lemonade, nodding at their conversation, the dog asleep at his feet. The afternoon had cooled and the breeze in the branches of the old tuart clacked and swished. It was hard to say without X-ray confirmation, but Marion had examined Pascoe and felt that he was physically stable, as long as he didn't exert himself. His heart was strong and his blood pressure within the range. He could go anytime, but then again he might have months. Marion offered to take leave to look after Pascoe, but Swann refused. If she told him what to do, how to administer the morphine and manage the pain, he would nurse the old man, wash him and clean up after him, until the end.

Swann didn't know how well Pascoe would fit in with his daughters, but the signs were good, so far. Pascoe liked to tell a story, for one thing, and he appeared to be a good listener. Swann watched him make big eyes at a story young Jock was telling him about a sea lion that they'd watched that morning, sunning itself on the local beach.

It was Jock's mother, Sarah, who asked Pascoe to tell them about his early years. He took a deep breath, put on a brave face, tried his best to smile – then began to talk. He didn't gloss over it and he didn't romanticise it either. He was born during the Great Depression that made both his mother and father unemployed. Pascoe's father had gone out to the gold mines and died in a shaft collapse. Pascoe's mother had also died young of tuberculosis. During his teens, Pascoe had been raised in South Fremantle by his paternal grandfather, by then a very old man, who'd come to the colony as a convict in 1868. He was transported from

Scotland for theft and did his seven years at Fremantle Gaol, working on the roads and reclaiming land for the port. He was a good man, Pascoe said, but damaged by his time as a convict, and Pascoe had grown up wild and unsupervised. He also inherited his grandfather's resentment and hatred of authority. Pascoe had made some bad choices. He loved his grandfather but had never learned the significance of family.

Pascoe looked at Swann when he said this. Louise put her hand on Pascoe's shoulder. Each of Swann's daughters knew the score. They'd had an unusual upbringing. Housing a wanted man didn't faze them. What made their first meeting with Pascoe difficult was the knowledge that he was dying.

It was only a look from Pascoe, but Swann felt it more deeply than he expected. It was a new feeling, and one that was going to take some getting used to – for both of them, he could see that. As though Pascoe had read his mind, he looked at Swann again, and this time held the look.

'You're a lucky man, Frank,' Pascoe said. 'You've got each other. You also got the best of your mother. I can see her in these kids too.'

Swann and Pascoe hadn't had that conversation. How Pascoe and his mother had met, why he'd abandoned them. If Pascoe was true to his word that he'd learned to be straight with others, then that was a conversation for another time. Neither had they talked about the coming months, what would happen when it ended. Pascoe had only said, 'Go and speak to Des Ryan, down there on Harbour Street. He knows what to do. Give him some of the gold I took off Tremain, tell him to give some of it to his neighbours. He'll know what I mean. Leave it up to Des. He knows my spot. Long as I'm buried outside those walls, I'll be free.'

Swann brought over the food, placed it on the table, caught the end of Pascoe's conversation with Marion.

'I like your garden,' Pascoe said. 'Anyone using that planter box at the back fence?'

Marion shook her head. 'It doesn't get much light. We planted vegies there for years, until the tuart grew.'

'I've got some ideas,' Pascoe said. 'Fresh parsley. I can eat buckets of the stuff. I also want to bury some things.'

'Like buried treasure?' Jock chimed in.

Pascoe grinned. 'From the mouths of babes, eh? But yeah, like buried treasure.'

Swann thought about the weight of gold in the Gladstone bag, tucked beneath the old man's bed. It made sense to bury it. It'd be a good nest egg, going forward.

'Where did you get the treasure?' Jock asked.

Pascoe shrugged, winked. 'From a goose who laid a golden egg.'

Swann shook his head at the bad joke. He sat beside Marion, who put her hand on his knee. Swann draped his arm around her and leaned in, raised his glass of beer. 'To family,' he said. 'Old and new.'

'To family. Old and new.'

'And to stopping and smelling the roses,' added Swann, to groans from his daughters.

He shrugged defensively. 'I mean it. Since I quit smoking, I can smell Salvatore's roses.'

Tony Pascoe raised his glass, touched with Swann. 'Doesn't make it any better, but yeah, here's to smelling the roses.'

ACKNOWLEDGEMENTS

All characters appearing in this work are fictitious. Any resemblance to real persons, living or dead, is purely coincidental.

This book is dedicated to Mark Constable for the decades of sharing stories over campfires and pints of Guinness; for his jokes, harmonica-tunes and songs, and for his fact-checking eye cast over each of my novels.

Thanks always to my publisher and editor Georgia Richter, and to all the great team at Fremantle Press. Thanks to Artsource for the continued use of my writing room. Much love to Bella and my three children – Max, Fairlie and Luka. Fairlie and Luka, I hope you're happy knowing that when I read certain passages of *Shore Leave* aloud, Mya will prick up her kelpie ears in recognition.

ALSO AVAILABLE

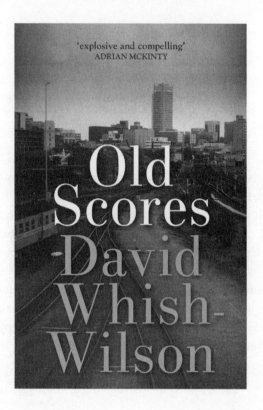

'explosive and compelling'
ADRIAN MCKINTY

Old Scores
David Whish-Wilson

It's the early 1980s: the heady days of excess, dirty secrets and personal favours. Former detective Frank Swann is still in disgrace, working as a low-rent PI. But when he's offered a security job by the premier's fixer, it soon becomes clear that someone is bugging the premier's phone – and it may cost Swann more than his job to find out why.

'[Perth] is indeed one of the key characters in the novel, a remote wild-west mirage with more money than sense ...' *Australian Book Review*

'Whish-Wilson has again delivered a fast-paced, entertaining and smarter than average crime novel.' *The Weekend Australian*

'In the Frank Swann series, David Whish-Wilson has done for Perth what Peter Temple did for Melbourne with Jack Irish.' *Westerly Magazine*

'As the plot unfolds, Whish-Wilson's text pulses from the pages at an escalating rate, building tension and suspense as the story hurtles towards its surprising resolution.' *Farm Weekly*

FROM FREMANTLEPRESS.COM.AU

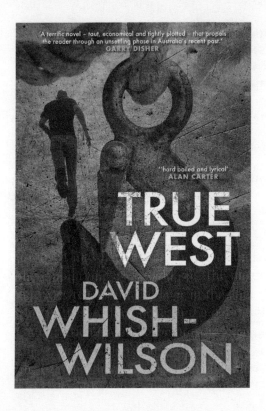

First published 2020 by
FREMANTLE PRESS

Fremantle Press Inc. trading as Fremantle Press
25 Quarry Street, Fremantle WA 6160
(PO Box 158, North Fremantle WA 6159)
www.fremantlepress.com.au

Cover image: istockphoto.com/au
Printed by McPherson's Printing Group, Victoria, Australia.

 A catalogue record for this
book is available from the
National Library of Australia

ISBN 9781925815986 (paperback)
ISBN 9781925815993 (ebook)

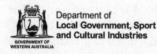

Fremantle Press is supported by the State Government through
the Department of Local Government, Sport and Cultural Industries.

Publication of this title was assisted by the Commonwealth Government through the
Australia Council, its arts funding and advisory body.